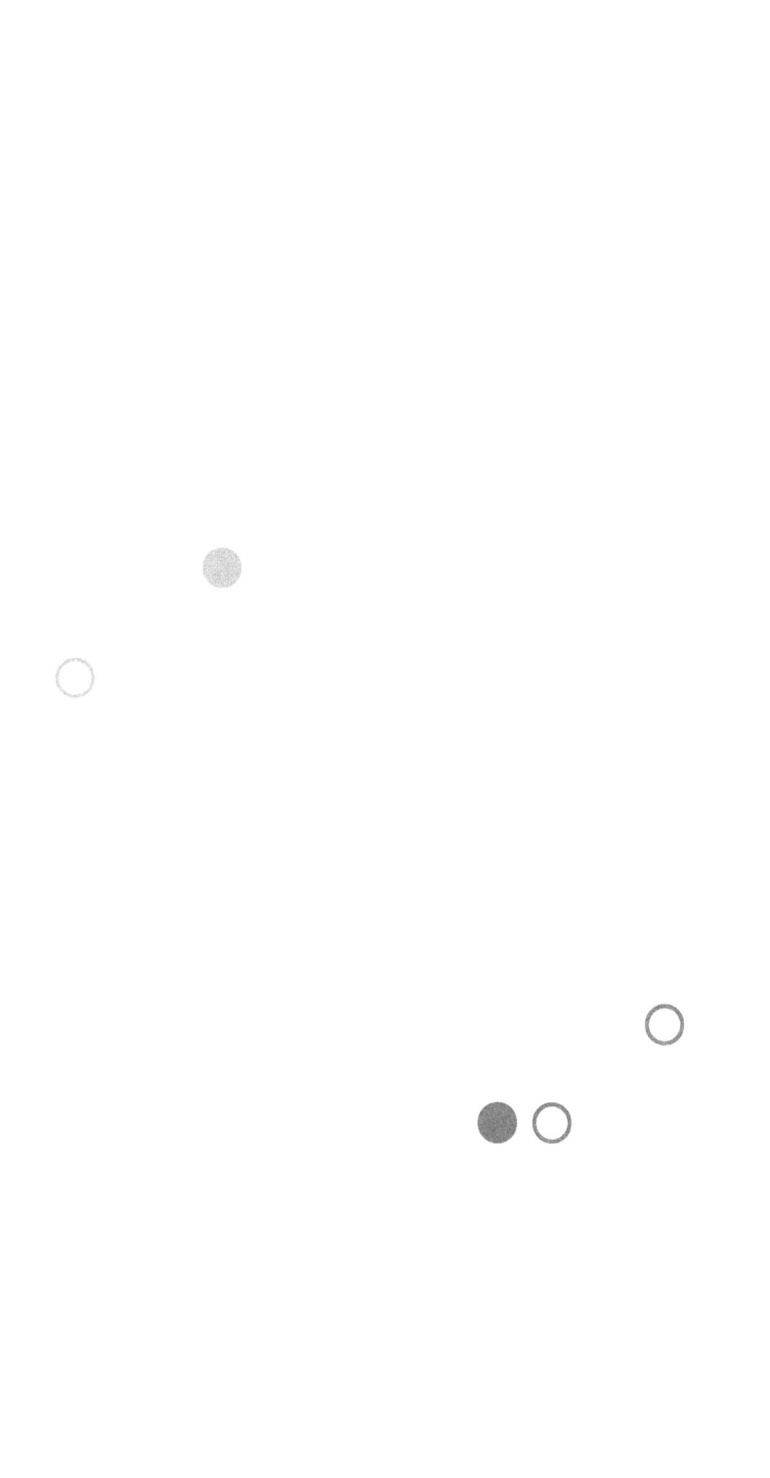

THE GLASS PARACHUTE

VILLIPEDE
publications

ISBN-13: 978-0615675626
ISBN-10: 061567562X

THESE STATEMENTS PASS ALL
CRITICAL SCREENINGS FOR THIS MEDIA
AVO: AC1019b-0329S.L

Those involved with the making of this book would like to honor the life and work of two brilliant men. We are grateful for your contributions to literature and for your lifelong inspiration.

You will be missed.

Ray Bradbury
August 22, 1920 – June 5, 2012

Harry Harrison
March 12, 1925 – August 15, 2012

CONTENTS

ILLUSTRATIONS

Introduction

If you're reading this, there's a good chance you're in the percentage of the population that feels compelled to read introductions out of a kind of literary OCD. Even if you know from experience that they're rarely entertaining—and all you really want to do is skip to the good stuff—you still find yourself reluctant and even fearful at the prospect of not reading the beginning of a book entirely.

Is it a sense of betrayal that holds us to it? Responsibility? Or is it just that we're afraid of missing some key insight.

Well, whatever the reason, if you're reading this: let me empathize with your condition now, and also vow to make this as short and sweet as possible.

Actually, so that you know, I've invented a device that will prevent me from digressing into any dialogue that may bore unnecessarily or steer us away from the subject at hand—

A thing to keep us on the straight and narrow, you see?

It's quite simple: I've attached the cable from my wet-wire implant (yes, they do amazing things in Tokyo nowadays) to this clever little apparatus, which is about the size of a household sewing machine. The primary machine monitors brain waves, measures synaptic activity, rips a mean basting stitch—et cetera. Some basic 220 wire connects from said machine into a gateway component (yes, it may *vaguely* resemble my old modem) separating a car battery from another set of gator clips that are presently biting into the tender, fleshy area behind my knees.

See? Simple.

Essentially, as I write, my thought processes will be monitored by this device, and any divergence from the primary subject will be rebutted with a good swift shock from the car battery.

Let's give it a try, eh?

I remember when I was eleven and standing in the local mall's only book shop—yes, the yokelish yellow-bricked one; the one by the soft-serve yogurt shop—utterly transfixed. Staring with googly-eyes, I was, at the lot of comic books and science fiction novellas occupying every nook of the—

GzzgzZZZt!

Wow—okay! That works fabulously. Well, then, let's *really* give this a genuine try now.

The Glass Parachute: it's an interesting title, wouldn't you say? I believe it's a title, however, that requires a bit of explanation—especially considering there is no story in this book with that title (as one might expect there to be) and, in fact, no other reference to any parachutes of glass aside from this.

You see, when the idea first occurred to me to assemble this anthology, I felt the first thing it needed was an enticing title; and so, from the inspirational ether, I pulled *The Glass Parachute* (I know, I know—pure awesomeness. You don't have to tell *me*).

What began as a simple-but-cool working title eventually worked itself into the folds of my subconscious, where it set roots into the soil of my mind and eventually sprouted as an idea for a short story.

Days later, around three o'clock in the morning, I abruptly sat straight up in bed (scaring the dickens out of my wife, naturally), and exclaimed with great fervor: "I've got it! A story that'll change the world!"

Frantically I scratched the basic ideas into a nearby notebook—or was it my wife's daily planner?—and, to my surprise, the jabber still held some loose coherency when I looked at it the next morning.

I worked on the story for a couple of weeks. It seemed to be going fairly well. And when it was all but finished, I set it aside to focus on other aspects of the anthology.

No problem there, right?

Well . . . about two months later I figured it was time to dig out that ol' *Glass Parachute* manuscript and give it the final touch-up before it went on its way to editing . . .

Confusion gripped my soul. Looking back over the story, I was perplexed—why, there were holes in it big enough to fly a fleet of class R Hagalian freight liners through!

Impossible! I exclaimed. *Outrageous!* I screamed . . .

Alas, it was true. I tried smoothing over the rough edges: no luck. No easy fixes for timeline conflicts, no quick patches for the monstrous, jagged holes.

Not to mention, I had also begun to fear (in that it shared the same title) that the story may be dubbed the "feature" of the anthology (I'm not so pretentious as to desire such a thing, I assure you. Borderline . . . but not quite there).

And so I must apologize: the title remains, but the story to accompany it must remain a mystery . . .

For now.

Fear not, however, for within this tome there is ample SF to satisfy all manner of enthusiasts.

For your tempered tastes, we offer some delicious cyberpunk (exquisite!), some lovely dishes on terraforming and futuristic drama (outstanding!) . . . or perhaps some fresh material on cloning and genetic manipulation better suits you? It's the day's special. And for dessert we boast a bit of fantastic satire— tangy and robust in all the right places.

Dear me, have I mentioned the authors yet? Well, they're all fantastic. Some have appeared in weighty venues such as *DailyScienceFiction.com*, *Foundation*, *Lightspeed,* and *Digital Science Fiction*. One has twice been a finalist for the Writers of the Future award, *and* had a story accepted by *Analog*. For a couple authors, this anthology will be their first published work.

Regardless of whether they are seasoned players or rookies to the game, I anticipate more great things to come from them all. And not only are they great writers, they're also optimistic and outgoing people.

I would like to single a few of them out for special thanks. Alex J. Kane didn't hesitate a moment before agreeing to be the anthology's first volunteer, and he went on to suggest the majority of the other writers as candidates. He has been both helpful and positive throughout; I can honestly say this book would differ greatly from the one you're holding in your hands if Alex hadn't been involved from the beginning.

Now, Grayson Morris and Jasmine Michaelson have both assured me that copyediting is not normally a function that is outwardly praised in literature, but I feel their hard work and contribution *must* be given credit. I think you'll agree: we've blurred the lines of literary taboo enough as it is—why stop now? After all, what is literature if not a device for the freedom of all humans to provoke their inherent nature and bravely embark on outlandish—

GzzgzZZZt!

Wow! Okay—who was I again? Smoke alarm is going off now. Hmmm . . . *note to self: adjust the amperage and sensitivity of the Track-Assurance Machine.*

Okay, then—right as rain and back on track!

I've known Jasmine Michaelson since elementary school. Come to think of it, I remember the two of us being involved with a group project in something like the third grade. We were presenting a wonderful cut-and-paste picture of an alien world accented with meteors blazing in the sky and futuristic cars zooming around in the foreground. I recall those hot pink and neon green cars so gleefully now; so sleek with their—

Gzzt . . . gz . . .

Right . . . of course. Just a warning there—but still a jolt to be respected. Now, where was I? Oh yes—

Jasmine and I hadn't seen each other for many years, and then I noticed her FB profile listed Orson Scott Card's *Ender's Game* as a literary favorite.

We chatted a bit (what? Is something wrong with a man *chatting*? Grown men can chat), and I asked if she would be interested in the book. She was excited to submit a story, and offered her editing support as well. I took her up on both; she accepted the task of copyediting and writing and did both with great finesse—all the while battling fits of nausea and overwhelming cravings for chocolate-salmon casserole.

Grayson Morris optimistically lent her expertise to the cause as well. A seasoned soldier of the profession, Grayson was there to illuminate a path of reason and guide us back to solid ground when we found our-selves lost and wandering haphazardly through the dark swamps of G'ram-mar.

Well, let's see . . . we've covered the title thing, the authors and contributors . . . what am I forgetting?

Of course. The artwork.

The contributing artists did a magnificent job. It can be unbelievably difficult to anticipate an author's desire for their illustrations, but the artists did ex-ceptionally well. Most of the authors were instantly thrilled with the art created to accompany their stories . . . and the ones who weren't? Well, some may have needed some *persuading*—threatening letters, ransom, blackmail—but rest assured it was mostly friendly and all in the name of fine fiction.

And when it comes to fiction—

Dare I press forward? . . . Yes, gently now . . .

When it comes to fiction—really *superb* science fiction—you will come to know that Villipede Publications will continue to evolve into an unstoppable juggernaut of literary excellence hellbent on nothing short of world domina—

GzzgzGzZZZZZt!

Mother of Daneel Olivaw, that is one *intense* sensation! It feels as though juvenile Ewoks are gnawing at my patellar ligaments! So . . . *painful . . .*

Well, it was worth a try—but let's just wrap this up simply, with some vestige of respectability.

SF: good.

Non-SF: good, but not *as* good.

This book: (inherent in its being SF)—good.

Enjoy.

—Matt Edginton
Villipede Publications

ΠΟΤ ΑΝΟΤΗΕR VΑCUUΜ STORY

Martin L. Shoemaker

Look, what you *don't* want to hear is another vacuum story.

Oh, we've got plenty of them here in the Old Town. They're older than this bar, older than Tycho Under, older even than space travel. They're our "essential folklore," as my old lit prof called it: tales that teach you how to survive in your culture. The most important lesson on Luna is: Keep your vacuum on one side, and you and your air on the other. So our essential folklore includes lots of variations of "How I Almost Breathed Vacuum" or "They Screwed Up, and So They Breathed Vacuum."

But you've heard them all before. *You* could tell *me* all the same stories. So while I may spin you a tale now and then, the one thing I promise I'm *not* gonna tell you is another vacuum story. Ever.

But sit down, order a drink, and I'll give you something different. Let me tell you how a young smartass—OK, it was me, back when I was younger and more of a smartass than I am today—got in trouble from *too much* air.

The story begins when I was hanging in the door of a short haul flyer, looking for a soft place to land without breaking my neck when I jumped.

Well, no, I think it's important that I be honest here, because I don't want you to miss my point. The story *really* begins a couple days before that, when I snagged myself extra homework by mouthing off to Fontes. Again.

Sergeant Armand Fontes, Lunar Defense Reserves, Lead Instructor at Lunar Survivor School, Tycho Under Campus. I always figured he hated me because I was an extension student from McAuliffe University, and all my classmates were from Defense or Rescue or the other services. I figured he saw me as a college punk, wasting his time. Now I know he just loves to mess with vac-heads, and I was the king of the vac-heads.

It was time for the solo practical exam in prefab shelters. I had two hot dates lined up for that week-end—*one* woman is more than I can handle these days, but I was young and stupid—and I was more interested in them than any exam. Plus it sounded like a cakewalk, and I wasn't shy about saying so.

"This is such a waste, Sarge. We should test manual thermal control, or something even more challenging. Who uses prefab shelters these days? They're as safe as a home cycler."

Fontes looked at me with distaste. "Mister Morgan, how many injuries were reported in home cyclers last year? How many fatalities?"

"I don't know, Sarge."

"Well, you just earned yourself a homework assignment. And I've pushed a restriction to the AI Net, so they won't help you with your research. I want a full summary, cross categorized by root cause, severity of injury, and how each might've been avoided. By Monday.

"Now for those of you who aren't the daredevils that Mister Morgan is . . . Prefab shelters date from the earliest days of the Lunar Era. The modern versions can be found in the cargo decks of half the shuttles and freighters operating in Lunar space, maybe more. They're also common at mine excavations and other sites with no permanent structures. They'll keep one person alive for a full Lunar without resupply, and they're simple to set up, just follow a checklist. *But you have to follow that checklist!* And then you have to monitor your gauges—not just your idiot lights!—keep on top of your controls, and be alert for variances. Don't assume that 'basic' equipment works as promised. Here's your cheat sheet for this exam, ladies and gentlemen: *This exam is all about following directions and taking care of the details, even when you're bored.* Those are your two most important survival skills, and you don't graduate to 'challenging' until you learn 'em. Got that, Kenneth?" When Fontes switches to first names, it means you aren't respectable enough to be "Mister" or "Miss."

I had no intention of a long homework assignment interfering with my dates, so I planned to get the exam out of the way quickly. When Fontes opened the list for testing slots, I practically sprained a thumb pushing my name into the first slot. The tests were staggered in groups of five, starting every four hours. If I got the exam out of the way, I could be watching Earthset with Mary Sue Reilly before the last group started.

The goal of the solo practical is to survive for two days under simulated emergency isolation conditions. You can't rush it, except by failing. If for any reason you don't last the full two days, you fail, and you get to repeat that whole unit. So the test starts when the timer starts, and you're done when it elapses.

Two days is barely a shakedown cruise; but knowing Fontes and the rest of the instructors, I was sure it was plenty of time for trouble. We'd all heard the scuttlebutt: Every practical exam has a bit of instructor sabotage thrown in, some zinger in the equipment or the scenario that would force you to improvise. If you flubbed that zinger, you shortened the exam the only way possible: hitting the panic button and flunking the exam.

I was sure Fontes wanted to see me flunk so I buried myself in research on prefabs and prefab accidents. Those case studies . . . Man, talk about your vacuum stories! I studied them all, and all the common causes. A hard ass like Fontes is the best teacher for someone like me, I guess. I'd even *study* if it would wipe that grin off his face.

And I studied that checklist. No, smartass that I was, I *memorized* that checklist. I could recite the list, forwards or backwards, by Wednesday morning when Fontes called my name.

"Mister Morgan, front and center. You're with me and Schultz, flyer 3. Suit up, and head down tube J to the flyer. Miss King, flyer 4, also tube J."

Sarah King and I went to the suit room and suited up, checking each other's suits and seals. Then we headed down tube J to our respective locks. We wished each other luck, and we boarded.

I strapped in and was soon joined by Fontes. Rita Schultz strapped into the pilot's chair and requested a launch window. The tug clamped onto our nose hook and pulled us out onto the launch pad. As Schultz went through her prelaunch checklist and Fontes made notes on his comp, I reviewed my lessons. Soon enough, we launched; and once we were off primary boost, Fontes pushed a map to my comp.

"OK, Mister Morgan, take a look at that map. You trainees get it easy for this test. Later on, your testing ground will be a large crater or more; but your prefab is somewhere in that square." Yow. Some restriction. That square was half a klick on a side. "But not *too* easy. To make it more challenging, we're going to simulate crash conditions."

"You're going to crash land the flyer?"

"No, rookie, we're going to crash land *you*. You'll pick an approach vector, Schultz will fly low over the testing ground, and you'll jump out."

"*What?* We haven't covered free jumps yet."

"Oh, don't piss your suit. We won't be high enough

up for any serious damage or injury, just enough to dust you up and make you nervous—I'll bet you are already! This way, the test is completely unbiased. You can't claim we set you down far away from the prefab, because you're picking the drop point."

So that brings us back to me hanging out the door of the flyer, boulders and regolith passing by beneath me. Oh, I was nervous, all right, but no way would I let Fontes see.

Part of the test is simply *finding* the prefab. Since Fontes wouldn't let me use my emergency locator while I was in the flyer, I was eyeballing as best I could. The testing ground was a semi-rugged section of one of Tycho's ejecta rays. It was late First Quarter, so the sun would be low in the west, casting shadows east over the ejecta debris.

Schultz interrupted my analysis. "Sergeant, we're at drop altitude on Morgan's vector. The flyer's depressurized, and he can drop any time."

"Thank you, Schultz. OK, Mister Morgan, your clock starts when you jump. Pick your spot. Take your time, but if Schultz exceeds our fuel budget while you're working up the balls to jump, I'm charging you for the extra."

We were over the debris field, moving slowly for a flyer, but still with enough forward momentum for my plan. I figured I would have time to run the locator as I fell, and that forward momentum meant I would pass over a lot of prime hiding spaces. I might just ping the prefab's beacon before I hit the lith, as long as I had the presence of mind to run the locator. As we approached the right spot, I breathed slowly: *Trust*

Fontes, don't worry about the jump, focus on the test. And then I jumped.

My relaxation trick worked. I was free falling, but I wasn't panicking. I turned on the locator in recording mode, and then I concentrated on where I would fall. By the time the regolith was rushing up toward me and I braced for a roll, a beep told me the locator had found the prefab beacon.

Modern suits are almost as sturdy as a prefab, relying largely on thinner layers of the same material and without the hard helmets common in the early Lunar Era. Fontes was right, LSS trained us in falling and tumbling in our Physical Training classes, and this fall wasn't that much faster than those. So I rolled three times and into a face dive, absorbing the last of the impact on my forearms. Then I used that momentum to bounce backwards to my feet. One simple pivot, and I was loping back to the beacon. That move could've gotten me into the Tycho Under Ballet.

It was another smartass move, really, but that move made me feel ready for anything. As I ran, I started mentally working my checklist and thinking on possible zingers.

STEP 1: SEARCH. I didn't even try a visual search. With the sun in my eyes, even max polarization left me plenty of glare, so the beacon was my guide. When I was practically on top of it, a hill-sized boulder gave me enough shade to see the prefab package, wedged into a cleft between two boulders. I had to wiggle it back and forth to work it out. When packed, a prefab is nearly as tall as me and equally wide and thick—a mass of fabriglass and plastic and consumables that would be impossible for me to budge on Earth. On Luna, I could lift it, sure; but moving it is a matter of mass, not weight, and it's massive. Once it was un-wedged, I rolled it onto its cage base, a smooth sled that would allow me to push it over regolith as long as I didn't hit any really large rocks.

STEP 2: SITE SELECTION. Fontes was almost kind to me in this step: Big Bertha (my new nickname for the hill-sized boulder) gave me plenty of shade. Out in exposed sunlight at Full, the prefab's cooling system would have more work. The fabriglass is largely reflective (and also photovoltaic for power), but far from a perfect reflector. It could get hot in there.

STEP 3: UNPACKING. The prefab has a thick floor disk and a thinner dome top. You pack it by collapsing the dome onto the floor and stacking the consumables package in the center. Then you fold the sides of the disk in, left then right then back, until it's all in a long, thick strip. And then you roll the strip into a massive roll, and assemble the plastic cage around it. I just had to reverse that process.

The cagework disassembles and telescopes to become support struts, which go into sleeves on the dome, a ground ring and a top ring and support struts between them. You lock these all together to make a skeleton for the dome. In case of a catastrophic leak, the skeleton holds the dome up so it doesn't collapse on you while you patch. I opened and disassembled the cage and laid the struts out in rays around the fabriglass.

One easy zinger comes in Unpacking: missing

parts. Or you can create your own zinger by losing parts. I had memorized the parts list, too, and I confirmed they were all there. I put all the fasteners into my utility pockets on my thighs.

STEP 4: UNROLLING AND UNFOLDING. I dealt with less and less fabriglass with each round, so unrolling got progressively easier. Then I unfolded the roll to either side and stretched it out. At the innermost center for maximum protection is the consumables package: air bottles, water bottles, liquid nutrients, and vacuum resin for seals. I set them aside.

Unrolling and Unfolding is an unlikely step for zingers. As long as the fabriglass was properly collapsed and folded, these steps should be trouble free. I looked for any tangles or creases, but found none.

STEP 5: STRUT ASSEMBLY. I put the upper strut ring in the sleeves around the upper dome, and attached the vertical struts. The verticals would also snap into the lower ring once the dome was sufficiently inflated. Next I assembled the lower strut ring in the sleeves around the flooring. I saw no cracks in the struts, nor any other sort of zingers.

STEP 6: ENVIRONMENT PREP. I unpacked the environment package from the sled. This was a single-module unit, air pump and water pump and recycler and solar power storage all in one. I opened the lid, visually inspected every component, and ran through the diagnostic circuits. No zinger there.

STEP 7: INITIAL INFLATION. I unzipped the outer and inner doors of the airlock, so the vacuum wouldn't stick the dome and the flooring together.

Then I propped up the struts nearest the airlock, creating just enough of a tent to let me crawl inside and close the lock behind me. I installed the air bottles and water bottles into the environment package, hooked up the feed lines, and hooked the whole package into the solar power line. I opened the first air valve, and prepared to start the inflation cycle.

Wait. The lack of any zinger so far nagged at me and made me expect the worst. What would be the most difficult thing to repair? That would be where Fontes would hide my zinger.

The snuff box. Those prefabs are made from the best fabriglass Corning makes, but even fabriglass will tear if it gets pierced by a shard of metal in a crash. Worse than a tear is a pinhole, large enough for a slow leak but too small to eyeball. Someone who's tired and maybe injured might fall asleep thinking he has good pressure, sleep through the pressure alarms, and asphyxiate. So LSS protocol recommends both an eyeball inspection and a dispersal density test—only we call it the "snuff test," not because it could snuff you out, but because of the dust or snuff involved. When the dome is inflated, you turn off the air recirc, get everybody out of the dome, and start the test. A little snuff box in the top center of the dome fires out a fine spray of reflective dust in all directions inside the dome. Then a camera matrix tracks the falling dust, and the AI in the snuff box looks for signs of air currents. It'll pick up even the tiniest pinhole leaks and then laser spot them so you can apply patches. You don't *have* to leave the dome for the snuff test, but still air gives you the most accurate patches. I'd hate to fail over a shoddy patch, so I would leave for the test.

When the dome was fully inflated, the snuff box would be at the top of the dome, more than twice my height. If something went wrong there . . . Sure, I could jump up there, but I couldn't *stay* up there. I'd have to let out a lot of air, waste a lot of time, just so I could fix the box. I knew of only a handful of snuff box failures; but a handful is more than zero.

I needed to check the snuff box, which at the time was buried between the two layers of fabriglass, so I needed to inflate enough to reach the box. I started the inflation cycle, and five minutes later I could just squeeze between the dome and the flooring to get to the snuff box. I opened it up for inspection.

"Gotcha, Fontes." Snuff boxes have six charges, so you can run the test multiple times if needed. The first charge had fired prematurely while wrapped deep inside the fabriglass. It hadn't damaged anything outside the box, but the box was a mess. If I ran a test like that, it would fire askew, wasting a *second* charge. Plus the snuff jammed in the box unit would foul up the camera matrix, so that when I ran the third test, the results would be useless. It would take four of my six charges just to get one valid test. If that test showed leaks, I would need to use the fifth charge. That would cut it close. Here was my zinger.

So while the inflation continued, I disassembled the snuff box and carefully cleaned it with supplies from the sled. Some of the snuff was caked into the screen, and I couldn't get it clean with a utility brush. If there were enough pressure to take off my helmet, I could've just blown through the screen to clean it out. But no, that was probably a bad idea anyway. Spittle could stick to the screen, gum it up, and invalidate the test.

But I had another source of air pressure: two full banks of air bottles, each full of clean, dry air. I pulled an air bottle from the second bank, cracked open the valve, and manually tripped the regulator to send out blasts of air and clean the screen.

When the screen was clean, I closed the valve, inspected everything under the magnifying glass, and ran all the diagnostic circuits. One charge was lost, yeah, but they couldn't mark me down for a precondition of the test. I reassembled the box and snapped it back in place on the dome top. *Take that, Fontes!*

But I was behind schedule! I was trying to shave time for that homework assignment. I had planned to assemble the remaining strut work as the dome inflated. Now the dome was more than half inflated, and my struts weren't assembled yet.

Still, I had mentally budgeted two hours for a zinger, and the snuff box took less than half that, so I was still good. I patted the snuff box like a good luck charm, hooked the spare air bottle back into its rack, and cycled through the airlock.

STEP 8: STRUT INSERTION. It's hard to insert the struts in the sleeves at full assembly, and the dome had inflated quickly while I worked. Still, I refused to rush and maybe make a mistake. I checked each strut for a solid attachment to the upper ring and then snapped it into the lower ring. Once all the struts were elevated, I fastened down the lock rings.

STEP 9: DISPERSAL DENSITY TEST. By the time the struts were done, it was time for the snuff test. I picked up the consumables pack, unzipped the outer airlock door and zipped it behind me, and waited for the pressure light to go green. My impatience was growing, and it seemed to take a long time. Finally, I zipped in, dropped off the consumables, hit the master cutoff on the environment pack, and zipped back out. After another impatient wait, I was back on the lith. I turned to my suit comp and pushed the command for the snuff test.

Poof! I watched the burst of snuff, silent of course, and then waited as it settled. Soon the results popped to my comp: seventeen pinhole leaks.

Seventeen? That was more pinhole leaks than in any case study. Usually before that, there's an obvious tear. A zinger is one thing, but Fontes was being a jerk here.

STEP 10: SHELTER INTEGRITY. I zipped back in, waited to pressurize, entered, hit the master power, grabbed the vacuum resin, and headed to the laser spot identifying the first leak. There next to the leak, very small and practically transparent, was a little smiley face drawn in marker. If the laser hadn't pointed me in the right direction, I would never have seen it. Yeah, Fontes, screw you too.

I dabbed the leak with vacuum resin. In under a second, a small dot in the center turned light gray, indicating that vacuum had caused a state change and sealed the resin. I scraped most of the remaining resin off the fabriglass and back into the jar, and then smoothed down the last bit so no rough edge could get bumped and break the seal. Just like a lab exercise.

Sixteen more dabs of resin (and sixteen more smiley faces), and I was done. I sealed the jar and went outside to run the snuff test again. My impatience was mounting further (seventeen damned smiley faces!), but I wasn't going to let Fontes goad me into rushing. I climbed out, pushed the snuff test again, and smiled. No leaks.

STEP 11: EXTERNAL REINSPECTION. You don't *have* to reinspect, if there's some reason you need to get into pressure quickly; but even as impatient as I was, I was determined to work the whole checklist. I carefully circled the dome, checking the struts, checking the lock rings, tugging and twisting and looking for unexpected movement. I found none. And then I checked the fabriglass as high as I could. Aside from seventeen tiny dots of hardened gray resin, I saw no flaws at all. Then I checked the airlock and its attachment to the dome and all the zippers and gaskets and seals. No flaws, all clean and functioning properly.

And then I had one more tiresome wait for the repressurization. And when that was done, I inspected the inner airlock. All clear.

STEP 12: INTERNAL REINSPECTION. Once I was fully inside, I was tired and hungry; but aside from a quick gulp of water (dehydration is a serious survival risk), I put biology aside. If I postponed reinspection for food, well, liquid nutrients make a lousy last meal. So I checked the environment pack, and all lights were green. I checked the solar power cable and the lighting (LED lights woven into the fabriglass). And last I reinspected the fabriglass itself, particularly the seventeen pinholes. All clear. I doubt Fontes himself could find anything to report.

And finally, I sucked down some nutrient compound and some more water. Then I lay back on the raised mat molded into the floor near the airlock. I tried to work on my homework assignment, but I was more tired than I realized. I was asleep in under ten minutes. Every two hours, my suit comp woke me for a spot inspection: all lights green, check the temperature, check the sealed leaks. Then back to sleep.

In the morning, I woke ahead of the alarm, and grabbed an early breakfast. After relieving myself, I hooked my suit's waste disposal tubes to the recyclers. I had plenty of food and water for more than two days (barring yet another zinger), so there would be no need for recycled water and nutrients. Still, I didn't want to carry the wastes in my suit, so into the recycler they went.

I was almost through my morning inspection when my suit radio spoke. "Mister Morgan."

"Sarge, what's up? I didn't hit the panic button."

"Oh, I know. This is merely an unofficial 'good morning, how ya doing?'"

"I'm doing fine. Just settling in to wait for my 'rescue'."

"Nothing unusual to report?"

"Oh, just routine stuff. My snuff box lost a charge, and I had to clean it. Oh, and I had to patch a few leaks, seventeen or so. Just routine." The smile on my face said: *I beat you, you bastard.*

"You're a clever one, ain't ya, Kenneth? Got it all covered. Well, then, I'll just leave you to your waiting. Fontes out."

I was so pleased with myself, I could barely finish my inspection, but I wasn't going to slip up now and give Fontes the last laugh. After I was done, I settled in and started seriously attacking that homework assignment. It's not like I had anything else to do. Outside of the two-hour spot inspections, I had time to kill.

And so my day went, and my night like the night before. Boring homework mixed with boring inspections. Boring squared. But I remembered Fontes's lessons: Boredom kills. So I broke up the monotony with some game sims, some music, and a few comic book files.

When I woke on the second morning, though, something was different. It took me a while to realize what it was: The air recirculator was barely running. In an emergency, it manufactures air from electrolysis and reclamation of volatiles from waste storage; but even in non-emergencies, it's supposed to run in low-energy CO_2 scrubbing mode. This was low energy, all right, but it seemed too low. Was this a *second* zinger?

I checked the recirculator, took it apart, checked every part and sensor and circuit. It was operating correctly based on its sensor readings. It read a very low ambient carbon dioxide level, so it was running accordingly.

Why would carbon dioxide concentration be low? I knew I was breathing. But just as I was pondering this, my suit radio sounded again. "Good morning, Mister Morgan."

"I'm a little busy, Sarge, no time to chat."

"CO_2 levels a little puzzling?"

"Huh? How do you know that?"

"Tell me, boy genius, when you so brilliantly

diagnosed the snuff box yesterday and cleaned it up, did you use an air bottle to clean the filter?"

I'm not *completely* clueless. "You have spy eyes in here."

"We have spy eyes in there, cameras woven all through the fabriglass. Other sensors, too, and I doubt you'll ever notice them. You think we want rookies dying on their first practical? Besides, we have to watch you to grade you."

"But now you're interrupting my test *again*, just when I've got an equipment anomaly. That tells me I've got a problem—not an immediate danger, or you'd flunk me now."

"I can't comment."

"And these calls come suspiciously close to being a hint."

"Oh, now what sort of test would it be if I gave you a hint? In fact, to be sure I *don't* give you a hint, I'm signing off. But Morgan, one thing, and this is *very important*: You call me before you try to leave the prefab. *That is an order.* Got me?"

"Got it, Sarge." He disconnected.

So the calls *were* a hint. He wanted me to know he could see me. And what he asked about: Did I use an air bottle to clean the filter? Yes, I did. And then I put it back in the rack.

I checked that bottle and immediately I saw my error. I had forgotten to close the regulator when I racked it and clamped it into the feed system, so the bottle fed into the air system, right along with the bottle I had already opened. And since it was the first bottle in its bank, when it emptied, the next bottle in that bank fed right out through the regulator, too. For nearly two days, I had been pumping twice as much air as I expected.

And that would explain the CO_2 concentration. There was twice as much air, but I wasn't exhaling twice as much carbon dioxide. If the CO_2 level gets *too* low, you can hyperventilate; so the scrubbers cut back to keep CO_2 within a livable range.

But if the air pumps were putting out double air, shouldn't the pressure reflect that? I checked the console. All green lights. But then I looked at the pressure gauge. It was reading 1.96 standard; and the red zone where the light would change was at 2.0. I'm not sure why twice the air didn't make for twice the pressure. Maybe the dome expands under pressure just enough to keep below the limit. But whatever the reason, the light stayed green. Oh, Fontes was going to mark me down for that! He *hates* idiot lights.

And I hadn't noticed the air pressure. Oh, my ears had popped once or twice, but when you're in and out of suits enough times, you get so you hardly notice your ears popping. Other than that, the human body mostly equalizes internal and external pressure if the change is gradual, so it's hard to detect. After all, if it were easy to detect, we wouldn't need pressure gauges.

Or even idiot lights.

I turned off the second regulator and checked the air bottles. Well, I was going to get marked down more for all the wasted air, but I still had air to last more than a week, plus the air plant in a pinch. I could breathe through the end of this test.

So why had Fontes warned me to call before I left? I would lose a lot more air during my exit, get marked down some more. But he made it sound more serious than that.

So since I had time to spare, I tied into my suit comp. To simulate isolation, my comp was locked out of all Lunar nets for the duration of the test; but I had an encyclopedia chip in storage for my homework. I looked up pressure. And what did I find?

Well, I've saved this bottle of beer for just this point in the story. Let me open it, and . . . See those bubbles appear inside? See that head when I pour? That's carbon dioxide, dissolved into the liquid under pressure. When I released the pressure, it bubbled out of solution. When that happens in beer, we call it the best part of the beverage. When that happens in your body, especially nitrogen bubbles in your joints, we call it the bends, horribly painful and sometimes fatal. Caisson workers and scuba divers first discovered it, and died from it, until people learned how to gradually depressurize. It takes a long time, based on how much pressure and how long you were in it. The US Navy put a lot of work into dive and depressurization charts, but none in the encyclopedia covered my case.

I called Fontes. "How long?"

He chuckled, and I cringed. "We don't quite know, Mister Morgan. There aren't many cases where someone spent two days in double standard. The docs are sure you'll live, but you're going to stay there a while. We don't have a lot of scuba divers here on Luna, so they're consulting with experts Downside.

Best guess is you'll be depressurizing much of the weekend. And then you'll have one long incident report to fill out. And *then* . . . Well, this doesn't get you out of your assignment for Monday. That'll take up the rest of your weekend, I expect."

"And you didn't call and warn me."

"And make you flunk your test, Kenneth? Never. Your suit comp told us your vitals were good. Our dome sensors and the environment pack readings said you were in no danger, as long as you decompress before you leave the dome. And you could've saved yourself the trouble if you'd ever wondered why the airlock cycles were getting so long. Or if *even once* in your inspections you had *read the gauges instead of relying on your goddamn idiot lights!*"

And with that, he laughed again and disconnected.

Later, I received a program for the environment pack to manage the decompression in gradual stages over the next twenty hours. That was longer than anyone had ever heard of for decompression from double standard, but with such a long exposure, the experts didn't want to take any chances. And I think Fontes tacked on extra hours "just in case." So I was locked in the dome right through my date with Mary Sue Reilly. But at least I finished my homework during decompression, so I made Sunday brunch with Janelle Brooks. Not a total loss for the weekend, then.

And as for my incident report? Well, I wanted to make up some points from my exam, so I was extra thorough there; and when it was done, Fontes grudgingly acknowledged that it was a good case study and a good set of lessons learned. He even helped me submit it to the Lunar Survival Journal, and it's required reading today. So I guess that's my own contribution to our essential folklore: *Being a smartass is hazardous to your health.*

Headcase

Alex J. Kane

Jed's girl is sprawled naked on the floor of my apartment, her bare legs tangled in a soft black blanket, and she says, "I want what you have, Dax. To shape and polish and steer the world for a buffered credit line. I want you to make me a mod."

My eyes fall on the expanse of flesh glowing in the false candlelight, and it takes a second for her request to sink in.

"Not a chance," I say, feeling a knot on my forehead.

Sasha's been sneaking across town for these little rendezvous for over two months, and this is the first time she's shown an interest in my work. In my mastership over the virtual realm, instead of my prowess in the bedroom.

"Oh, *come on*," she says, craning her neck to look at me over her shoulder, "you did it for that prick, Nelson. Even Jed says you did."

I tell her, "Nelson wasn't my best friend's girl."

She grunts, and rises, stretching her arms in a crooked Jesus Christ pose. The blanket drops to the floor, and my eyes crawl along the full glory of her. Exposed.

Her dark breasts point accusingly at me. An intricate circuit-board pattern tattoo snakes down her ribs, does a triple-helix twist across her navel, and then disappears into the soft shadow along her inner thigh.

The yellow flicker of a reflected LED winks at the edge of her eyes, which I notice are shiny with moisture as she draws near.

"You'll do it," she says, "or I'll tell Jed we've been sleeping together."

I say, "Go to hell."

The slap rattles my skull, and one of her fingernails carves a warm slit across my cheek. Blood drips, tickles my face.

"You can tear down skyscrapers and rebuild them out of dust," she whispers. "You can erase entire data trails. Alter avatars. You could fucking *stop time*, if you wanted." Her teeth are an ivory cityscape inside her mouth. Her lips are a pair of rolling hills, the kind corporations buy up to plant endless rows of corn and hemp and soybean crop in.

Her entire face is exactly the sort of monopoly the old city used to be, back before WorldNet's pioneering neuroware went live, global, and in control. Before Lachiga towered over the heartland, its electro-chemical heartbeat the new lifeblood of civilization in the Americas.

Sasha's a relic of the distant past, and I shudder at the thought of her manipulating even the smallest facet of cyberspace. The digital realm needs a headcase like her in control like I need Jed finding out about the two of us.

"You're cruel," I tell her, holding my arms out, fingers splayed. I force a gentle laugh, still feeling the trickle of blood on my cheek. "But you don't need *me* to tell you that. I love you to death, Sash, but seriously—I'm not licensed for that shit."

She takes another step toward me. "You can do it, and you *will*."

I stammer the start of an unintelligible rebuttal, the words caught in my throat—

She cuts me off. "Now. Today. I'm tired of spoon-feeding the sick, wiping shit off the bedsheets of old, *dying* men."

It's not like having administrative capabilities will earn her a job; if anything, it'll only land her in prison, and perpetual debtorship. "Sweetie, please—"

And then she's got her left forearm held out, upturned to show me the knockoff touchpad she had installed, discernible only by the small black alpha-numerics tattooed along her wrist. An illegal street job, but impressive nonetheless.

She keys in Jed's online alias, pauses with her finger over the *send* command. A threat.

"All right, all right!" I yell, my own words a

stinging venom on my tongue. "I'll do it."

The green light visible beneath her skin winks to red, signaling a canceled transmission. I exhale, feel my head lighten with equal parts relief and fatigue.

Sasha's crazy-talk bullshit is moving from endearing to downright terrifying, and I wonder whether she's gradually gotten worse from all the time spent together or if she lost her mind long before Jed dragged her home.

I breathe a silent curse.

"What if Jed drops by, finds me digging around inside your head, and you're unconscious and blood's spewing out all over my hands and sofa?" I imagine his hand curling into a fist, rising up to eye-level, ready to smash my teeth.

Ouch.

"In that case," she says, "just tell him the truth. I asked you to give me the upgrade, and you said okay. Not the end of the world, jitter-boy."

"You say so," I sigh, then cross to the window and ease it open. The smell of a nearby coffee shop wafts in, along with the distinct stench of industrial pollution, on a stiff breeze.

Every year, the UA surgeon general puts out a report on the carcinogenic toxicity of each major metropolitan district in North and South America. Stars glitter across the night sky, obscured here and there by a brushstroke of gray-black cloud, and I wonder when my own cells will go kamikaze to escape the factory filth.

"Got any tranq?"

She does. No surprise.

I tell her to just get dressed and lie down.

"Take it now?" she asks.

"Wait." I hesitate, wince. "First, let me . . ." I kneel, bring my lips up to meet hers. Taste of wet, cherry-cola pink. Surge of electricity. Her eyes are a pair of crescent moons, blurred by the darkness.

She pops a lozenge from her candy-store purse collection into her mouth, swallows. "Love you, Dax. Like hell."

All that's beautiful in the human race sags into a lifeless sack of meat on my bed, and I heave a long, sharp exhalation that ends in a hiss.

Silently, I pray her trust isn't misplaced. My hands are shaking.

In the front room of my apartment, where the broadcast throne sits amid a mess of fiber-optics and various server components strung together in a semicircle, I dig through my toolbox and retrieve a surgical laser.

It's small, and fits my hand like an ink pen. It weighs about the same as a handgun.

The overhead lamp stutters alight; the milky flesh of Sasha's neck becomes semitransparent. A flick of the switch on the tungsten instrument in my still-quivering hand, and a blinding beam splits the skin along her upper spine.

Her implant is a centipede, a parasite, its tiny legs sunken deep into her brain stem. A single tube pumps and filters cerebrospinal fluid through the center of the device to prevent blockage or infection. The biochip itself sheds a soft halo of blue-green luminance.

In the harsh lamplight, a ghostly white cyst is visible underneath the implant. No doubt the result of a half-assed installation.

"God*damnit*."

How long, I think, *would it have been before Sasha saw a doctor? Before she discovered the infection?*

Tampering without a license is a felony right up there with dealing firearms. If I don't get the damn thing treated, she's dead; if I take her to a doctor, I'll face incarceration, guaranteed.

But everyone's heard the horror stories, how infections like this one kill. Fragile things, too— puncture it and the fluid spreads along the spine, paralyzing the body or destroying the brain. It all depends on the location.

This one's right under the occipital lobe, beneath the implant itself. Shit device, mostly: a testament to the unreliability of cheap black-market builds. Untold toxins.

Maybe I can phone in a favor, I think.

Except I don't know any street surgeons, or at least not any I'd trust with Sasha. With Jed's girl.

And an accomplice is really just a witness, just one more wild card stacked against you; under enough pressure, even your best friend will collapse into a confession.

Still shaking, I've got no choice but to finish out the operation myself.

Cut the omni out, scour the cyst with antibiotic spray, and install the new one. Slow and easy. Clean and careful.

By holding down the laser's switch, the beam intensifies and I burn away the links hardwired into

Sasha's brain stem. The fibrous hooks melt away, curl, and clatter to the floor.

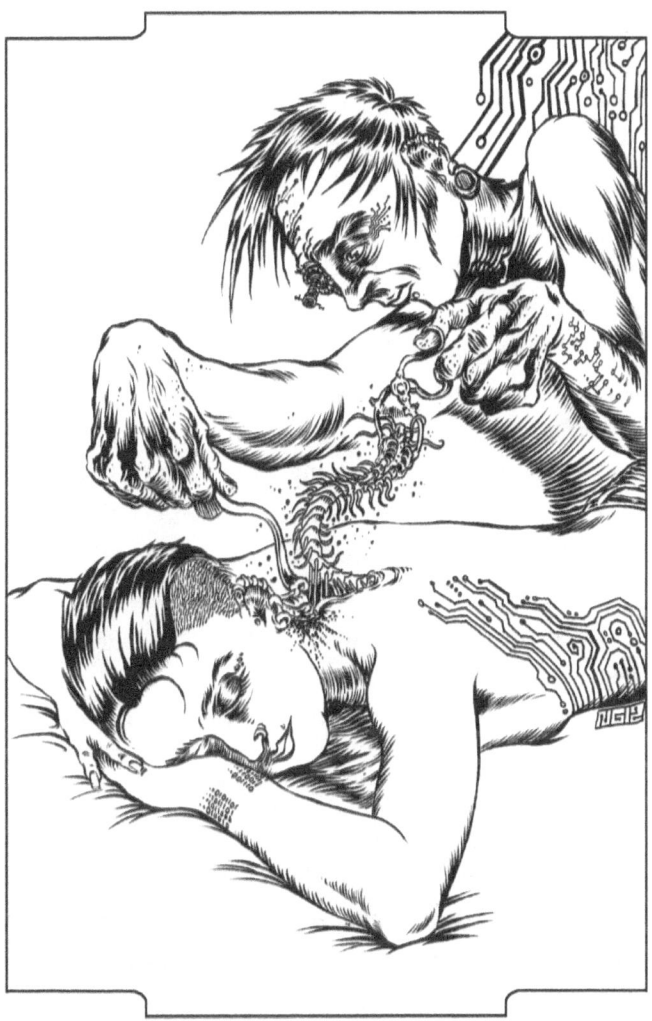

Blood seeps out from the tiny voids left by the omni, and I set the device down on the tray beside me. Fortune has favored me with a full bottle of antibiotic.

I spray.

Until the whole damn bottle's gone.

Staring at the bloated white sac of pus in the light, I glimpse its black roots. Veins. Legs sprouting from the bottom, twisting and searching, making their home in and about Sasha's spine.

I shiver, flick the surgical laser back on and go to work on the infectious bulb. As I burn away the black threads at the base, I reach for a paper towel to blot away the pinkish fluid that's starting to leak out in pearly gobs.

And then, just as the cyst is coming loose and the peculiar black veins are starting to break away, the bastard breaks—*pop!*

A quiet hiss follows, letting loose a deathly stink.

The breach in her spine where the infection sprouted is a tiny black hole, a hollow opening.

Bleeding the brain dry. Empty.

I look down at my hands, feel my breath catch in my throat. *My* hands.

Hands sticky with red, sticky with sweat, red with death.

Still unconscious, Sasha trembles, twitches.

Hemorrhaging.

The broadcast throne is meters away. Less than a minute is all it would take to track down Jed online, summon him over to my place, in the flesh. He's got a Magnetrak pass on him at the office, could easily ditch work and help me get Sasha to a hospital within a half-hour.

Except that I know, gazing at the bloodied hole at the base of her skull, at the mattress flecked with red, at my hands sticky with the heat of life falling away, there's no hope. She will die, is maybe dead already. I feel myself nod solemnly as I watch her go still.

What I've done is unforgivable, and I feel the weight of it on my chest, the oppressive dark of midnight stifling my every breath.

What'll Jed do when he sees this? I wonder. *Will he kill me first, or himself?*

I pray silently for the former. I think maybe I deserve it, not only for betraying my friend and sleeping with his girl, but for all the lying and deceit. For listening to Sasha's wishes just to save my own ass. A dilemma of my own choosing, I realize.

Yep. I fucking asked for this.

Under my arm, holstered, is a contraband Xing-Barron .45 handgun. A hazard of the underground apps sales business is, people will sometimes try and kill you. In general, competition is a good thing—except in my industry, where every participant is a social pariah.

I've never been forced to fire the thing, but now I give the idea careful consideration. A hole in my own head seems a swift path to exile, to freedom.

Jed will be home in a matter of hours. Cleaning up the blood, thinking up an alibi . . .

Impossible.

The pistol feels heavy in my hand, the smell of cold steel repugnant. I draw the muzzle up against my skull, and look once more at the lifeless beauty lying on my bed. Marred by ghastly blood, motionless as a statue.

Then Jed's in my mind's eye, his face twisted

with fury.

I holster the gun, and bolt for the door. After a moment's hesitation, I turn back to check Sasha's eyes. To my relief, they're closed. Peaceful, even.

Under my own suddenly immense weight, I collapse.

By the time I'm able to stand, I glance down at the bloodstained sheet to see my own face painted in tears next to Sasha's hand.

My thoughts are too erratic to operate my own neuroware interface. I can check my credit balance later, I decide. I see only the faint time display in my field of vision: *12:39am.*

The vacuum-shuttle to London leaves in about an hour. The train to Lachiga leaves in fifteen minutes.

Lachiga it is.

My status as a mod will immunize me somewhat against the tiresome protocols of Lachiga's security drones, making it easy to land a new apartment outside of Jed's tighter budget. There I'll be able to hide, resume work with some degree of normalcy.

It'll be up to Jed whether or not he wants to turn me in. I imagine him finding her, the inevitable scream as he apprehends that she'll never wake.

I lift Sasha's hand, kiss it one last time. And then I'm out the door, into the chill dark of night.

A bass-drum pulse thudding in my ears, the whisper goes unheard: *Forgive me, man.*

Final
Relocation

David Tallerman

Dom was in his cubicle when the announcement came.

It didn't seem important at the time; just another announcement, not even the first of that day. The crisp female voice was accompanied by a crisp female face, too perfect to be real. She began with her credentials: She was a SocAd announcer, and this was a priority message. It was redundant information. All announcements were from SocAd, all were priority.

"Everyone knows the manifold benefits the versaTile has brought to our lives," she said. "Now, new from SocAd labs comes versaTile v.5, a radical development in the field of personal space allocation. Here to tell you more is professor Lanstern, speaking directly from SocAdCen."

Lanstern, his name untraceable without his full designate, could have been anyone. He was neither young nor old. His features were undistinguished. Yet he projected an aura of benevolence and intelligence; in his own way he was as attractive as the female announcer. Lanstern proceeded to discourse about v.5, striking a fine balance between technicality and vagueness. The gist seemed to be that these new tiles could move under their own power, though the specifics eluded Dom. Finally the announcer returned, and informed him that sometime soon he would be allocated a v.5 PAD—whatever a PAD was. Further personalized announcements would follow.

When Dom went to the cafeteria, everyone was talking about it. The general tone seemed enthusiastic, but it was Chas who collared him first. Chas was built like a bundle of wire, with his graying head stuffed clumsily on top. Everything about him exuded tiredness except for his fiercely glittering eyes, which latched onto Dom and held him. "It's not such a big deal. V.4 was a letdown, what did it really do over 3.7? A few interface upgrades, that's all."

Dom had no extreme feelings either way. He was impressed by the remarkable versaTile technology, but not interested enough to discuss, let alone defend it. He excused himself, found a corner where he could eat alone, and listened instead. No one seemed any wiser than he was. There was general agreement that the new tiles were in some way movable, and speculation as to how this might improve things, but nothing that was more than guesswork.

●○●

By the next day, Dom had forgotten about the v.5 announcement. The talk in the cafeteria had moved on to other subjects: highlights from the entertainment channels, the crisis in GLA shell, the still-persisting rumors regarding the LUNA expansion. Messages from SocAd easily became background noise, for it was difficult to tell what might be important and, with the exception of eccentrics like Chas, no one much tried.

When, five days later, the announcements of relocation began, it surprised almost everyone.

Dom, amongst the first, was alarmed when a tile close by began to reel off his designate. He looked up, following the noise, but there was nothing to see except the text of the message that was currently being voiced from thin air.

"Your Private Adaptive Domicile, hereafter PAD, is now available for residence. All personal properties have been transferred in your absence. Address of PAD is as follows: UKLIV 34/S71-B4/6L3. This address has been mapped to your designate, and a printout will follow. Please do not attempt to return to your former residence, as deconstruction is in process."

He looked at the square of paper spooling from the wall. It was in the standard format of shell code, block number, corridor, and room. For a moment he tried to process the idea that it represented what would be his home from now on. Then, giving up, he crumpled the sheet into a pocket.

Throughout the day, Dom heard the echo of other personalized announcements from other cubicles.

Obviously the upgrade project was well on its way. Realizing that it would be busier than usual on the shuttles and in the corridors, with everyone hunting new addresses, he decided to leave early.

The ploy paid off. The crowd for his new shuttle was already large, and swelling, but Dom was small and succeeded in maneuvering quickly to the front. When the patchwork rectangle of the shuttle slid noiselessly against the platform, he managed to leap aboard and clutch a rail before the press behind him burst into the carriage.

The doors whispered shut and the shuttle's imperceptible motion began. Tiles spaced along the inner walls lit with a display of the next station number. There were thirty two stops before his. His new address was a greater distance away than his old one, and he'd have to allot more time for the journey—or rather (since the actual traveling time amounted to next to nothing) for the lengthy embarkations and disembarkations at each additional station.

Dom waited patiently through the riots of arrivals and departures at each stop, through the brief intervals of silent, unfelt travel between, until the number of his station appeared on the display tiles. It was harder getting out than it had been getting in. Once on the platform, however, Dom quickly slipped free of the press. He edged towards the wall and looked around for his block exit.

Once he was into the wide block arterial the going became easier. All the corridors looked the same, just as all the stations and arterials looked the same, and only the Universal Addressing System made navigation possible. But Dom hardly noticed it, and found his turning with only the faintest flicker of conscious thought. The maze of interminable white-tiled passages didn't bother him, and it made the relocations simpler, since apart from the range of letters and numbers along the walls this could easily have been his old corridor.

When he finally found his PAD and stepped inside, his reaction was much the same. The shape was different, noticeably smaller; the bed was in a different corner and so was the sink. But in a few minutes he knew he'd have forgotten these dis-similarities. For a short while it would be as if his mind was playing tricks, misleading him with false memories. After that the room would be the size it had always been, the sink and bed in their familiar places. That was how it went.

He began by inspecting the versaTiles that composed his new PAD. They were the same pristine white as the v.4s that made up his office, the passages outside, the shuttle and everything else. Or were they perhaps a faint shade darker? Certainly, he thought that they were fractionally smaller.

Dom decided to test the interface system. He tapped twice in rapid succession with the tips of his fingers upon a tile halfway up one wall. Sure enough, the familiar menu flickered up. There were a couple of new options, others missing or listed under different categories. It wouldn't take long to work that out. He turned on vocal command and used that to call an entertainment channel, resizing the screen to cover most of one wall. Apart from a brief meal from the dispenser, he spent the rest of the evening watching listlessly, occasionally changing channels or being interrupted by SocAd announcements.

As he watched, he remembered what Chas had said all those days ago. He'd been right; v.5 was no big deal after all. The handful of improvements were probably just there to sugar the pill of another relocation into smaller apartments. It didn't bother Dom, who didn't expect much. Others would be up in arms for a day or two; the optimists always took these things hardest. Still, no one could deny that SocAd had delivered on their promises to reduce congestion.

By the time Dom fell asleep he'd all but forgotten about the relocation, had become as minimally accustomed to his new room as he'd been to his old one. He slept the same blank sleep as every night.

When he woke the next morning, however, confused and bleary-eyed, the room *did* seem different. At first he thought it was just the last vestiges of nostalgia for his previous home, and staggered to the sink to splash water across his face, sure the feeling would pass.

It didn't. It wasn't just that the room was smaller than he'd been accustomed to; it actually seemed to have shrunk in comparison to his memories of the previous night. The wall had been further from the door. When he glanced up, the ceiling seemed closer to his head.

Dom stripped and bathed himself with water from the sink, watching thoughtfully as the tiles at his feet drank the excess liquid. Using voice command he set a row of tiles for moderate heat and stood beside them, steam misting from his thin body. When he was dry enough he pulled on fresh clothes from the dispenser.

It was just his imagination, he told himself, probably a natural reaction to the stress of yesterday's move. Steeling himself with a deep tug of breath, he went out into the world.

● ○ ●

At lunchtime the canteen was in an uproar, a running battle between optimists and naysayers. The fierceness of opinion and the aggression it brought out in his otherwise placid colleagues bewildered Dom. He knew his views would make no difference to anything, so why have them? But others obviously felt differently.

Just as he was getting up to leave, he overheard a conversation that startled him, and stopped, distracted.

"You know, I'd swear my room got smaller in the night."

"What? Don't be crazy."

"What's crazy? They said, didn't they? Moving tiles, tiles that rebuild themselves. Don't you remember?"

"Crazy. No, I don't remember."

"I suppose you've forgotten what the A stands for too?"

But at that point others began to leave and Dom, caught in the jostle, was forced to abandon his eavesdropping.

● ○ ●

Dom, used to discarding information as rapidly as he learned it, was surprised to find as he walked the last distance home that he was still thinking about the overheard exchange. He did remember, suddenly, what the A stood for—the A in PAD, as he'd realized. What exactly was an 'Adaptive Domicile'? Had his room really shrunk while he slept; could they do such a thing? The thought unsettled him, more than anything had in years. As he turned into his corridor it seemed narrower, the ceiling fractionally lower. Could they *do* that?

When he looked, almost fearfully, through the open door into his room, it was undeniably smaller. Not only that, it had changed shape, was now more square than oblong. It took a surprising effort of will to put his foot over the threshold. When he did, a wave of disorientation washed through him. The floor might as well have been the ceiling; the walls could as easily have been the floor. Dom glared at them with distrust, wanting to steady himself, not daring to for fear that the room would somehow betray him. He stood for a long while, rocking unsteadily on his heels.

Nothing changed. Slowly he began to wonder if it might have been his imagination after all. The space before him seemed undeniably, unalterably solid.

Yet, the A had to mean something. He was willing to admit that he might be going crazy, that the speaker in the canteen had been as well, he knew of enough people who had—but the A must mean something.

He would have to not think about it. Not thinking

about things was the best way to stay sane. He sat on the bed and called up an entertainment channel, tried to follow and laugh along with it. After an hour he went to the food dispenser and requested a meal. He felt a little better after that. Perhaps the room was changing in size; perhaps he was losing his mind. Either way, what was the use of worrying?

● ○ ●

Though Dom wasn't pleased when Chas collared him in the canteen the next day, he didn't try to resist. There was no question about v.5 anymore. Dom had woken in an undeniably smaller space and had gone out into a corridor barely recognizable from the previous day. The dimensions were completely different, as were those of the arterials and stations. Only the consistency of the universal addressing system had made the journey possible.

Everyone had woken to similar experiences; it was the one topic of conversation. Chas looked pale and gaunt, more so than usual, and obviously hadn't slept. Dom, expecting a tirade against the new tiles and subsequent decrease in space, was surprised when instead Chas said, "Do you remember when they last mentioned LUNA?"

Dom shook his head. For a while, the proclamations about the planned LUNA expansion had been optimistic, and almost daily. When the last one had been, though, he found impossible to say.

"That was it. The last chance. You know that, right? If they're not talking about it anymore, that means there's no hope anymore."

Dom, noncommittal, didn't answer. It was true that silence from SocAd on a particular topic was generally bad news. Yet there had been occasions when the opposite held true, where some significant new development appeared with no fanfare at all.

Chas didn't press for a response, and Dom assumed their conversation was done. Then, just as he was about to start eating, Chas—his voice more thin and shaken than before—said, "Do you ever dream, Dom?"

Thrown by the change of subject, all Dom could think to reply was, "What?"

"Do you even know what it means? You're young, you wouldn't. Dreaming is . . . is pictures in your mind when you're sleeping. Like your brain is telling itself stories, or . . . you wouldn't understand. You couldn't. I used to dream when I was your age, but I don't anymore."

Dom, not understanding or wanting to involve himself, just nodded.

"There were good dreams and bad dreams. And after a while, you'd always work out you were dreaming—that you were having a nightmare—and then you'd wake yourself up. Do you see?"

Dom nodded again. Then, realizing Chas wasn't paying attention to him anymore, he concentrated on his food. He finished his meal in silence, conscious that he was the only one eating. When he got up to leave and said goodbye, Chas didn't answer.

● ○ ●

After that, things became normal again for a few days. The tiles continued to rearrange themselves, silently molding the world into a fresh pattern for each new day. It never happened when there was someone there to see. However, diversions had become commonplace in public areas, and PADs were altered during allocated sleeping hours. Almost everyone began to accept it. A few tried to stop sleeping. Dom grew used to waking each morning to find the walls a little closer together, to new shelves and alcoves having materialized to compensate for the ever-diminishing space.

Then, late one evening, the announcement came—a female face again, as beautiful and subtly unreal as all the SocAd announcers. The message began with Dom's designate and continued, "You are advised that your workspace has been deemed non-critical and is closed to access. Please do not attempt to reach your workspace, as deconstruction is in process. Facilities to continue your work function are available via versaTile link. SocAd asks for your patience during the process of restructuring."

It was a hard blow to Dom. He wasn't sociable, since the nature of his existence had made it so difficult to make or maintain relationships. Nevertheless, his office space—indeed, his half hour in the canteen—had been his only opportunity to be in the company of other human beings. No one spoke to each other in the corridors and arterials, no one socialized after work hours because of the difficulties inherent in travel. Dom had no idea what the dimensions of UKLIV were these days, except that they were vast. Without the shuttles, transit would be inconceivable. But, he thought, the shuttle tubes took up space, just like the offices, like the corridors and arterials. And there was no space to spare. Presumably they would be cannibalized by the versaTiles, for new PADs or some other purpose. He could understand the necessity. Yet the idea of losing that half hour of interaction, which he'd never consciously valued, twisted his stomach now.

On a whim, he went out into the corridor. The ceiling was very low, mere centimeters above his head. If he'd stretched out his arms he could have touched both walls. He set off in the direction of his station. Though only a few hours had passed, it took much longer to reach the arterial than the reverse journey had earlier in the day, and when he finally came to it, it was only twice the width of the corridor. A few days ago, two dozen people could have comfortably walked abreast there.

In the direction of the station he could see that the passage came to a dead end; or, rather, to a line of apartment doors. He'd never been in the other direction, and didn't dare to now. The disadvantage of the Universal Addressing System was that unless you knew exactly where you were going, it was practically impossible to find your way. Was there any exit from the block now? Were there any stations left? Could he reach one if he tried, if he had the courage to try? And where was there to go if he did?

Dom started back in the direction of his PAD. After a few minutes he was suddenly gripped by the irrational fear that it would have disappeared while he was away, and for the first time in years he broke into a run. But the door was still there, and even the inside of the PAD hadn't noticeably changed.

● ○ ●

For the next two days, Dom worked diligently in front of a versaTile screen, following the work hours he'd kept in the office. He didn't try to go outside. It was pointless, and he was afraid to. He slept no more than four hours each night, and not according to the allocated times. Nevertheless he woke on each occasion to find that the walls had edged closer together. The room was growing cramped now, and—even for Dom, who'd never known anything except confined spaces—was becoming claustrophobic.

There had been no more announcements from SocAd.

On the third day he woke to find that the door had disappeared. He knew it hadn't led anywhere, that there was nowhere it could have led. Nevertheless, there was something to be said for the illusion of freedom, even knowing it was an illusion. It took a great effort not to panic, to start beating against those blank, unbreachable tiles.

Instead, Dom forced himself to sit on the bed and watch an entertainment channel. He found himself hoping for an announcement, an assurance that this was only a temporary measure—that soon things would return to some semblance of normality.

None came. That night he drifted in and out of something like sleep, partly rousing himself again and again, staring around in terror each time and then falling back exhausted. In his confusion, he knew he

was scared of the walls, though he couldn't remember
why.

Dom finally fell completely asleep in the early
hours of the morning. He didn't realize it. He was used
to transitioning from wakefulness to wakefulness, and
there was nothing in his experience for this: He was
still seeing and, on some dim level, still feeling. It
should have been alarming, and wasn't. Rather, he felt
at peace, unafraid in a way he'd never consciously
known.

He was suspended freely. There were no walls.
Most of what he could see was darkness, though
patterned everywhere with countless, shuddering
pinpoints of brilliance. Directly before him, a gray orb
hung, its face pitted and marked without apparent
pattern. Though he had no frame of reference, he felt
sure it must be vast beyond anything he'd witnessed
or could have imagined; more vast even than UKLIV.
Staring at it, the effect was something like being very
close to a pale-irised eye, if the sclera were black
rather than white. It was beautiful—incredible in its
beauty.

Dom woke. For a moment he managed to hold on
to the image clear in his mind, and then it was gone.
Forgetting, too, that he had no workplace to go to, he
lurched out of bed, struck his head on the ceiling,
stumbled and jarred his elbow against the wall. He fell
back. The room was tiny now, less than a third of its
original size. There was space enough for the bed, the
food dispenser and sink, but nothing else. He couldn't
stand up. Sat in a crouch, his head brushed the ceiling.

Dom lay back and covered his face with his arms,

trying very hard not to think.

After a long while he dared uncover his eyes. The room was, at least, no smaller. His body ached with stillness. He became suddenly aware that he would have to cope with this somehow or soon lose his mind. Once that happened, he'd begin to forget fundamentals such as eating and drinking, and to defecate only in the corner where the tiles could more easily absorb it. He didn't want that. He had to keep hold of the hope that this was temporary; that SocAd had some plan and that it included him.

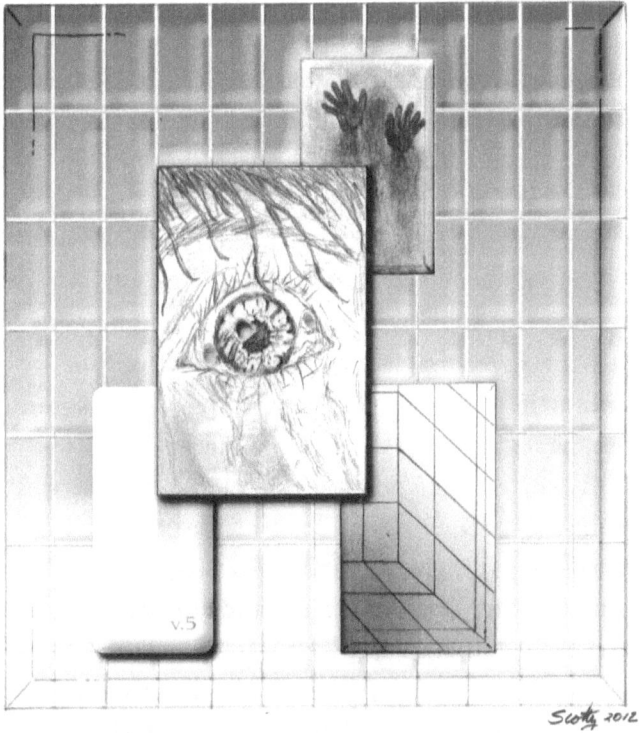

He forced himself to get up. He ordered food from the dispenser and ate it sitting on the end of the bed.

Then he stripped and washed, hunched beside the sink. There was no point trying to work, even if he could have maneuvered into a suitable position. Instead, he voice-activated a set of tiles, deciding to leave a channel on permanently in the hope that an announcement would be made and that he'd be awake to hear it.

Dom ate again in the evening, although he had no appetite. A few hours after, he fell by stages back into half-sleep. There had been no message from SocAd, only the endless drone of an entertainment channel.

The next morning there was no longer space to sit up. The room was as wide as the bed and a little longer, with a gap at the end beneath the sink. If he could have wriggled into that gap he might have been able to wash, but it would have been awkward and uncomfortable. Realistically, there was nothing he could do except lie back, arms tucked by his sides.

Though Dom knew he should be terrified, he couldn't find it in himself. It occurred to him that he'd been afraid for most of his life—of everything, of nothing in particular. Now, when it was too late for fear, he had nothing to be except numb.

By voice command, he moved the channel screen to the ceiling. He couldn't concentrate on it. He was conscious of weight, a tremendous weight above him—whether it was his imagination or not, he couldn't say. In his mind's eye was an image, a hallucination perhaps, of hundreds, thousands of PADs, stacked beside and upon each other. He could sense it, *feel* it: the presence of other people beyond his head and feet, above and below and beside him, in countless rows and layers.

Unbidden, a memory came to mind, something Chas had told him once. He'd said that, years ago, people had chosen sometimes not to cremate the dead; that instead they'd been buried in the ground and left to decay. Chas hadn't bothered to explain why anyone would do such a thing and Dom had never wondered, until now. He lay staring at the ceiling, thinking about it.

At some point in the evening, the entertainment channel shivered and went dead. A few minutes later the lights guttered and dimmed, fading to a meager glow.

It didn't concern Dom. He was waiting for an announcement from SocAd, and nothing else mattered.

● ○ ●

The message that he had been hoping for came, finally, in the early hours of the morning. There was no image, only voice.

It said, "Please prepare yourself for relocation."

Dom lay back and did as he'd been instructed.

Putting Down Roots

Grayson Bray Morris

My name was posted to the Tau Ceti Three crew list, along with my mother's. Two sixth-years saw my broad grin and came over to look.

"NiIIIice," the girl singsang, dripping puffs of lavender lashglitter onto my shoulder with every blink. "But don't get stuck alone with *that* pilot. He's soOOOoo boring."

Her boyfriend—he had to be; he was dusted in lavender lashglitter—hooted. "She won't have a choice. It's her first survey. She'll be ship-bound."

"Well, don't encourage him. Wear earplugs at aaAAaall times."

I raised an eyebrow.

"You don't want him to think you're listening. He's

got this thing about filling up empty silence with what he calls conversation. The inner workings of the com system. The proper descent vector for using minimum fuel. Like that."

The girl tapped her right ear with long nails finely splayed into fans. "Earplugs."

The boy laid a proprietary hand around the girl's neck, and I saw his nails matched hers. Oh, *honestly*. "They'll keep the Raging Bore at bay. And if worse comes to worst, you can always let in a spider."

They walked off with the razorblade laugh of the in-crowd bully, and I decided I liked the pilot on principle.

●○●

Time seemed to dilate until hours were years, but launch day finally came. I was going to a *planet*! Never mind that I would be confined to the survey shuttle; I would be off the *Ceiaides* for the first time in my life. Even a psych eval droid for pilot couldn't have dampened my spirits.

The Raging Bore turned out to be a soft-around-the-middle young man named Mart Jansen with curly blond hair and a thick beard. Dr. Egil Parnum I knew; she was my mother. Our fourth and final crewmate was a tiny, honey-skinned woman named Dr. Bjalili Okara.

The two-light-year trip down to Tau Ceti Three took forty-six hours: thirty-nine wormhole and seven straight-space. The pilot was in the cockpit for a few hours at each end to maneuver us away from the station and onto the surface, but the ship was on autopilot for the rest of the trip. The four of us spent our waking hours in the mainbay. Despite the sixth-years' stationside warning, the pilot was quiet as a mouse, and I felt smug. He'd turn out to be fascinating when you gave him a chance, and we'd be fast friends by the end of the trip. Watch their glitter-addled brains wrap around *that*.

"Hey, Mart, why don't you join us for a game of cicce?" I waved my hand of cards.

"No, thanks. I don't know how." He looked up briefly, then reburied himself in his reader.

Or maybe I'd be spending the eight planetside days talking to myself.

"I'll be interested to see the numbers on the higher animals this year. We're getting close," said Dr. Okara. "Another few decades and Teasy Three will be ready for colonization."

"Dr. Tresnik told our class that Epilepsy Five was going gangbusters. He said it might outpace Teasy Three," I said.

"Could be. But the Alpha Cen system is going to win this race by a light-year. I hear they're opening up the colonization roster on Acey Twelve next month. Or Nivenia, I should say, now they've named it. Apparently it's filled with woody Iridaceae." Dr. Okara chuckled at her own joke.

"They say it's a beautiful world. Even more beautiful than Earth." I glanced at my mother. "I'm thinking of signing up."

"You are? That sounds exciting." My mother snorted air but Dr. Okara went on unperturbed. "Have you ever been to the Alpha Cen system, Laru?"

"No. I've never been to a planet, period. The thought of *living* on one makes me feel like a pioneer."

Mart had stopped reading to watch us.

"The real pioneering work is taking a hunk of dead rock and turning it into a living, breathing ecosystem," my mother sniffed.

"Oh ho ho." Dr. Okara grinned. "Looks like I've stumbled into a family can of worms."

Mart stood up and plucked rapidly at the curls of his beard. "Can I, uh, get anyone some coffee?"

Were we making him nervous?

"Me," Dr. Okara said, raising a finger.

"Me, too, please," I said, smiling my friendliest smile. My mother nodded, and he trundled off to the galley.

"What are you signing up as?" Dr. Okara asked as she pulled her feet up under her on the smaller mainbay couch.

"They've got eight slots for biologists, but I won't be finished studying in time to apply for one of those." My mother snorted again; I ignored her. "They have a lot of slots for elementary school teachers, and not enough people to fill them, I've heard."

Mart returned with four cups of coffee. He placed two cubes each of sweetener and tannin binder in front of me, then watched intently as I dropped both cubes of binder in.

How very odd. Okay; okay; odd was okay. We were still going to be friends, or at least decent acquaintances, because I was *not* going to agree with the opinions of two snot-for-brains trend-lemmings.

"Oh, Laru," my mother sighed. "I can't believe you

want to throw away a promising career on the cutting edge of exobiology to go put down roots on some primitive planet just being colonized. You're only nineteen. At least finish your education first."

We'd been having this conversation for months. To my mother, planetary life was for placid, stupid people who lacked imagination. The real thrill was out among the stars, playing God on the natural satellites orbiting them. There were twelve Ceti Sector planets in various stages of terraforming, and she had a hand in them all. Epsilon Eridani Four was just developing a greenhouse-gas cover; Tau Ceti Two had gotten its first injection of cyanobacteria. Tau Ceti Seven was scheduled for plant life later in the year. When my mother wasn't out surveying the progress of gestating worlds, she conducted research on nanite-enhanced terraforming strategies back on the space station. Her work was varied and complex, and she loved it. She said it was exhilarating.

It sounded interesting. It sounded mentally stimulating. But exhilarating? I thought creating a community of human beings from wildly different places on a brand-new world with wide-open vistas sounded exhilarating. I'd watched plenty of old vids of Earth and Mars. I wanted to live in a place with sunrises and sunsets, rain that fell at non-programmed intervals, forests to lose myself in, hills and mountains and rivers and lakes. I wanted the planetary experience.

The distance was the only thing that gave me pause: It took two weeks to travel the wormhole network from Alpha Centauri to the Ceti Sector. I'd be lucky to see my mother once a year. I'd seen her wrestling not to throw that in my face just to keep me on the *Ceiaides*. I loved my mother for that, for fighting fair.

● ○ ●

Mart touched our ship down with a dancer's grace just after breakfast. Automated sensors collected the first routine samples of atmosphere; by lunchtime, the ship's bioanalyzer had manufactured antibodies to the local airborne pathogens, and doctors Parnum and Okara went out on survey. I sat twiddling my thumbs in the mainbay with Mart for the five-hour wait; until my mother and Dr. Okara returned with the first samples to process, I had no duties.

"So. So, uh, Miss Parnum, this is your first trip planetside?"

Okay, see? He was opening up. Let the bonding begin. "Yes. I'm a fourth-year. Biology."

"The same field as your mother."

I nodded. He nodded. He drummed his fingers on his thighs, then pulled at his beard. "Biology. I was terrible at biology. I'm not good with animals and plants. Machines are more my thing. I would have liked to go into nanotech, but my scores weren't strong enough."

Nanotech was very complicated stuff; almost no one had the scores for it. "How'd you decide to become a pilot?"

"My dad would take me out sometimes. I liked sitting in the cockpit, reading off all the monitors. One hundred and thirty-eight individual pieces of information that let you predictably control a complicated machine. And the precision! It's a thing of beauty. For example, do you know how a retroflux thruster works?"

"No, I don't." The words *Raging Bore* popped into my brain before I could stop them.

"It detects changes in temperature down to the picokelvin, and changes in density down to the milligram per cubic meter, and uses a series of nanosecond measurements to determine the vehicle's distance from the surface *and* the amount of friction to apply to the landing pads. See, the measurements form a Gerrison curve, and based on the tangential acceleration of the curve vector, the retroflux unit can tell what kind of surface material it's approaching—titanium alloy, organic matter, bioasphalt, whatever—and adjust accordingly. It's incredibly precise, and completely predictable."

"I see."

"I can show you how it works, if you'd like." He stood up and gestured toward the cockpit.

I saw an hour sitting in the pilot's chair—no, standing behind it while *he* sat in it and pointed out dial after dial after button after switch. "That's nice of you to offer, but to be honest, I'm not really a fan of shuttle tech. Besides, I've got some reading to do for class."

"Oh, yeah, of course," he said, almost before I'd finished speaking. He pulled at his beard and looked around the room. "Well, I'll leave you to your books." He pointed at my reader on the table. "Can I at least get you a cup of coffee, or something?"

I looked up at the disappointed blue eyes in his pale, pudgy face. He seemed angry with himself, and that made me angry with the sixth-years—and myself. "Coffee sounds good. Tell you what—why don't I teach you how to play cicce?"

I thought he'd say no again, but he surprised me. His eyes widened as he smiled and ran a hand through his hair. "Sure. Why not?" He turned toward the galley, then turned back with a frown. "I have to warn you, Miss Parnum, I'm not very good at card games. I haven't played much."

"That's okay," I said, tapping controls to raise the low table to card-playing level and lift the smaller formfoam couch from its floor recess and inflate it. "Everybody has to start somewhere. And stop calling me Miss Parnum. Call me Laru."

● ○ ●

My mother and Dr. Okara returned with a rollcrate full of samples and some kind of skin rash. "I'm itchy all over," Dr. Okara complained.

Mart looked really alarmed.

"It's not that unusual," my mother said. "The analyzer only screens for serious pathogens. Survey crew come back with sniffles and rashes all the time. Biodiversity makes for a healthy ecosystem."

"This is the first time anyone's gotten sick on my run," Mart said. "That's twenty-two trips. One in twenty-two doesn't sound common to me."

"Relax, Mart. It's normal." She put a hand on his arm and smiled at him. "Trust me; I've been doing this for a long time."

Mart nodded, and she let go of his arm.

After dinner I suggested we do some singing. I love to sing, and my mother and I can belt out a pretty nice duet.

After our third or fourth song, Dr. Okara sniffed, coughed, and stood up. "Well, lovely as this is, I'm going to hit the sack. I'm bushed, and this damned itch is making me cranky."

"You do that," my mother boomed. Singing always put her in a good mood. "Rudolph the red-nosed reindeer."

I laughed beside Mart on the larger mainbay couch and let myself fall against the rounded armrest. Dr. Okara looked at me like I was sprouting woody Iridaceae from my nose. "It's an old Terran song," I explained through my laughter. "Your nose is a little red."

"Aha. Charming." Dr. Okara raised a hand and turned toward the cabins. "I'm out of here. Good night, all."

"Where did you learn all these ancient songs?" Mart asked as we readied the table for a game of cicce.

"My father was a music buff. After he died, we played his collection as a way of remembering him. We learned our favorites by heart. It's a lot of fun, singing together."

"If you can call it singing," Mart ventured, his eyes darting from one of us to the other.

"Good one, Mart," my mother said, thumping him on the leg with a laugh. "I knew you had it in you." She played a card. "And you're very good at cicce."

Mart blushed, looked at me with a shy grin, and

ran a hand through his hair, and I wished those sixth-years could see us. Raging Bore? Hardly.

I slapped a card triumphantly onto the table. "But not good enough. Cicce!"

My mother groaned. I stood and threw both arms into the air, eyes closed, head bobbing, hands in the old-Earth victory *V*.

Mart gathered the cards and looked at the clock.

"Oh! It's late. Past protocol."

My mother looked over. "Just twenty minutes. Relax, Mart. I don't sleep much back on the station, either. I'll be fit enough for duty tomorrow." She winked at me.

"Still, it's protocol." Mart plucked at his beard.

"That it is. Hup, off to bed with us all. Don't stay up reading, Laru." My mother leaned across the couch and plucked a skinboot from the floor. "You've got your work cut out for you tomorrow, analyzing the sequencer results. A hundred and eighty samples will take longer than you think." She yawned and held up a hand. "Good night."

"Sleep tight, Mama," I said, standing and stretching. "Good night, Mart."

"Good night, Dr. Parnum, Miss Parnum." Mart smiled at me. "I mean Laru."

I lilted to my cabin, happy for the way Mart was responding to a little friendship and eager to stretch my biologist's wings in the lab tomorrow. In ten hours I would be touching things that had grown on this planet.

● ○ ●

My professors on the *Ceiaides* had taught me to expect mutations in the Terran organisms transplanted to Ceti Sector worlds. Over the years, my mother had described many unexpected, and often beautiful, adaptations to which the older terraforming worlds' unique variations from Terran gravity and atmospheric pressure were beginning to give rise: the enlarged butterflies of Tau Ceti One; the swaying, lace-like plants of Alpha Centauri Sixteen. But the mutations in front of me were improbable beyond reason.

"Laru? Lunch is ready." Mart stood at the entry to the survey ship's lab. "What's wrong?"

"These samples. The DNA isn't consistent. They're like bizarre hybrids."

Mart cocked his head. "Like what?"

"Two species intermingled. Like, say, two types of rose bush. But these are beyond possible. Take this one—this is a spider crossed with a birch tree." I angled the sequencer's screen toward him.

His expression of worry turned to stone before he looked away. "Ah. I get it. Little Miss Funnypants. I'm not *that* gullible, whatever they told you about me."

Oh, crap. Why did I have to mention spiders? I opened my mouth to apologize, but he was already gone. I stood up and shouted. "Hey! You know I'm not like that. I'm not joking, Mart."

I heard him pad back toward me, then saw his face peer in. "You're not?"

"No."

"Oh." He took another step in. "How is that possible?"

"Exactly. How is that possible? I don't know." I waved him closer. "All the birch tree samples Mom and Dr. Okara brought in yesterday have two kinds of DNA, from two completely different species. They're *Betula papyrifera* everywhere except in the mitochondria. And there, they're something else. An arachnid. An amphibian. Each one is different. So far, I've found two species of fungus, one protist, four plants, and eight animals encapsulated in the mitochondrial nucleotide barcodes."

Mart was watching me intently, and I realized he was trying to understand what I had said. My ears began to burn: I'd just given my own retroflux thruster speech, to a much better audience than I had been.

"It's like finding a . . . a com unit speaker inside a thruster," I started again. "Not stuck onto the side of the control panel, but deep inside the thruster itself, wired in like it belongs there."

His eyes registered comprehension. "That's very odd."

"It certainly is." I stood up and prowled the tiny lab. "The birch samples are the only ones like this. Everything else is what it's supposed to be." I stopped pacing and stared at Mart as if the answer to the riddle was written in miniature script somewhere on his face.

"Come eat lunch?" he said, squirming under my scrutiny. I nodded and followed him to the galley.

"How did all this other DNA worm its way into the birch cells, Mart?" I watched him peel back the steamy polylactide film on a serving of fungoid tetrazzini, then funnel the condensing water into two cups of granulated strawberry. I wasn't really asking; I was thinking out loud. He surprised me by answering.

"Dead spider scraped off the birch trunk?"

I shook my head. "All the foreign DNA was *inside* the birch cells. If it had been a dead spider, the spider DNA would be outside the birch cells. Like this cup on the table." I picked it up. "Touching, but separate."

"Dead spider that got inside the tree through a crack and disintegrated into the birch cells?" He slid my lunch over to me.

"Still wouldn't work. That would be like spilling juice on your clothes—even if it sank into the fabric, it wouldn't become part of the cloth." I speared a forkful of gummy tetrazzini. "The DNA in one wouldn't mix with the DNA in the other."

"Not even if it was there for a really long time?"

I swallowed and shook my head. "Most cells can't penetrate another cell and release their DNA into it. Only viruses and gametes."

"Gametes?"

"Reproductive cells."

Mart cocked his head. "You mean sperm and eggs?"

I nodded. "In animals. In plants, it's pollen and ovules."

"So breathing in pollen is like breathing in sperm?"

"Yes, actually." I'd never thought of it that way.

"Another reason to be glad I don't go outside," Mart said into his cup. I snorted, and a second later we were laughing like hyenas.

"You'll make a really good teacher," he said when we finally got ourselves under control. "You explain things really well."

I was moved far more than I'd have expected by his words, and I realized I was actually really worried I'd be awful at it. "Really?"

He nodded. "You made all that make sense. I'm terrible at biology, but you turned it into thrusters. Nobody's ever done that with me before."

● ○ ●

"They aren't answering," Mart called from the mainbay. "Probably in the com's null spot. I'll try again in thirty minutes."

My mother and Dr. Okara wouldn't be back from survey for another three hours. I'd redone all the birch samples and driven myself crazy trying to figure out what my results meant. I was desperate to hear what they thought. Maybe we were sitting on something enormous here. Some new evolutionary mechanism. I'd never heard of anything like it, in class or from my mother, which meant she'd never heard of anything like it, either. Which meant it was BIG.

A major discovery like this could make me a very desirable commodity. How could I possibly wait three more hours? "Let's try them again."

Mart raised his eyebrows and looked at the panel clock. "It's only been five minutes."

"So?"

"So protocol is to wait thirty."

I was buzzing with adrenaline. "Jesus, Mart, stop quivering on the altar of the holy gods of protocol.

Move over. I'll do it." He took a hurried step back and I sat down at the com panel. No answer.

I was too preoccupied with myself to register the look on his face when I turned around. "How big is this null spot you mentioned? How long before they're out of it?"

"That depends on their distance from the ship, and their orientation and velocity."

I looked upward and sighed.

"Generally at least thirty minutes." His politely unspoken *Duh* hovered in the air between us, but I was too wound up to acknowledge that I was being a jerk. All I could focus on was how impossible it was to wait a second longer when I was sitting on something THIS BIG!

"Well, that's too long." I walked to the storage cabinet behind the galley and pulled out a helmeted exosuit, way bulkier than the flexible skinsuits my mother and Dr. Okara were wearing. Mart was right behind me; he grabbed my arm, and I read real panic in his face.

"Laru, you can't go out there. It's against protocol."

"You want to go?" Of course outdoor-phobic Mart didn't want to go; the horrible snideness of my comment finally cut through my adrenaline hyperbuzz. "I'm sorry. That was completely uncalled for. But I'm jumpy, and sitting around waiting on protocol isn't my style. This might be something big we've discovered. I'm going to find Mom and Dr. Okara." I finished pulling on the exosuit and checked the air tank, then eased past Mart toward the airlock.

"Why are you wearing *that* suit?" His voice was shrill.

I turned and laid a gloved hand on his shoulder. "Relax, Mart. This is all there is; I wasn't issued a skinsuit. Besides, it's good protocol, right?" I squeezed his shoulder, then let go and stepped into the airlock, excited but also just plain thankful for an excuse to escape the cramped, windowless ship after sixty-eight straight hours and giddy at the thought of setting foot on an honest-to-goodness planet.

Mart waved frantically, and I opened the inner door. He looked faintly golden through my helmet's nanowire visorplate. "The null spots," he said. "One's off the nose, one's off the tail. They start out narrow, and get wider the further you go from the ship."

I beamed at him. "Thanks, Mart. I didn't know that." Then I closed the airlock, waved, and stepped out onto the surface humming *Zippity Doo Dah*.

● ○ ●

I walked to the edge of the bioasphalt landing strip and paused. My left foot came down onto the leafy soil, which gave gently under my weight; then my right foot touched down. I took a slow, reverent breath and looked around. Damn the helmet and its muffling, goldifying barrier, marring my first taste of life outside a space station. Without it, I would have heard birdsong, and the wind through the trees, and the rustling of small animals pattering away in search of cover; with it, I heard only the subdued crunching of my own footsteps. I reached up to loosen the neckline seal, then paused: I wasn't supposed to be outside at all. Let the review board see I'd broken the rules responsibly. I dropped my hand and started walking.

The smooth, even ground was covered in last year's leaves. Most had turned a decaying brown, but here and there, tips of orange and yellow dotted the forest floor. Tau Ceti Three was well into its spring season, and the space above me was a vibrant green canopy through which sunlight filtered, dropping bright specks onto the ground in gently bobbing patterns. I stepped through the swaying net of light and ran my gloved fingers along the trunks, tracing lines in the fine layer of pollen that covered them. The oldest tree here was no more than forty; the last to be introduced were in their first reproductive season, and younger than me.

The chuckle of running water filtered through my helmet, and I walked toward the sound. I squatted and peered eagerly into a middling brook, but no shining silver fish betrayed their positions; I saw only brown and gray pebbles lining the bottom, distorted in the swirling current. I longed to unlatch my exogloves and dip my fingers into living water, home to a trillion trillion trillion individual organisms too tiny to see, living out their microscopic lives in a miniature world within a world. Right here in front of me, within arm's reach. For the first time, I truly understood the thrill on which my mother had so often waxed exuberant. I *did* feel like the creator standing before my creation, watching as it unfolded and grew and lived.

The temptation to touch it all made my fingers itch. But I was already walking a very fine line, and an unfounded disobey on my record would keep me permanently out of the colonization rosters. My stomach clenched; was there really a reason I couldn't have waited for the others to return? Would the review board agree that three hours—no, *thirty minutes*—was too long to sit on my results?

I ran back to the ship, seeing nothing, hoping I could talk Mart into keeping my transgression a secret, knowing before I'd gone twenty steps that I wouldn't ask him to.

● ○ ●

All my adrenaline had turned to churning acid in my gut. By the time I finished the UV bath and stripped off the suit, Mart was waiting outside the airlock. He was visibly relieved to see me, which, irrationally, pissed me off. "You were gone twenty-six minutes. The others aren't back yet. I've been comming them every six minutes. I should get through to them soon. I should have explained the null spots better. They're fairly narrow. I'll show you the RF patterns. You look worn out. Let me get you something to eat." He was hovering solicitously beside my right shoulder, and I shoved him away. His eyes widened and I closed mine in instant and thundering regret.

"I'm sorry, Mart. It's not your fault. Food would be great. I'm just mad at myself for torpedoing the thing I want most because I can't frigging think two steps ahead."

He didn't answer. I opened my eyes and saw his cabin door closing.

Was there anything, *anything*, I could possibly *not*

fuck up today?

I sank to the formfoam couch and kicked the table, then picked up the cards and threw them at the galley wall with a long, hard yell. Mart didn't come ask me what was wrong, or if I wanted a cup of coffee. I was all alone with my reckless, idiot self.

●○●

I didn't have to wait three hours after all. My mother and Dr. Okara returned less than half an hour after I did, both coughing and feverish.

Dr. Okara pushed the rollcrate into the mainbay and leaned against it, panting. "All I want to do is sleep."

"Ditto," my mother said. Then she frowned at me. "What's wrong, Laru?"

I shook my head. She looked really sick; her skin was splotchy and sweaty, and she was breathing in short little pants. All the excuse I needed not to dump the day's failure in her lap quite yet. "Just bored. Want me to make you some tea?"

Neither of them wanted tea; just enough water to down an analgesic before getting supine. Dr. Okara lurched toward her cabin as I kissed my mother's burning cheek. "Sleep well, Mama."

"You too, sweetie. Oh—how'd it go with the samples?"

"Fine." I smiled brightly. "I'll tell you all about it tomorrow."

She nodded and shuffled to her cabin.

And then I was all alone with my reckless, idiot self again.

I wallowed in misery for a while; then I tried to read for Terraforming II, but I couldn't get the words to stick. Eventually hunger was the only thing I could focus on, and I knocked on Mart's door.

"Mart?" I tried to hear movement, or even breathing, but it was quiet in there. "I'm really sorry about pushing you. I'm just mad at myself, and I took it out on you. I'm really, really sorry." No sound. "Look, um, I'm going to eat something, and I thought you were probably getting hungry, too. I'll make us some dinner, okay? Come on out in fifteen minutes and it'll be ready. Okay?"

After another thirty seconds of silence, I trudged off to the galley and managed to heat up two foodpacks without burning down the ship. Mart didn't show. Maybe he was just sleeping. Or maybe he hated me now.

One thing was sure: Sleep was out of the question for me. I cleaned up my galley mess and pulled the day's rollcrate of samples into the lab.

● ○ ●

Mart shook me awake. "Were you here all night?"

I blinked my eyes and looked around. "What time is it?"

"Oh seven hundred local."

"I guess I was." Then it hit me: Mart was talking to me. "Hey, look, I am so sorry about what happened yesterday—"

"It's okay."

"No, it's not, I shouldn't have—"

"It's okay. I'll make breakfast." He padded out and

I blinked at his receding back. Then I unstuck myself from the chair and followed him.

"The others are sick," I said by way of conversation. "Sicker than they were, I mean. They had fevers. They came back early and went straight to bed."

Mart looked up at that. "Fevers? What do they have?"

I shrugged. "I don't know. Some local variant on the common cold, I guess."

"Can you test it?"

"You mean run it through the analyzer? I guess, but I don't see why."

Mart had forgotten all about making breakfast; he was looking at me—more like through me—as if he saw some giant six-armed ogre bearing down on us swinging spike-studded clubs in every hand. Poor Mart, so scared of things that were alive, and nobody who took him seriously. Well, *I* could take him seriously. Especially after yesterday.

"Hey, sure. I'll get a sample from my mom and run it through. Then I'll have the synthesizer make up a batch of antibodies. Like a vaccine, to keep you from getting it. Wait here."

I got a swab kit from the lab, then swung back into the galley on my way to my mother's cabin and handed him a disposable face mask. "Here. You can wear this till everyone's well again."

He took it like a starving man being offered a four-course meal.

My mother was still sleeping. I tiptoed over to her bunk and whispered "Mama?" but she didn't wake.

Her breathing was still short and rapid; her skin was mottled, with specks of white among flushed streaks of red. I touched her arm; still feverish. Then I touched it again: The specks of white were hard and smooth, like flattened grains of sand. I shook her again, harder. "Mama? MAMA?"

I wasted no time getting the sterile swab out of its pipet. I wormed it between her slightly parted lips and waved it around inside her mouth, then practically fell over myself getting to the lab. "Okay, thing, analyze. Analyze. Analyze," I chanted after I'd loaded the swab into an input tray.

A thousand years later, it pinged. No culprit: just the usual cornucopia of oral microbiota. "WHAT?" I shouted—which, of course, brought Mart running.

"What's wrong?" he said through his face mask. "What is it? Is it bad?"

I shook my head. "It's nothing. Literally. The analyzer didn't find anything making her sick. But she's really sick, Mart. She won't wake up." I looked at him. "We've got to go back to the station. Let's go, right now."

Mart's eyes were wide and he was close to hyperventilating. "We can't."

"We have to!" My shout ended in a wail.

"Protocol. Section eighteen point four. Sick survey crew will be denied station reentry until the source of the illness has been identified."

I wanted to scream. "But there's nothing *there* to identify."

"There has to be something. People don't just get sick for no reason."

"I *know*."

"So there's something." Mart all but stamped his foot; his eyes were wild.

"Okay. Okay. Let's think. It isn't a virus. It isn't a bacterium. It isn't any kind of infection."

"Cancer."

"Too fast." I shook my head. "And both of them. It

can't be cancer."

"But something like cancer. Cancer's not an infection, right?"

"Right, but—"

"Can you test for that with the things in here?" Mart swept his arm across the lab.

"I don't know. But I'm telling you, Mart, it can't be cancer. Cancer doesn't just spring up overnight. The way they got sick is classic infection."

"Maybe this planet has fast cancer. It has all kinds of crazy things. It's got birch trees infected with spiders. It's—"

"Wait a minute," I said. "Hold on. You said birch trees *infected* with spiders."

"Yeah, just, you know, a figure of speech."

"Maybe not," I said. "Oh, my god."

● ○ ●

The only DNA in my mother's saliva was her own. So I went back and carefully scraped a sample from one of the hard, smooth, white patches spreading across her skin and ran it through the analyzer. Again no identifiable infectious agent; but the sequencer told a different story.

The mitochondrial DNA was my mother's. The nuclear DNA—the only DNA that mattered, the DNA that made the cell what it was—was *Betula papyrifera*.

My mother was turning into a birch tree.

"It was a figure of speech," Mart said. "I don't— how can this be happening?"

"It's called transduction," I said as I pounded out commands on the lab console. "We've been doing it in the lab for centuries, using viruses to move new genetic material into host cells to overwrite faulty genes. To make crops more resistant to station blight, or just to make them use less water. It's also how we've gotten rid of most hereditary illnesses, like cystic fibrosis."

Mart had that intent look again.

"Say you have a program with errors in one of its routines. You write a new routine without those errors and stick it in where the old routine used to be. That's transduction."

"Ah. Only the birch trees are rewriting the whole program."

I nodded.

"I don't understand how birch trees can do that."

"Neither do I. But I just spammed the station with every bit of data we've got. There are some really bright minds there." I chewed on a fingernail. "Someone will figure out how to make it stop."

●○●

I checked on Dr. Okara first; she was just like my mother. Short of breath, feverish, and splotchy skin with patches of smooth, hard white. I didn't know what to do for either of them. I sat with my mother, singing songs and telling her about yesterday's colossal fuck-up. That made me weepy—not because I'd made such a mess of things, but because I didn't know if she would ever actually hear about it. I leaned against her after that and cried for a long time.

Mart was sitting at the mainbay com station when I came back out, still wearing his face mask. "No news yet," he said before I'd even opened my mouth. "I've been waiting, but nothing's come through."

I nodded. I walked over to the couch and sat down, then stood back up again and looked around the mainbay. I didn't know what to do with myself.

Mart swiveled to look at me. "You'll probably feel better in the lab. I'll make us something to eat."

●○●

Mart shook me awake in the lab chair. He looked like I felt: His cheek was creased where he'd slumped against the com panel in the mainbay when he fell asleep, and his eyes were bleary. My eyes groped for the lab clock. Twelve hours since I'd sent up my mother's DNA.

"They've got something. They want you."

I jumped to my feet, instantly awake, and followed Mart to the mainbay.

"Laru Parnum here," I croaked into the com.

"Rikkel Smit. Miss Parnum, we've developed an immunoglobulin that will protect you and Mr. Jansen from infection. I'm sending the blueprint now. Synthesis should take about six hours."

I looked over my shoulder and smiled at Mart in relief. "That's great news! Thank you so much, Dr. Smit."

"We're continuing to work on a fix to the invasive genome, but that will take some days longer. In the meantime, the immunoglobulin will protect you down there. We do need you to stay planetside until we have the delivery vector ready, so you can administer it."

"Understood."

There was a brief silence. "Miss Parnum, as I'm sure you understand, the immunoglobulin will only prevent future infection. It won't cure your infected crewmates."

"Right. I understand finding a way to reverse the infection will take longer. Do you know how much longer? My mother and Dr. Okara are very ill."

Dr. Smit didn't answer; I thought I'd lost the connection. "Dr. Smit?"

"Miss Parnum, there won't be a cure. There is no way to reverse what's happened."

"But when you correct the birch pollen—"

"It will stop infecting new organisms. Period."

I began to gasp air in sharp, sucking breaths that brought no relief. Mart crept toward me and rested a tentative arm around my shoulder, no doubt afraid I would hit him again. That act of bravery nearly undid me. I clung to his hand and clamped my mouth into a thin line to still it.

"Miss Parnum . . . Laru, I am so, so sorry for your loss. Look, I know this is cold consolation, but your discovery will save the planet's ecosystem from ruin. Five generations on the *Ceiaides* have invested a hundred and sixty years into terraforming Tau Ceti Three, and the last seventy would have been wasted. This kind of infection spreads exponentially . . . by next year's survey, there would have been precious little but birch trees, and they'd have been doomed without other life to maintain the carbon-oxygen balance. We'd have had to raze the forests and reintroduce everything from the microbes up."

I nodded, though Dr. Smit couldn't see me. Mart

cleared his throat and said, "Ah, Miss Parnum is nodding." I laughed at that, and Mart's right hand tightened on mine, as if he knew my laugh would open the floodgates.

"It was brilliant work, Laru, especially for a fourth-year. You have a bright future ahead of you."

I didn't answer, and Mart didn't describe the way I was shuddering with the effort not to cry or his left hand gently patting my arm. The com remained silent for several seconds more, and then Dr. Smit signed off. I let myself go, howling and screaming and throwing things and curling up on the floor and kicking at the air. And when I finally rolled onto my back, bruised and hoarse and spent, Mart was still there with me.

● ○ ●

My mother died later that night. That is: She stopped breathing with her lungs, and I could no longer find her heartbeat. The birch patches continued to spread until they consumed her skin, so something inside her was still alive.

"I can't seal her in a hazmat bag," I told Mart when I came back out. "I just can't."

He squirmed. "The protocol is very specific. Crew members who die on survey have to be sealed and returned for incineration."

"I know. But it feels like suffocating her."

He didn't say anything else, and I didn't push it. We still had some time; protocol gave us forty-eight hours.

● ○ ●

We played a lot of uninspired cicce that day and the next, waiting for Dr. Smit's team to send us the birch fix. I gave Mart a double dose of the immunoglobulin when it was ready. We were in no danger of infection inside the ship, which is the only place Mart was ever going to be, but I knew swallowing two cupfuls of bitter medicine would make him feel safer.

I still hadn't sealed my mother and Dr. Okara in hazmat bags. I told myself I'd bag them as soon as they started to smell. Mart and I didn't discuss it again; I didn't know if he was unaware I was planning to violate protocol that grossly, or unwilling to fight about it. Maybe he was just working up the resolve to walk in and bag them himself.

On the third day of our wait, my mother began to sprout new growth. A load fell off me when I saw the pale green buds dotting her former torso. She *was* still alive. Maybe not in any way that recognized me, but that didn't matter. What little doubt I'd had about keeping her on the planet was gone.

I came out of her cabin intending to tell Mart, but when I saw him bent over the cards, nudging this one and that one with a finger until they were precisely aligned, words failed me. He looked up, and two things I should have noticed earlier leapt out at me: the way he searched my face to see if I was okay, and the way he bit his lower lip to keep from speaking.

"Hey." I smiled and walked over to him.

"Want something to eat?"

I shook my head. "I was wondering. Do you think you could show me how a retroflux thruster works?"

For an instant his eyes lit up; then the light went

out and he looked away. "But you're not a fan of shuttle tech." He had remembered my cut-him-off-at-the-pass word for word. Ouch. "I don't want to bore you, Laru. I know the things I talk about bore people."

"You do?"

"Yes." He looked at me with a sour smile. "I'm the Raging Bore. Hadn't you heard?"

This moment needed complete honesty.

"I did hear that. And I believed it that first day, when you started to tell me about the thrusters. It's true, they don't interest me. Any more than plant DNA interests you. But you listened to me anyway, because you aren't a shallow, self-absorbed ninny." I waited until that sank in and he looked at me in surprise; then I said, "I'm really sorry, Mart. I was an ass. And you are *not* a bore. You're a friend."

He nodded, tears close to the surface.

"Shuttle tech still doesn't interest me, but it interests you. And I really do want you to tell me about it."

He searched my face then, looking for some sign I was atoning for my self-absorbed sins or otherwise little-white-lying to him. He didn't find any: I was honestly eager to hear what made him sing, after all these muted days.

● ○ ●

We stayed up talking, deep into the planetside night. Really talking, back and forth and at the same time, about everything and nothing. Mart did have a tendency to long monologues in excruciating detail on subjects that fascinated him, but I was quick to tell him when my attention started to wander. That broke through the last damper on his enthusiasm; he knew that if I was listening, it was because I was engaged in what he was saying.

For my part, I talked more openly about myself than I ever had with anyone besides my mother. It was a really good night, so rare and freeing that neither of us wanted to end it, even long past bedtime protocol, long past the point of fatigue.

I woke hours later on one of the mainbay couches. My face was swollen and sticky, my bra dug into my back, and I was cold, though Mart had apparently covered us both with blankets at some point. I looked over at his puffy, slack-jawed face on the couch across from me. He was dreaming, his eyes darting beneath their lids, his brow jerking lightly. I eased off my couch and tiptoed toward the galley, but I wasn't quiet enough; he was sitting up when I came back with my coffee. I handed the cup to him and went to make a second.

"I'll help you do it," he said as I walked back in.

"Do what?"

"Plant your mother and Dr. Okara."

I stopped cold. I hadn't told Mart about the new growth last night, despite all our heartfelt talk. The self-absorbed me of a day ago would have done it, angsting about what it meant for *my* life; but I'd rounded a corner yesterday, and I wouldn't saddle him with that damning knowledge. I was only going to torpedo one future here. "No. It's a blacklist offense. You stay here and file a report that you disagreed with me."

"It's only blacklist if it's an unfounded disobey. Section thirty-two point nine of the fourth Terra-forming Convention: Survey crew will not transport viable specimens from their planet of origin. I looked it up."

"You looked that up?" I was moved. "When? Why?"

"Yesterday when you were in with your mother. You were gone longer than usual. I figured you must have seen something new."

I nodded. "She *is* viable, Mart. She's sprouting leaves. I can't believe you found a way to keep her here legally." It wasn't just my record he'd saved; I was pretty sure the *Ceiaides* would send someone to dig up my illegally planted mother as soon as we got back. "Unbelievable, Mart. You're brilliant."

Mart wasn't sharing my relief; in fact, he looked pretty miserable for someone who had just kept the door to my newly bright future from swinging shut. Then it hit me.

"Oh, Mart. It's okay. I'm strong enough to pull them outside by myself."

He shook his head, looking queasy and even paler than usual. "It's not the physical weight you shouldn't bear alone. I'm going with you."

"Thank you," I managed to say, just before I burst into tears and spilled my coffee all over the floor.

● ○ ●

Mart and I carried each body into the airlock; then he coached me through rigging two rollcrate trolleys together on the landing strip. He breathed heavily the whole time, and more than once I said I'd do the rest alone. He didn't listen to me.

Then the moment of truth arrived. He pressed the release to open the outer door and stepped up to the edge. I held out a hand to him. We stood there in silence, side by side, close to the shuttle for several minutes, until he clicked on his com mike. "I'm okay."

He sounded awful, somewhere between passing out and throwing up lunch.

"Mart," I began. He walked over to the doubled-up trolley and pulled it toward the airlock in response.

We brought my mother and Dr. Okara out one by one and lowered them onto the trolley. Then I led us toward the creek I'd seen before.

This time I noticed what I had missed in my innocence four days earlier: Very few fungi sprouted among the leaf litter; no moss covered the stones; only scant algae grew on the pebbles in the eddyless pockets of the brook. For every oak or maple we passed, there were a hundred birch trees. The youngest of them had oblong trunks woven of fused, ficus-like trunklets rising up. We saw countless apparent logs sprouting new growth along their lengths. At every one, I wondered *what were you before?*

I pulled us to a halt at a wide bend in the creek. "I think this is a nice place."

Mart nodded and gave me a bulky exoglove thumbs-up. His hand trembled.

"Mart—"

He shook his head.

I loosened the dirt in a wide patch of creek bank,

and we laid my mother and Dr. Okara out, careful to avoid crushing the new shoots. Fine roots were beginning to grow on the side of their bodies that had lain against the cabin bunks; these we patted gently into the loosened soil, working side by side on our knees in silence. Then Mart clicked on his mike and I heard him humming, off-key but recognizable. I stopped patting and looked at him.

"I thought you might want to sing your father's songs to her. As a kind of ceremony."

My throat closed up as I tried not to cry again.

My first words came out as twisted croaks, but as I went on, my voice stabilized. Mart hummed beneath my words, something soft and tuneless and mostly in time with me. I sang song after song and lost count; the light dappling the forest had deepened toward sunset by the time I fell silent.

By next year's survey to this location, my mother would be a young bonsai birch reaching toward the sky. I knew I would be on that survey ship; I would come and sing to her again, then and every year, until I died.

Someday, a hundred years from now, Tau Ceti Three's first colonists might chop her down to build a home, or to burn a fire. My mother had never wanted to end up on a planet, but she would have been glad she was still useful, even in death.

"It's ironic," I said through my tears. "*I* was the one who wanted to put down roots on a colony world."

Mart turned toward me with a horrified look, doubly golden through our two visors. "It's okay," I said, half-laughing, half-crying. "It's a terrible joke in horrible taste. I know. But it's funny, isn't it?"

He wrapped his arms tightly around me then, and I cried my heartbreak into the verdant woods.

Acts

S.C. Wade

Tammi stood on the second floor of the ballroom and peered down at the sea of assorted colors before her. Per standard formal attire, the damsels at the meetings wore gowns that matched their natural-born hair color—some shade of violet, orange, or green. Formal attire for gentlemen who lived on Nobile never bred variety, because each one was required to wear a two-piece silver suit.

"This turnout is repulsive," she whispered just loud enough for the communicator in her ear to transmit.

She looked to her right and saw two damsels in conversation. Tammi glanced at their forearms and saw that each of them had a red band embedded beneath their wrist.

"The new Nobility Act is more repulsive," her consort, Westin, responded through the communicator. "Limiting the number of times a year you can take a space tour of the neighboring planets?"

"I swear, if we don't relocate soon . . ." Tammi let her statement trail off and she walked toward the stairs. "I hope this to be my first and last Act Announcement Meeting. I feel out of place with all of these Upper-Bloods."

Upper-Bloods was the term for anyone who had a color around their wrist that indicated a higher level of class.

On the planet Nobile, after each birth, a surgery was implemented to input a mechanical band beneath the layer of skin on everyone's wrist. That band received signals from the government and changed depending on the person's adherence to the Nobility Acts—the laws of the planet.

The color of the wrist decided who was allowed entrance to certain areas within certain cities and even who was allowed into any districts at all. It was a method that Tammi thought was beneficial if one had obeyed the Acts for the majority of their lives. But for someone like her who had taken part in unfavorable things in the past, the Acts offered little forgiveness. Her wrist never seemed to surpass the color blue.

To be a Blue Citizen on Nobile wasn't the worst, as decent residences of living were possible, but it was nowhere near the grandeur, safety, and cleanliness options that Green, Yellow, Orange, and—the highest class—Red Citizens were given.

Being a Blue Citizen also meant that only two classes of people were beneath you—Purple and Black. And any misstep could force regression. Any time a Nobility Officer conducted an arrest, they inputted strikes against the citizen. And once that information was forwarded to the government, the wrist band would be updated accordingly.

"We'll be free of these Upper-Bloods and the entire Nobility Act nonsense soon enough," Westin said.

Tammi stepped carefully down the steps, holding onto the gold-plated hand railing. On her way, she spotted Westin in the crowd. His black, slicked-back hair was a standout among the array of vibrant hair colors.

Then a freckled face drew Tammi's attention. It was more the length of his bright green hair he wore in a ponytail that made him noticeable. Very few Nobilian men fashioned their hair with length. But it looked good on this gentleman; worked well with his round face.

"Jasen's coming your way," she whispered.

"I see him," Westin said.

Now on the lower floor, Tammi slipped between two people and kept her distance. Because of her history with Jasen eight years ago, it was important he not see her until the time was right.

Tammi heard everything through the communicator.

"Gentleman Personal Relations," Westin said with enthusiasm.

"How are you living, sir?" Jasen asked.

"Excellent!"

"You suck up so well," Tammi whispered.

"I know you're a busy man, but because of my Citizen status, a public Act Announcement Meeting is my only chance to even approach you."

"What can I do for you, sir?" Jasen asked.

"Westin," he said. "My name is Westin, and I actually have a card."

Tammi leaned against a wall and watched as Westin pulled out a business flex-card they had printed the day before. "My consort and I would like to submit an objection to the Nobilities Act regarding one of their laws, and we would love to have your support."

Jasen chuckled. "I'm flattered you believe I have some sort of sway to their opinion, but I'm merely a spokesman. An employed face. I relay their decisions, nothing more. My objection would be just as effective as yours."

"But you would have a greater impact because you're an Orange-Blood. You and I don't intermingle, so if the government sees us together on a subject, they're sure to notice."

Tammi listened with eagerness as her consort wove the web of stories to her ex-lover. If she didn't know any better, she would've thought Westin *actually* cared about overturning the Act. She was impressed.

Jasen asked, "What are you objecting to?"

"We want to change the offspring counts implemented by the Nobilities Act. We believe the color of one's wrist shouldn't determine the number of children a couple is allowed to have."

"A lot of people have submitted that objection.

None succeeded in getting the government to alter the Act."

"Yes," Westin said," but all of them were Blue-Bloods and below. And none of them teamed up with someone of your stature."

Tammi and Westin knew that even submitting an objection to the Nobile government to change one of their laws was futile. Even if they were partnered with someone in Jasen's position, they had no chance.

But to draw in Jasen, they had to make him believe they weren't going to give up. That they had to at least try. In reality, they weren't even interested in remaining on the planet, and Jasen was just a link to help them attain their goal.

"I can't commit to anything," Jasen said.

"Commit to have dinner with my consort and me," Westin smoothly worked in the invitation. "Bring your consort and we can all discuss it without the pressures of time."

Tammi made her way toward the two.

"Oh, here's my consort now."

When Tammi stepped beside Westin, she kept her eyes deadlocked on Jasen's to monitor his reaction.

"This is your consort?" Jasen asked, his mouth barely moving.

"Yes." Westin put his arm around Tammi's waist.

"Hello, Jasen," Tammi said.

Jasen didn't reply.

Westin said, "I understand that you and Tammi have a bad history, but I hope that has no bearing on any decisions you make."

● ○ ●

After Jasen and his consort, Claudia, put the twins to sleep, they climbed into their own bed. She cuddled up to his chest, one arm around his ribcage. He sat against the headboard, reciprocating the hold. He had mentioned the dinner invitation to Claudia earlier, but hadn't been able to truly discuss it until now.

"It'll only be awkward if you let it," Claudia said.

Jasen sighed. He had a hard time coming to grips with the fact that he was just face-to-face with the damsel he loved nearly a decade ago. A damsel whom he originally thought he had a future with.

"Of all people, though . . ." Jasen said.

"What are you finding so hard to believe?" Claudia asked. "That you crossed paths with her after so many years, or that she's actually bonded to someone?"

"Both . . . and why they came to me."

"Probably because she knows you. Chances were better than going to a stranger."

"Well, the previous relationship may cost them. I liked Westin but when she walked up . . ." Jasen shook his head, not knowing what else to say.

The relationship he shared with Tammi, in the beginning, was everything to him. He wasn't sponta-neous and he lived his life according to the Nobility Acts. Tammi, however, constantly flirted with the law, and at times completely disregarded it. What Jasen had loved about the relationship was how he was able to vicariously take part in the adrenaline of crossing boundaries. Hearing her wild stories enthralled him. He thought it was love until he found out she was a liar.

"Maybe we won't go to dinner."

"Why?" Claudia asked.

"Why are you even entertaining this? Any other damsel would be loathing the idea of having dinner with her consort's former lover."

"That's why you wedded me—I'm not like every other damsel." She lifted her head the slightest and kissed Jasen's chest. "But what they want to do, you have to admit, is admirable."

"And a complete waste of time."

"You don't know that," Claudia said.

"You don't know if my name on the objection with theirs will even help."

"That's why they want to try."

Jasen realized he sounded childish, but he thought he had let go of the pain Tammi caused him. Seeing her again only made the anguish resurface. "She's an old part of my life I don't want to bring to the present. My life consists of you, Marlene, and Gregory. I don't want to include her. At all."

"Okay."

"You just want to meet her, don't you?" Jasen strove to find a lighter mood.

She laughed. "You think I have an ulterior motive?"

"I'm just saying you've expressed on numerous occasions your desire to hospitalize her for aborting children without telling me."

"That was when I was younger." Claudia sat up and dangled her legs off the side of the bed. "I'm older now. More mature. More forgiving." She walked to the sink to get a glass of water. "And you should be too,

Gentleman Personal Relations."

"Forgiving her isn't my forte."

"We're all adults, Jasen," she said. "You and I know their predicament firsthand . . . just think about that."

Jasen and Claudia had their twins when they were still considered Yellow-Bloods, and they were only allowed two children. But when Claudia conceived, she was pregnant with triplets. The dilemma of keeping all three and being demoted to Green-Bloods or aborting one and remaining Yellow-Bloods weighed heavily on their minds. If they reverted to Green-Bloods, they wouldn't have as much provision, and Jasen's journey toward becoming the spokesman for the district's government would have been hindered.

Jasen didn't know the exact similarities between him and Claudia and Tammi and Westin, but he figured that Tammi and Westin wanted children. Since they were Blue-Bloods they were allowed one child. He hadn't asked if they had a child already, or if Tammi was pregnant, but if they were going to submit an objection to the government, they had to know that the process was lengthy. It had many channels to go through. If Tammi was pregnant now, even if the objection was given any merit, it wouldn't go into effect until after Tammi gave birth.

"So, you want to help her?" Jasen cringed.

"*Them*," she corrected, returning to the bed. "It's just dinner, Jasen."

Jasen wasn't looking forward to sharing a table with Tammi. Eight years wasn't nearly long enough to erase the hurt of what she had done. He knew when he looked at her all he'd be able to see would be the two abortions that had put an end to three children he hadn't known anything about.

●○●

A couple of nights after the initial dinner invitation, Tammi and Westin arrived at the bistro early. They wanted to be sure they were given a private booth in an isolated room. Reservations were one thing this bistro didn't allow for Blue-Bloods. But this was the classiest place that allowed Blue-Bloods to eat.

Westin rested his arm on the back of Tammi's seat and took another drink from his glass. She watched him take his generous sip and then gave him a quick kiss on the cheek.

He smiled. "I'm excited too. But they've only agreed to dinner. We'll see how they react when we tell them the real reason."

"Still . . ." Tammi leaned in for another kiss. "We're getting there." This time their lips met.

After Jasen and Claudia arrived, introductions were made and dinner was ordered. Tammi felt the unspoken tension emanating from Jasen, partly due to the fact that he hardly looked in her direction. She knew the bad feelings were justified, though. She had betrayed him.

When Tammi and Jasen were together, Tammi had a dependency on drugs to the point that when she discovered she was pregnant, she didn't even consider quitting. She figured the babies wouldn't have grown to full term anyway, so aborting seemed like the logical choice. She had regretted not telling Jasen and keeping the relationship honest, but she accepted that she was a selfish person.

"Thank you both for coming," Westin said.

"Our pleasure," Jasen said.

"I love the food in this restaurant too," Claudia said.

Tammi wasn't sure if Claudia was genuine or was overcompensating. Tammi was positive that Claudia wasn't thrilled to be having dinner with a former lover of her consort. But if it bothered her, she played it off well because Claudia made more eye contact than Jasen.

"Good," Westin said. "I'm glad you like this place, because we wanted to take you someplace classy."

"As classy as a couple of Blue-Bloods can be," Jasen added.

"Speaking of . . ." Westin said. "Would you two like to eat first or discuss our objection?"

"Whichever," Jasen said.

While waiting for their food, they discussed general topics, and Claudia inquired about Tammi's activity the past few years and asked how she became sober from drugs. Tammi attributed a lot of her strength to Westin.

Jasen was the quietest during the conversation, but once dinner was consumed, he clasped his hands together and said, "On to the objection?"

Tammi and Westin looked at each other.

"Westin and I want to start a family," Tammi said. "But the Nobility Acts have that ridiculous clause about no more than one child for a Blue-Blood."

"I wouldn't call it ridiculous," Jasen said. "You get rewarded for the lifestyle you live; the rules that you follow."

"A child's life should never be in the category of a 'reward,'" Westin said.

"Do I agree with it?" Jasen said with a shrug. "No. But it's the law."

"Nobile is the only planet in these systems that even has such asinine laws."

Tammi looked back and forth between the two men. She sensed the tension mounting.

"It's disgusting," Westin added.

"Then why don't you leave the planet?" Jasen asked.

"Jasen," Claudia chided.

"That's what we want to do!" Westin blurted.

Silence filled the room. Tammi looked from Westin to Jasen to Claudia. Westin looked as if he had made an error; Jasen and Claudia looked confused.

"Then why are you here if you're going to relocate to another planet?" Jasen asked, scratching his chin.

"Because we need your help," Tammi said.

"Claudia, you work in the hangar bays, and you have direct contact with the ships that come and go from the planet."

"I oversee the manifests. Yes," she said.

"Could you arrange for me and Westin to be aboard one of those ships? We want to go to Kartigen because Westin has an uncle who lives there."

Jasen shook his head. "You two planned this. You want Claudia to illegally place you as passengers on a ship to get off the planet? Why not just buy two tickets?"

"Westin has made a few mistakes in his past as

well. Only his were the kind that gave him a record."

"A lawbreaker record?" Jasen asked, and Tammi swore it was in snide.

"We applied for approval to relocate, but we were denied," Tammi said. "The government isn't keen on granting transferences to those who served time in the penitentiary."

"I don't understand," Claudia said. "Most conceptions yield two or more children, but twenty-five percent of the population have one." She shrugged. "I would see where you are after conception before you want to jump to another planet. You may not have to leave."

"Trust me, those statistics are what we were counting on," Tammi said. "But I'm pregnant with twins."

● ○ ●

Jasen and Claudia stepped out of the room and took a seat on a bench that was halfway down the narrow hall that led to the public area of the bistro.

"What do you think we should do?" Claudia asked in a low voice.

"We can't defy the Nobility Acts."

"They want to have a family, Jasen. They don't want to abort." Claudia sniffled.

Jasen knew exactly why Claudia was getting emotional—she was allowing herself to empathize. Which wasn't a bad thing; it was one of the reasons he was attracted to her. But just because they knew what it felt like to be in Tammi and Westin's situation didn't mean that breaking the law for them was a good idea.

Jasen took a deep breath because a knot started to form in his throat. "If we had to abort one of our own, Claudia, what gives Tammi the right to skirt the law? And to use *us* to do it? That's obnoxious."

"She made mistakes," Claudia said, "but she's reaching out for a helping hand."

"And who's going to help us? Claudia, supporting them in an objection is completely different than helping them illegally transfer to another planet."

She had tears steadily flowing down her cheeks, and it was hard for Jasen to see her cry. He slid closer to her and wrapped his arms around her.

"No one should have to abort a child to remain in the government's good graces," she said. "No one."

Jasen detested seeing Tammi again and despised her more when he found out that she and Westin wanted to use Claudia to get a free ride off of the planet. Jasen was feeling many emotions, but the strongest was spite. He wanted Tammi to know that if she lived a certain way previously, she should have to live with the present consequences.

"We have to think about our children, Claudia," Jasen said. "Providing the best life for them that we possibly can. They're who everything has to come down to. Reconnecting ties with Tammi to break the law is not going to benefit them. We are Orange Citizens because of our obedience to the Nobility Acts. If we help them and get caught, we'll be looking at repercussions. And she isn't worth it."

● ○ ●

Tammi and Westin waited patiently for Jasen and

Claudia to return to the room.

Tammi rapped her fingers on the table and sighed. "What if they don't even come back?"

"Then that's their answer," Westin said simply.

Tammi crossed her arms over her chest. She didn't want to have to do this to Jasen and Claudia, but it all came down to the best thing for her family. Her kids. It was obvious that the hangar bays had more than one manifest overseer, so they didn't have to choose Claudia and Jasen. But Tammi and Westin chose them because of their pregnancy similarities, hoping that would make them sympathetic.

And if they weren't moved by sympathy, Tammi and Westin also chose them because Jasen and Claudia had the most to lose.

Jasen returned to the room alone, standing behind the chair that he had sat in. "Might as well make it quick, but we won't be assisting you." He left abruptly.

Tammi lowered her chin to her chest and took deep breaths to keep calm. With Jasen and Tammi refusing to help, they had to fall back on the alternative plan; the plan she'd wanted to avoid.

Westin gently squeezed her hand in support. "You know what we have to do now."

She raised her head, hoping that Jasen would come back in and say that they changed their minds.

"I do."

Neither Tammi nor Westin had been convinced Jasen and Claudia would agree to help, but Tammi had pleaded with Westin to try the civilized approach. And now that it was rejected, there was no choice but to resort to Westin's initial concept.

"Are you going to be okay with it?" he asked, leaning forward to see her face.

"I just have to not think about what it is we're doing."

Westin kissed her on the temple. "I know . . . I was actually hoping by some miracle they would help us. I didn't want to have to do this."

Tammi looked at him and a tear crept out of the corner of her eye. "Tell me again."

Westin placed a palm on her cheek, wiping the tear away with his thumb. "We're doing this to save our children. No one else is standing up for them. We're their parents. We need to. What we're about to do won't be easy, but in just a few short months, we'll be a family of four, not three. A beautiful family of four."

The picture he painted brought more tears to her eyes, nearly blinding her to the blue band around his wrist. Knowing what had to be done to be free of such limitations motivated her. She wrapped her arms around his neck.

"I love you," he whispered.

"I love you," Tammi said and regained her composure with a few breaths. "Jasen's going to hate us forever."

They released their hug and Westin said, "But he'll hate from afar . . . you have their schedule memorized, right?"

"Yes," Tammi said. "When should we do it?"

Westin hesitated with a stilted breath before answering. "Tomorrow."

That was the answer Tammi's ears weren't

prepared for, but it was the only answer her maternal instincts would accept. She had to get her growing children away from danger, distant from the Nobility Acts.

What they were about to do went against who they were as people. They both were adamant about making their lives better every day, separating from the stench of their pasts. Because of that decision, Tammi and Westin hashed and rehashed ethics and morals and whether what they had to do would completely negate the goals they wanted for their future. But it all came down to what future they had in a place that imposed limits on family.

Tammi and Westin weren't surprised Jasen refused to defy the Nobility Acts for them, but they had a very strong feeling he would break them for his children.

● ○ ●

The next day, when Jasen arrived home, he set out ingredients for dinner. Claudia had gone to the doctor and would pick up the twins from Educational on her way home. He wanted to have the meal halfway done.

Around fifteen minutes later, Jasen received a video call from Claudia.

"The kids aren't here!" Claudia's voice cracked.

"What do you mean they're not there?"

"I mean—"

The feed disappeared, and that never happened. With laser communication and auxiliary relays, the only way it would cease functioning would be if it were deliberately turned off.

Jasen heard steps behind him, so he turned

around. Westin was standing in the kitchen's entryway.

It didn't take long for Jasen to assume Westin and Tammi were behind Marlene and Gregory not being at Educational for Claudia to pick them up.

Jasen stared at Westin and neither made any sudden movements. It was a staring match until Jasen glanced at the knives on the counter.

"How did you get in here?" Jasen asked.

"That's irrelevant."

"I guess this is what your past consisted of? Breaking and entering?"

Westin stuffed his hands in his pockets. "Go ahead and ask the question you really want to know."

"Where're my kids?" Jasen dug his fingernails into his palms. He wanted to grab a knife and hold it against Westin's throat, but he didn't know if Westin had a weapon on him.

"They're safe," Westin said. "And they'll remain that way, but you and Claudia need to help us off of this planet."

"You kidnapped my children."

"Only to persuade you," he said.

Jasen eased his way around the counter, slipping a small knife beneath his sleeve as he went. He stood five feet from Westin.

Westin smirked. "If you're going to attack me, Jasen, just do it. I've been in these situations much more than you have."

With surprise no longer possible, Jasen dropped the knife into his fingers and swung at Westin. Westin grabbed Jasen's arm with one hand and then struck his wrist, forcing Jasen to drop the knife.

Jasen landed an uppercut to Westin's jaw. Westin stumbled backwards but quickly rebounded and punched Jasen in the face. As Jasen recoiled, Westin picked up the knife, gripped Jasen's neck and backed him up against a wall.

"You think you'll get away with this?" Jasen muttered as he tried to release the hold on his neck. "The moment you leave, I can have Nobility Officers after you and Tammi."

"No, you can't. We've been in the wind for a while, and we're good at not being found." Westin tightened his grip and flaunted the knife. Jasen saw the pain in Westin's eyes. "I really wish you would've just helped us willingly. We didn't want to do it this way."

"You mean hold my kids ransom?"

"Well, a guillotine is effectually being held over mine."

"You can still have one child, Westin." Jasen struggled but it was useless.

"And abort one of them?" Westin's face twisted in disgust. "What man would kill his child to save himself? Oh . . . I'm looking at him."

"Don't judge me," Jasen said.

"You don't judge me! You claim to be about family, but you want to abide by the Nobility Acts more than anything."

"It's called providing for my family."

"Very little I've seen so far tells me you're a true family man, Jasen," Westin said. "You're a law man at heart. It's convenience that your compliance with the Nobility Acts harmonizes with your children's provision. The real test is what you'll do when the law and your children's well-being are on opposite sides."

"You think I don't love my children? You think I *wanted* to abort a child?"

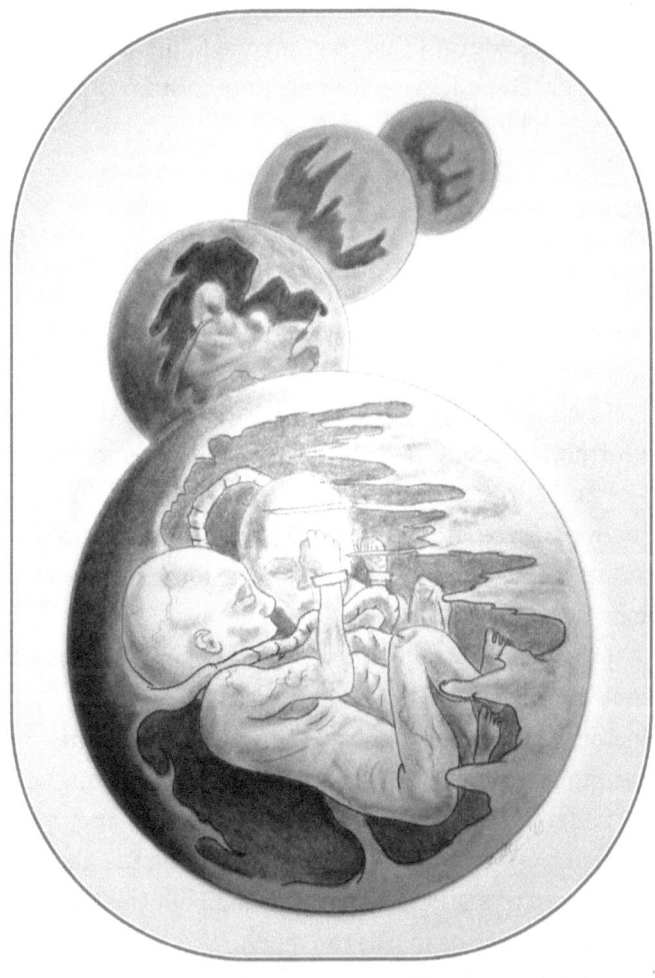

Westin yanked Jasen from the wall and pushed him to the hardwood floor. Jasen's chin hit with a thud, and Westin placed a knee on his back to keep him down. He grabbed Jasen by the hair and showed him the blade of the knife. "Do you know one difference between you and me? When you realized I was involved in your children's disappearance, you probably wanted to use this knife only to subdue me, to scare me. Me? If I find that anyone in my family is being threatened, I wouldn't hesitate to stain this knife with blood."

"I guess that's how you got your lawbreaker record," Jasen mumbled.

"Believe it or not, you are not my problem," he said. "You're part of my solution. Now, do this for us, or we'll make it public knowledge that Claudia is pregnant . . ."

Jasen was wide-eyed. He and Claudia kept the information about her being pregnant close-mouthed.

"And correct me if I'm wrong," Westin said, "but I'm pretty sure Orange-Bloods are only allowed two children . . . huh, maybe there's hope for you yet, law man."

Jasen couldn't get over the shock of how Westin knew information that only he, Claudia, and her doctor were supposed to know. He guessed Westin was more resourceful than he had originally thought.

Westin banged Jasen's head into the floor and jumped from on top of him, quickly exiting the house. Jasen tried to stand to chase after him, but the throbbing pain in his head was too much.

He remained seated on the floor for a while, riled up. When Claudia arrived home, they both sat at the kitchen table and discussed every option.

"We have to do what they ask," Jasen said.

Blackmail worked. If it got out that Claudia was pregnant and so far along, it would damage them tremendously. They hadn't aborted it because they were hoping they would be upgraded to Red Citizens soon. They were playing the odds, especially if the government had no intentions of upgrading their citizen status within the allotted timeframe. But they needed to be upgraded to Red Citizens shortly so they could legally have a third child. If they weren't . . .

"Do you think they'll hurt the kids?" Claudia asked, her eyes red and wet.

"I don't know."

"Would it be so bad if the news of my pregnancy did come out?"

"The government won't like the presumptuous-ness of the whole thing," Jasen said.

"It's not like we planned this, though."

"It wouldn't matter. They could see it as being too sure of ourselves, as if we *expected* to have a higher level of citizenship. They don't want their citizens, especially their employees, to conclude something before them . . . we can't risk it."

Claudia banged the table. "But we're already in trouble, Jasen! Even if they upgraded us today, the math will show that we conceived before we became Red Citizens. And it won't be long before I start showing!"

Jasen flared his nostrils, upset with himself for getting his family into this predicament. If only he had used safety, if only he hadn't assumed he'd been an Orange Citizen for so long that they'd render him a Red Citizen soon . . . if only.

He just couldn't bear to go through another abortion.

"We have to deal with one thing at a time," Jasen said.

"So, you want to go against the Acts?" Claudia asked.

"I want our children back."

● ○ ●

Tammi and Jasen were instructed to be at Claudia's workplace the next night.

They entered the main foyer of the district's hangar bays with one bag of belongings each. This part of the structure housed all of the offices, and this was also where crowds went through security before proceeding to the ships which they had tickets for.

Tammi took Westin's hand, interlocking her fingers through his. There were a few security guards at the far end of the foyer, waiting to validate tickets and search people's belongings before allowing access to any of the terminals.

But they wouldn't be going that way.

They approached the information desk and asked for Claudia. After a few moments of verification, a security guard escorted them through Personnel Only doors until they reached Claudia's office. The guard knocked and used his badge to let them in.

Tammi and Westin stepped inside Claudia's office and saw her seated at her computer; Jasen leaned against the front of her desk, arms crossed over his chest. Neither of them looked as if they'd gotten much sleep.

Tammi glanced around the room. There were pictures of Jasen and the twins all around. More than pictures—recorded moments in time. Silent video snippets played in continuous loops. Tammi caught Westin looking at the images as well.

"Thank you," Claudia said to the guard. "If you can just make sure their bags get onto Shuttle 226, I'll escort them from here." The guard nodded, took the bags, and exited.

Tammi knew that taking the bags was part of the requirements, but the knots in her stomach wouldn't rest. She looked at Westin.

"They still have to put your bags through check," Claudia said, barely taking her eyes off of her screen.

"We know. We trust you," Westin said.

Jasen's eyebrows raised. "That's more than what I'd say about you two."

"How're our kids?" Claudia asked, still not making direct eye contact. Tammi noticed she wasn't as engaging as she was at dinner.

"They're good," Tammi answered. "They're really sweet too. You two are doing a great job."

"Really, Tammi?" Jasen asked. "You're complimenting our parenting skills while you're holding them hostage?"

"Yes, Jasen, because contrary to your belief, I do have a heart. I can see when children are being raised with love and affection. I can only hope Westin and I can have kids as precious as yours."

"Thank you," Claudia said, finally making eye contact with Tammi for a brief second. She typed a few more commands into her computer.

"Thank you for doing this," Tammi said.

"Don't take this as if I'm being a jerk, but we're not doing this for you," Jasen said. "Understand that."

"I do. But I still feel a great deal of gratitude."

Westin said, "If we had met under different circumstances, I think we all could've been really good friends."

"I doubt it," Jasen said. "But under different circumstances . . . who's to say?"

Tammi was taken aback to hear Jasen say that, especially after Westin broke into his home and threw him to the floor. But Jasen was always someone who appreciated family, and he respected those who stood by their family. So, even though it was clear he didn't agree with Westin's methods, perhaps he developed a fraction of tolerance for him.

"Shuttle 226 is the last ship out for the night," Claudia said. "It'll get you to Kartigen before morning. We'll bypass security because I'm classifying you as VIPs, so I'll escort you directly to the ship. Meaning, I'm assuming responsibility that all of your paperwork and identification is checked and you are departing the planet under legal conditions."

Her computer beeped, and she reached beneath her desk and came up with two passes.

"Here are your security passes." Claudia stood, walked around her desk, and handed one to each of them.

Tammi and Westin had to get Claudia to issue them security passes because if they had bought their own tickets, their names would have been on the registry. Security passes required no name, as the assumption was only very important people who wanted to remain anonymous were given those.

"You're saving our children's lives," Westin said. "And I assure you, when you see your kids you'll hear phenomenal stories about the fun they had."

"When will you tell us where they are?" Claudia asked, her eyes pleading, arms wrapped around herself.

"I pre-recorded a message to you. It's scheduled to transmit when we're on our way to Kartigen."

"Follow me," Claudia said, hastily exiting her office and heading down the corridor.

Minutes of silence followed and Tammi's heart beat with excitement. They eventually came to the end of the corridor and walked through a door.

Tammi smiled as the engines of their shuttle made a satisfying roar. This was reality! She grabbed Westin's hand. He pulled her close and kissed her cheek.

They approached the ship and only maintenance was around. Tammi was beaming.

"This is it," Jasen said, stopping at the ramp with Claudia at his side. He stretched out his hand toward Westin.

Tammi was surprised at Jasen's offer, but smiled when Westin took it and the two men shook hands. She looked over to Claudia and mouthed "thank you." Claudia nodded and looked down.

Tammi and Westin entered the shuttle and took seats around midway down. Very few people were on the shuttle.

"This is a weird feeling," Tammi said. "We're about

to fly away and they're not vowing to track us down and murder us? . . . What if Jasen turns on us the last minute?"

"He won't."

"How can you be sure?"

Westin put his arm around Tammi. "We're both just men fighting to protect our families. Neither of us will jeopardize the other's chances unless the other does something first, but both of us have stakes too high to let pride dictate our actions."

While basking in Westin's reassurance, Tammi felt guilty for all the illegal and deceptive things they'd done. Things she hoped she'd never have to do again.

Tammi leaned her head against Westin's shoulder and closed her eyes. She envisioned their lives on Kartigen months down the road once she gave birth. Maybe she and Westin would still be living with his uncle, but that would be okay because as they'd sit down and look at their kids, they'd be overjoyed and so thankful with the count—one . . . *two*.

Sᴏɴs ᴏғ Aᴛᴏᴍ

Ben Godby

The night Tommy and I were patched in, the gang
threw a party at the Deerskin & Bile. I think everyone
in town must've been there. We drank radium beers
with evaporation pond workers and did plutonium
shots off the waitresses—we'd gone to high school
with all of them. Weylan, the deputy from the local
PRNA chapter, came down and sat with us smoking
cinnamon sticks, and you could tell Kel—that's our
boss—was really happy about that. There were two
guys playing theramins on stage that Rico had found
in the next town over.

Yeah, it was a blast.

But the best part was when Tommy and I got
patched, obviously. We already had our powder blue

jackets, maroon slacks, and black bowlers with white hatbands, and we'd kept those duds spick and span just like we were supposed to. But we both knew those suits only really shone with a patch, and our faces must've been shining like lightbulbs when Kel and Negar—that's his second—got up on stage, kicked the theramin players offstage, and tapped the microphone to get everyone's attention.

The sound system wheezed and screeched and everyone howled. Then we all laughed and looked up at Kel grinning and giving us the finger, and Negar looming over his shoulder on the right (the guy never half-lifed; that's why we loved him).

"Thanks everybody for coming out tonight," Kel said. "The Sons of Atom love this town, and your support means everything to us."

There were cheers. The Sons of Atom meant something to Athabasca Lakes, too; that's why we were patching up, after all.

"Tonight we've got two really great guys patching in," Kel went on. "They've been hanging around with us a long time, and I think it's about time we rewarded them for all the stupid shit they've done for us."

Tommy and I, standing just behind the first row of the audience—which was all the older patch members, like Rupert and Stuart and Avi—traded grins. You can't dig that kind of excitement out of the ground. The guys in the front row hooted or jerked their thumbs at us and called us losers.

"I don't think these kids need any more intro-duction than that," Kel said. "Jin Kwai! Tommy Tellum! Get on up here, you two."

I remember thinking that was my only time as a hangaround with the gang that someone hadn't called us Jack and Tits; but other than that I don't really remember what it was like up there, because the stage lights flooded my eyes and the crowd seemed to go on forever. Everyone was laughing and hollering, and Kel and Negar and even Kel's wife Mireille were slapping us on the backs and shaking our hands. Mireille kissed us both on the cheek; she was kind of like a mother, like that, to all these guys in the gang, and especially to me and Tommy, what with our relationship with Kel.

Kel went to the back of the stage and used a key he had hung round his neck to open a balsa wood box. I didn't see what he took out until they slapped on our patches.

I looked down at it on my breast pocket and nearly teared up—too many radium beers and the heat of the moment, I guess. But, honestly, that little Bohr-Rutherford diagram never meant so much to anyone—I'll tell you that much.

● ○ ●

The party went late, but Tommy and I were jazzed as shit. Hours after we'd been patched—which felt like minutes, though we'd been to every corner of the D&B to arm-wrestle the whole Sons of Atom crew and hold gamma-ganja smoking contests and shoot beer bottles in the back parking lot and get blowjobs from the retrofitted automatons that did the dishes in the kitchen—everyone had finally left, but Tommy and I couldn't help but stick around. It was just the two of us plus this hangaround called Mike, Tommy's girl Cassandra, and the PRNA deputy Weylan sitting at the bar. Even the bartender—jones, we called it, though it couldn't give it to itself and it had to be lowercase because it was a necrotype and soulless—had gone home, though it was only early spring so the sun wasn't even up yet.

Kel and Mireille were the last ones to leave besides the rest of us, and they'd gone out just a few minutes earlier. Kel was a big man, the type that looked too big for his Sons of Atom jacket, and too mean for the powder blue. But he tucked all his muscles into it each day, and the man had more love than the rest of the gang combined: That night, before he left, he took me and Tommy into that vise-hug and embraced us. Then he pushed us back out to arm's length, snugged the brim of his hat low over his eyes, and looked us each in turn as he said:

"Now don't go getting into any trouble tonight. That patch isn't a privilege, it's a *responsibility*." He shook his finger when he said *responsibility*.

"Everywhere you go, you take the whole club with you. In this town, in that town, in the whole fucking world. Understand?"

"Serious, boys," Mireille said from the doorway, smiling—like she was trying to get us to crack and not man up to Kel's challenge.

But me and Tommy both nodded yes; Kel took club business seriously and, full members now, we did, too. But like he didn't trust us, like we were kids, he turned to Weylan and said, "Deputy, make sure these boys get home safe tonight."

Weylan laughed. "You sure you should be telling *me* that?" he asked. And then Kel turned to Mike, the hangaround, and said (though he was talking to us while he looked at Mike), "And don't hangaround hangarounds too often, boys. You're better than that, now."

We all had a good laugh, except Mike whose laugh was forced and got bitter as Kel walked out the door.

"You'll make it one day, Mikey," I said after Kel had gone.

And I felt sure he would, because Mike was a tough kid with ambition, and Kel was a good man. He'd been like a father to me and Tommy, and even though Tommy and I were so different, that sort of made us like brothers. Both our own pops had died fighting the Nuclear Holocausto, and maybe since they'd both been friends of Kel's, and Kel had no kids of his own, there was a psychological thing going on there—and what with his wife like a mom to us, our own mothers all shrivelled in the heart after the war. So maybe it's a head thing. Just don't ask me to understand it.

"I just can't believe it," Tommy was saying. His eyes were glowing softly in the way that means a boy's had a lot of rads that night. "I mean, you and me, Jack. We've been talking about joining the Sons of Atom for years. And here we are." He looked at me. "Sons."

"Sons," I said, and we clinked glasses, the heavy metal juice swirling to the rims.

"You guys," said Mike, holding his hands up like he was framing us, "are going to get *so* much more pussy now."

"Hey, jerkoff," said Cass. She looked up from

painting her nails laser orange. "I'm sitting right here."

"Yeah, my baby's more than enough woman for me," Tommy said, wrapping his arm around his girl's neck and smooching her.

"You hear that? You need to lose some weight," Mikey snickered.

The girl went to punch him and Tommy tried to get between them. I just smiled, shook my head, and put my nose in my glass.

"I'm glad to see you boys patched up," Weylan said, raising his cup to us. He was only a few years older, but it always seems like people who work for the People's Republic of North America just get older faster. He already had a little bald patch at the front of his head. "We may be on different sides of the fence, but we're playing the same game. Good to know I've got real brothers on the inside."

"The inside?" I laughed. "*You're* the inside, Weylan!"

"Shit. I guess I am," said Weylan.

Everybody laughed, and I went around the back of the bar to pour shots for everyone. I was feeling really good.

But then the door to the Deerskin & Bile banged open and interrupted our laughter. I looked up and everybody else turned, and we all really nearly let our jaws drop when we saw who was walking in.

In had come these two droopies. In their tongue they say *djrupi*, but that just sort of means 'man' in their language—and besides, around town *we* were the men and *they* were the *droopies*.

Their skin was sort of black and gray and bubbly all over, and it drooped off their faces a bit—which is why the nickname stuck. Their heads were very round, with big round eyes, little sucker mouths, and wide ears that were just as flat as saucers, without the fancy cauliflower cartilage of our own. They wore these snazzy double-breasted black and tan two-pieces, and went about with fedoras.

They just carried snooker cues, as if they weren't up to no good.

While we were all still staring like a bunch of dumb droopies (it's a real expression—it means with wide eyes—and obviously really appropriate; I'm not just being smart), trying to figure out what to do, Tommy jumped off his stool and swung his fist in the air.

"The hell are *you* doing here?" he shouted at the droopies. "We don't *serve* your kind here!" And he stabbed his finger at a sign behind the bar that read simply, "No ETs."

The droopies sort of looked at each other, though they only had to turn their heads the slightest bit to do it on account of their saucer-sized eyes; and then one of them—I couldn't tell which, their voices don't come from the normal places and you can never tell in a group which droopie is talking—began to speak. They spoke in a funny, high-pitched drone, like Tommy would sound if he dosed up on helium, and on the occasions when you had to talk to only one (which happened nearly never, since there were so many and they moved in packs) the words seemed to come from their ears rather than those little sucker mouths.

"Deputy?" the droopie said. "Isn't xenotic

inclusiveness a principle and policy of the People's Republic of North America?"

Weylan looked around at us, slowly, bringing in air through his nose like for a sigh. Then he shrugged. "This is a private place of commerce, mister. I can't tell them what to do."

"Yeah," Tommy said, swaggering. He tossed an arm around Cassandra, who helped him glare at the droopies. "And it's a private party, too. We don't need your ugly alien faces messing up our fun."

"Ugly faces," the alien mused. A green iris rolled across the flat black surface of its left eyeball and was gone. "What's the girl doing here, then?"

That cracked the room open like a supercooled piece of PVC. Mike and Tommy broke bottles on the bartop and sent radiated suds flying. The droopies drew back with their pool cues, holding them like spears. Honestly, I didn't know what to do, and later I thought that was a mighty poor way to act, like a coward, on my first night as a Son of Atom. Thankfully, Weylan spared us all the trouble and me the embarrassment: He rushed between the two sides, his arms flung out, the red of his epaulettes vibrant in the earthy common room of the Deerskin & Bile.

"Hey!" Weylan growled. Tommy and Mike were snarling, and Cassandra was hissing like a cat. The droopies were dead silent. "There's not going to be any trouble, so long as I'm here. Understand?"

"You heard what that droopie said," Tommy spat, his voice dripping with hate.

"And in *our* place, too!" Mike added.

"This is jones' place," Weylan snapped at the

hangaround, and Mike—for a change—shrank back. Then the deputy straightened a little and arranged the lapels of his red and black coat—satisfied, I guess, that the fight had been stilled. He turned to the droopies. "Why don't you all clear on out?"

And just like that, the droopies slipped out.

"Sons of bitches," Tommy swore.

"Bastards," said Mike.

"Did you hear what that alien freak said about me?" Cassandra shrieked. She slapped Tommy on the chest. "What're you going to do about it, huh?"

Weylan looked around at us again, at the mess of broken glass on the floor. The whole bar was filthy, I realized. There were walnut shells littering every surface that wasn't taken up by empty bottles, and great piles of ash marked the places where smokers had sat not long ago. It wasn't our fault, though in one sense we'd made it.

"I'm going back to the station to finish off some reports before I crash," Weylan said quietly. "You all ought to go home as well. No trouble, alright?" He looked around at us. "Please."

And then Weylan was gone, too.

We found ourselves back at the bar, and in the quiet I had more time to get angry at just how quiet I'd been throughout the little drama. I hadn't known what to do, not in the way that the other guys had it in them like instinct. It wasn't that I didn't want to defend Cassandra, or that I didn't care about my brothers; and it wasn't that I didn't hate the droopies, either. And least of all was it (before you go making any hypotheses) that I wasn't a real Son of Atom. If there was one thing I knew I was—was born to be—it was a brother, a member of that club. I knew that the situation called for Tommy's actions, and that even little Mikey had been braver than I; and that if things hadn't been so confused, I would've been flamed for my cowardice, and deservedly. But I thought then—even angrier at myself for the honesty—that maybe I just couldn't stomach it: the fists.

"I'll tell you what we're going to do," Tommy said quietly, and when I heard him I sort of came back from the place between my ears. He put out his index finger. "We'll hunt those droopies down." Then his middle. "And then we're going to show them a lesson."

"Damn right you are," said Cassie.

"Put 'em in their place," Mike agreed.

"Now hold on," I said. I started to speak, and the words started to get acidy as they came out, but I kept speaking them. "We'd better get Kel in on this. I'm sure he's got something to say about it. He's been after those droopies since the day they came to town. And the whole gang'll help, better than just the three of us."

"We don't need Kel," said Tommy. "Besides, think about it: He'd want us to handle it ourselves. He's gone home to bed with his wife. And this is just a couple of stupid ETs we're talking about. And we're Sons of Atom now." He grinned at me, but in a mean sort of way. "Don't tell me you forgot already."

I saw Mike grin, and the girl just stared at me. Her hair was very red, I realized then, like Weylan's epaulettes.

"It's not like I don't want them to get what they deserve," I said, "and it's not like I don't know what this patch means. But those droopies aren't going anywhere, and . . . and . . ."

"And?" Tommy demanded. I could only look at him pleadingly. And what? Did I just want Kel to clean things up like a dear old dad? That thought hurt, and it was my own. Tommy reached over and took my shoulder. "You know what you want to do. You know what we've got to do. Now I don't like violence any more than anyone else, Jack; but sometimes, there's a call for it. Athabasca Lakes is *our* town, and those droopies have got to understand that. Otherwise, there'll be hell to pay down the road."

I hated it. But, God damn if I didn't know he was right.

● ○ ●

Although I've never lived anywhere else, I suspect Athabasca Lakes is the nicest place anyone could ever live. There's hills, forests, and rivers for you to ride up and down along, and only a very little winter—which tonight was trickling off into ditches as the spring came.

We unhitched our bikes from the bike-posts out front of the D&B and set the little reactors thrumming. They were just like city bikes—thin wheels on superlite frames in hot colors (mine was an electric blue that inspired me to name the ride Hydromancer; Tommy's was waxed black and heavier than most, so we called her The Beast)—only difference was that, with those reactors going, you could zip around like you were on a dinosaur-burning motorbike. Mike climbed aboard his little green cycle, the one we called El Lizardero (to his chagrin), and Cassy straddled the back of Tommy's. We didn't have keys or anything to lock up the D&B, but everyone knew it belonged to the Sons of Atom, so it would be safe. With a nuclear hum, we set off into the night.

Our first stop was the girl's house. Cass must have thought she was coming with us, because she really howled when we dropped her off at home. It was the kind of racket someone totally radiated throws, which was weird because I hadn't seen her fuse all that much at the bar. Even if she was only putting on a show, it was good enough to draw her mother—a really shrivelled creature with iron muscles—outside.

"I want to see you kill it!" Cass was screaming as her old lady dragged her off. "I want to see you beat it to a pulp!"

"I will, baby," Tommy called after her. "Don't you worry."

And off we went, looking for droopies.

The droopies were new to Athabasca Lakes; they'd come down in the middle of the cold season—"just like influenza," as Kel had said. There were plenty of ETs in the People's Republic, and none of them were good for much, but the droopies in particular were sly. They'd tried to get their paws on stocks in the uranium mine just outside town, but ever since the Nuclear Holocausto (which happened when I was just a tiny bruiser), ETs had been forbidden from controlling nuclear resources. But the ETs that were sly, like the droopies, tried to find ways they could do it—legal finagling, back-door dealing, the sorts of strategies only dishonourable lowlifes will trade in—and so the PRNA didn't bother the Sons of Atom when we took our own measures to ensure the spirit of the law was upheld, and the ETs kept out of what was rightfully Earthlinger business.

We stopped in at Tommy's mother's place, and he slipped inside to get the old ray-gun that had been shipped home with his father's uniform. None of my dad's stuff had made it back—he'd been vaporized—but Tommy's old man had caught the Fissions and perished that way, so they still had a bunch of trinkets in the attic. We saw a light go on up there, then go off, and Tommy came back out and flashed us the gold and shiny piece with a grin on his face.

Mike laughed like the gun had told a joke. I was just glad: A ray-gun would make faster work than our fists.

●○●

The droopies lived in a squat little borough of row-houses off of Route 9, one of the tenement projects build a half-decade ago during the Malthusian Refutation that were emptied out when the PRNA needed fighters and they didn't all come back. We rode by there and didn't see anything, just all dark-ness and decay, broken windows patched up with planking and bricks lying around on the half-finished sidewalks like bums. But then coming out through a neck of woods on the other side—which was Route 202—we caught sight of some junky tar-burning taillights, and when we saw that dinosaur ride we knew that we'd found them.

How they'd got that old clunker to run we couldn't say, and how they fuelled it was even more of a mystery, but it was a noisy, bright old artifact and I knew it would be an easy thing to follow without giving ourselves away. Our bikes just made a little hum and let off the tiniest glow, and on all but the very darkest and most silent of nights you wouldn't notice the thing without it being right in front of you. We followed the car, having to crank back our throttles so we didn't overtake it.

We rode for a while, and I was convinced the whole while that daybreak was just over the horizon, but the night was longer than I expected or we just hadn't partied quite so hard as I thought. We swept through the tree-lined avenue of 202, passing more abandoned houses and some live ones, the corner store Le Pilon (it was a Quebecker place), and finally came back around the other side of town. The droopie car pulled into the lot of the bowling alley, called Great Balls of Fire, and we stopped across the road in a stand of hemlock. Still, we had to drag our bikes backward through the brush to keep hidden. There were a lot of lights on across the road. The bowling alley was one of those weird places that stayed open all night, I guess because ETs like to have something to do in the wee hours.

We all stayed silent and just watched as the droopies got out of the car, went to the trunk, and pulled colorful bowling balls from its depths.

"Ultimate gamers, there," Tommy snickered.

"Yeah," added Mike, "guess they're just looking for

some innocent fun, right?"

"Right," said Tommy.

"What do we do?" I asked.

"We go in and show them what's what," said Tommy, "that's what we do."

Mike nodded and reached over as if to grab the ray-gun off the little haversack Tommy had strung to his bike, then let his hand drop and touched the mini-bat he had on his own instead.

"Well, hold on," I said. "We know they're going to get kicked out of there, too. Nobody around here likes droopies, or any ETs for that matter. And we don't want to cause a scene inside. We know what Weylan would have to say about that."

Tommy shook his head. "He's our man."

"But he's still PRNA," I said. "They could fire him if they knew. You know, *knew* knew."

Mike and Tommy nodded. I rubbed my hands on the handlebars, thinking. There were just certain ways you had to do things, but I was sort of afraid to get too far from civilization before we faced those suckers. In the dark, by the tenements off Route 9, they might have backup.

"So, let's ride over there and wait for them," I said. "Then, when they come out, you let them have it with that blaster."

Tommy grinned and reached over and slapped my back. "I knew you were a Son at heart!"

"Of course I am," I said sharply, and then, hearing the acidity in my voice, said more softly, "Always have been." And at that moment it felt good to be a Son, to have a gun, to be able to make rights out of wrongs by just moving little obstacles with just a little force.

We stood in the parking lot, in full view (since we were Sons of Atom now, and Mike, well, he was our hangaround), and huffed a little einsteinium to bring us up and then a little argon to level us out. I started feeling really good and sort of realized that my lack of enthusiasm earlier had probably been the drags of the late-night half-life. Mike had his little bat down his pant leg, and I had a switchblade in my pocket (the switch actually didn't work anymore; you had to unfold it, like a pocketknife), but I asked to see the ray-gun again, and Tommy showed it around.

It was a beautiful gun, just like you'd expect, made for killing.

Then the droopies came out.

I'd imagined them stopping at the door, then scattering, but instead they walked right toward us.

"Well, look who it is," Tommy said sarcastically.

"Have you come to apologize?" one of the droopies asked as they stopped, a few feet from us and their car. I still couldn't tell which one had spoken.

"I don't think so," said Tommy. "We came to give you a little of this."

He'd had the gun at his side but now it was out, like a magic wand, and it made a sound, like the whole world was radio static. A violet band shot out its end and flanged around the droopies, encompassing both of them in a purple cloud.

Tommy released the trigger, the interference sound died, and the cloud parted.

The two droopies were still standing there.

"Ah," one of them said, or maybe both of them said

it. And then they split.

And I don't mean they ran away. I wish they ran away. I mean they *split*: They each tore in two, and made two more. Four droopies stood looking at us now, each wearing those slick tan double-breasteds as though it were just part of their organism.

"What!" said Tommy, but before he or anyone else could say anything more, the droopies swooped forward and grabbed him. The beautiful gun fell to the ground.

Mike and I had our little weapons, but suddenly they seemed so dull and pointless. I mean, if your best weapon just makes more trouble, what more have you got? The droopies all had bowling balls—all four of them—except now they didn't look to be bowling balls, but big stone fists fused to the ends of their arms. They were crunching them into Tommy, and he was crying, really crying, just sobbing, totally helpless on the ground. Me and Mike were just watching, and I was thinking, *This boy doesn't look like a Son of Atom*, and then I thought, *I hope I'm thinking about Tommy*—and then I killed the thought, the way you kill a thought you don't like to think about.

Time passed in slow-motion, like when you take too many hits of the gamma-ganj, and Tommy's face and the droopies' faces were really crystal clear in my eyes, and my heart was really loud in my ears. My thumb fingered the knife in my pocket, like it at least had the courage to consider options. But what really came through was the thought that we were all going to die.

Then the door of the bowling alley swung open

again, and a big guy in bowling shoes stepped out. I think his name was Richard, like *Risharde*, the Quebecker version, and I actually spent time thinking how to greet him. But he wasn't thinking that kind of stuff. He had an old fashioned shotgun, and the first thing he did on coming through the door was level it at the droopies and fire. With one big bang, he dropped one of them. Its blood was black and gray like its face and sprayed all over their car in a rush.

In another second the others had scattered, double-breasteds disappeared into the trees. Tommy had stopped crying, and when the droopies fled I saw him laying stretched out on the ground, his blood and his brains just sort of everywhere. The gun was still lying beside him.

Richard in his bowling shoes ran up to us, then stopped short and looked sick when he saw Tommy.

And me and Mike, just standing there watching.

● ○ ●

The first thing that happened after that was that the PRNA got called. The next thing that happened was that Kel heard about it all.

Mike and I wanted to run. It's hard to say it, and we didn't say it to each other, but I know we both wanted to. Not like we had a choice, though. The manager from the bowling alley had seen us, and he came over, the gun still cocked under his armpit, and nodded knowingly.

"Those bastards," he swore. "They think they can get away with anything!"

He turned around, and we all looked at Tommy

again. Mike shuddered, and I turned away. We'd grown up together; anyone you really care about, you sort of expect to die together. But I doubt that happens very often, except maybe in wartime.

The PRNA cruiser swooped in over the trees a minute or two later. Its reactor was silent, but it had red and blue lights on top and on bottom that flared over the forest, casting the trees and the underbrush and then all the crud piled up in the parking lot hallucinogenic in its weird glare. It settled down a dozen feet from us, blowing pebbles and garbage out from under its propeller, and just as its little feet unfolded to the blacktop and its engine quietly died, the gang rolled in: bicycles silent, hats drawn low over their eyes, and powder blue coats immaculately brushed.

Me and Mike stood dumbly as Deputy Weylan got out of the cruiser alongside Sheriff Ichibara. Both of them looked at Tommy and then looked grim, and I knew their stomachs were queasing; but I felt a lot worse, because, with the sheriff involved, this was serious. Then Kel, Negar, and the rest of the gang dismounted, switched out their kickstands, and came up alongside us. They looked grim, too.

Kel didn't stop next to me and Mike, though. He walked forward and just stared at Tommy. I don't know how you could do that, he was so messed up. Then he hunkered down and picked up his hat, and cocked it over Tommy's eyes—like he'd just gone for a nap.

"This is a crime scene, Kel," Sheriff Ichibara said, a fat cigar—a real tobacco kind, real serious—hanging from his yellow lips. "You're going to need to step off."

"It involved my crew," Kel said, standing slowly. He didn't look at me, but I felt like his mind's eyes were turned on me, and I shrivelled a little then, cursing myself for being afraid of Kel. But if he was like a father, I guess that meant I had to be a little afraid of him.

"And I'll be questioning them," said Ichibara.

"Me, too," said Kel.

Ichibara sighed. I looked at Weylan—the only face I could stand to look at—but he was just looking at Tommy and trying to keep his eyes from popping.

"You and your club ought to head home, Kel," Ichibara said, looking around the parking lot. "I don't want any more trouble here."

"We'll stick around, just the same," said Kel. He kicked the ray-gun, and then looked at me. His eyes were so cold they burned. "We don't want any more trouble, either. This is Athabasca Lakes, and we don't like to see anybody get hurt."

● ○ ●

Ichibara finished with me and Mikey pretty quickly— only really making any noise that you might think was approval or unhappiness when I mentioned me and Tommy had just got patched in—then moved on to the bowling alley manager. It wasn't the kind of investigation anyone expected to go anywhere, but sheriff was a political position and Ichibara had to go through the motions to keep it. He knew the Sons of Atom would deal out justice on the droopies; the PRNA had a hard enough job trying to keep ETs on paper, and if there was one less illegal, so much the trouble for them.

But I knew the worst was still coming. After I talked to the sheriff I picked up my bike and sort of stared at the handlebars for a while, and then Mike came over and got ready to go home. But Kel stepped up and grabbed each of us by one arm. "You, too," he said to Mikey.

We rode to the clubhouse in silence—really silent, because we only went at half speed (that's what you do when a member bites it, and I was glad for it, because I could hardly stay on my bike my heart hurt so much) and the reactors made practically no noise at that volume. Our spot was in the opposite direction from the droopie tenements, across dykes that separated rice paddies that were already filling with run-off, the winter-hardened seeds just shy of bursting into green sprouts. I could practically *see* the green—through the night, through the earth—and wondered if you picked up special powers, being close to death. Kel, who'd been in the war, seemed to have picked up something there: He'd looked on Tommy's corpse more easily than anyone else had that night.

Soon our clubhouse came into view: a squat log cabin attached to the nuclear refinery and reactor we owned just outside Athabasca Lakes. We parked our bikes and went in, me and Mike following Kel, the other guys just standing there watching.

We went past the billiard tables, the bar, the dart boards, and all the other fun stuff that a clubhouse is about. We went past the pin-ups of cute girls and Silent Shiny, the necrotype who keeps everything running around the clubhouse for us. He knew some-how—maybe because he had a connection to the other side—and we didn't have to nod or anything as we went past him into the conference room.

It was a big room with a big, solid table in the middle, and an engraving of our patch in the center. It occurred to me as we entered the room that I'd only been allowed in here once before, which was when the rest of the boys had voted whether I should be promoted from prospect to full member. Tommy had been there at the time, but now, it was Mike. The fact that he, a hangaround, was being brought in, was—as far as I knew—unheard of.

We all sat down and a few minutes of silence passed, with Kel sitting with a finger pressed to his temple and his hat laid down in front of him on the table.

"What," he said finally, "did I tell you before I left the bar tonight?"

"Kel . . ."

"Don't!" he snapped, and he pointed a finger at me.

"It was my fault," Mike blurted, and we both turned to look at him.

"No," I said after a minute of struggle. "He's not even patched. It was my fault. Those droopies just talked smack about Cass. I never should've let us go after them." I shook my head. "It wasn't worth retaliation."

Kel leaned over and took my head in his big hand. His face was old, lined, framed by gray hair and a fringe of gray beard. It was imposing with its age; how much had it seen? "No. You let me decide what's worthy of retaliation. You've only got one job to do. And that's to do what the club tells you. This isn't just about you, or Tommy, or Mike. It's about a whole gang of us. We make decisions *together*."

"I'm sorry, Kel," I said. "It's just that, there were

only two, and Tommy was riled about Cass . . ."

"It doesn't matter if there's one or a thousand!" Kel shouted, and he slammed the table. "It doesn't matter whether it's a one-word slur or if they murder everybody in the gang. We do things *together*. Or else guys get killed, guys like Tommy." He sat back and sighed. "There's got to be order. I told you. That patch isn't a privilege; it's a responsibility to each and every one of us." He put his hat on. "So what happened?"

I told him the story, and when I got to the part about the ray-gun he seethed. "Damn it, Jack. Those droopies are *radiation-eaters*. That's how they replicate. They're barely alive at all. They just absorb gammas and alphas and split open like amoebas. Didn't you ever wonder why they all looked the same? Why they wanted to get on the rad market so bad?"

"I'm sorry, Kel," I said again. It seemed like the only thing I could say, to try to put things back in the order they were supposed to be. I felt like such a kid, not two bits of data in my head. "I didn't know."

He pointed his finger at me again. "Because it's not your *job* to know. It's *mine*. That's why we talk, we share. That's why we're in this *together*."

We all sat in silence. "So what do we do now?" Mike finally asked.

"You do nothing," said Kel, "and *we* wait. We've got a brother to bury. And after that . . ." He steepled his fingers. "We retaliate." He looked at me pointedly. "Properly."

"Together," I said.

He nodded.

I took a breath. There was something gnawing at

me. I could still see Tommy's face, bashed in by those bowling ball hands. "Look, Kel . . . I know I did wrong. I hear what you're saying. But I was thinking . . . I can— I have—to make this right on my own."

Kel grabbed me again, and this time I thought he would tear me apart.

"Say that again, and you're out of this club. Violence has its place, Jack. But you don't get to decide on your own."

I nodded and looked down between my legs, then looked up at Mike. He nodded at me. I was wearing a patch and he wasn't, but I felt we were the same: on the outside because of where we'd been.

●○●

Kel wouldn't let me make it right on my own for the club, but I knew there was someone I had to make it right to on my own nonetheless, and that was Cassandra. I went the next morning, my bike gliding silently along the wet roads of Athabasca Lakes. The sun pattered itself along the route, lacing with the greenish glow from the reactor behind me, and before long I rolled to a stop in front of Cassie's mother's house.

It took something out of me to knock.

Her mother looked at me darkly. She was one of those locals who thought they'd be better off without the Sons of Atom, which is to say, she was one of those locals who'd never looked too closely at the PRNA. She probably couldn't tell the difference between me and Tommy, but it didn't matter, because Cassie was right on her heels.

Turns out there was nothing left for me to tell her.

"You bastard!" she screamed. She flew through the door. Her mother tried to catch her, but she was like a raptor. Her fists rained on my chest, and the morning cracked open, hot and white. "You son of a bitch! I hate you! I hate you! I hate you!"

"It was for you, Cassie!" I yelled back.

It wasn't what I had been thinking to say; I had been thinking to tell her how sorry I was, and how the club—or at least I—would care for her no matter what. But her onslaught brought it out of me, and suddenly the whole thing appeared starkly: How Cassie had been insulted, and she and Tommy wanted vengeance. How Cassie had said, "I want to see you kill it." And now Tommy was dead.

And now how I had the gall to blame her.

People sure take violence so much harder when it's done to them.

She stopped and looked at me.

"It was for you, you stupid bitch," I said again, and then I left and got back on my bike and rode.

●○●

The funeral was another day later. The club and everyone from town who'd ever been close to Tommy was there. His mother was, even though they'd never had any sort of relationship, and she laid the PRNA flag that had been sent home with the rest of his father over Tommy's coffin. Burying two men at once, I thought, and wondered how long she'd held on to her memories of Tommy's old man.

In the middle of the ceremony, while the priest

was saying the rites, some droopies came up the rise on the other side of the road that split the cemetery. There were many graves in between us, but some of the guys turned toward the ETs on the horizon and curled their hands, like they were ready to go breaking heads right then and there. Kel just gave one curl of his lip and they stepped back in line.

Afterwards, we held a party to remember Tommy, but it wasn't much of a party. Everyone who'd come knew we'd be planning something; they knew we had more important things to do than remember the dead. Tommy had been buried, and now it was time to bury others. After all the food had been eaten and the drinks drunk, we gathered in the conference room, the whole club, and looked at each other.

"These ETs," Kel said, "live in a bunch of houses off Route 9. They're radiation-eaters, which means we've got to use our fists—just like they used theirs on Tommy."

"How many?" Negar asked.

"Every one of them," Kel answered.

It took a minute for it to sink in that Kel had answered a question that was at least partially different than the one Negar had asked. I sat there looking at the boys, thinking how dumb a response all this was. This was order? This was a man's say-so. When Kel had held my head the other night and told me that things had to be done in a certain way, I imagined glory. I thought I was a soldier. It was the same thing when I went with Tommy. But now, sitting around a table, *contemplating* it, we were only exterminators.

"Early morning," Kel said, looking around. "That's when they're at their weakest. We'll meet off 202 at six A.M., sharp. Tomorrow."

I drifted out slowly, after the others, everyone going home to their old ladies or their kids. The nuclear reactor thrummed behind us. I wondered why the droopies didn't just come and take a bath in it, if that was all they were after; but I guess they were vulnerable to punches and kicks just like everyone else.

I was sort of letting the kickstand out on my bike, and feeling like the letting out of it was like letting the tension out of my chest—you can always ride, you can always run, you can always just move on from your thoughts and your thinking—when Mike came up from behind me.

"Oh, hey," I said. Something about him standing there was revolting; it reminded me too much of myself.

"Hey, Jack," he said. He looked around, all squirrelly, but the other guys had already left to rest up for the operation in the morning. "I was thinking about what you said."

"What did I say?" I asked.

"That it was our fault," he said, and hung his head. "About Tommy, I mean."

"You heard Kel," I said. "We've got to work together."

He raised his face to me. "So why don't we? You and me. We're the ones responsible. We can make this right. Then the rest of the club doesn't have to. No one else has to be risked."

I let the kickstand back down. It made sense. It made more sense even than the Bohr-Rutherford patch on my chest. Sort of a law of causality, something primordial. I just wanted to make it right; I wanted to take responsibility. How can you take responsibility in a group? You just get the guilt, and none of the share in the credit.

"Let's do it."

●○●

We rolled up Route 9 in the early evening, when we knew the rest of the boys would be sleeping. The sun cast oranges and yellows around the tops of the trees and leaked down into puddles along the streets between the rowhouses.

"How many of them are there?" Mike asked.

I realized for the first time I didn't know—anything, really. The enemy, who were they? Where were they? It seems like you shouldn't go into a war without being really sure of that. That's what the Nuclear Holocausto was supposed to teach us, according to the history textbook I had in high school. But we didn't have the privilege, so we'd just have to find out. The world could come to us; this would be a subjective thing.

We only had to roll up the street once. Those droopies must have been able to sniff the exhaust from our reactors, because a pair of them stepped out, those sucker mouths of theirs twitching, from one of the houses at the end of the line. We pulled up short and climbed off our bikes.

"Yeah, come and get us," Mike shouted. "We're

here for you. We're who you want. We're the Sons of
Atom."

I thought, then: Were we? Or only trying to be?

They came on, their hands bowling balls again, and
I saw they weren't balls at all but just flesh: metasta-
sized protrusions hard as rock.

Mike had brought an old .38 revolver with him,
and I had my switchblade. I didn't even have to do
anything at first: A few quick bangs rang out in the
still air, and the droopies dropped. They leaked some
sort of gray-black fluid. It was like they were made of
just one thing, the whole way through.

"What do you think?" Mike asked. His face was
both pale and full of blood, and he held the gun with
shaking hands. He'd fired four times. "One more, by
my count. Am I right?"

A door opened down the street, and six more
droopies spilled out.

"Shit!"

We tried to get back on our bikes, but the droopies
were fast. Mike snapped off the last two rounds in
his gun and knocked over one more of them. I kept
hoping that someone would appear from a nearby
house, like the manager had at the bowling alley,
shotgun in hand, ready to tackle anything. But this
was droopie territory; it was like they had just
swallowed up all the neighbours and turned them into
more droopies. I cut out with my knife a few times,
and I felt some fleshy thing give way—just beneath
those dapper tan duds—that wheezed and sighed as it
released its alien fluids. Mike struck out with the butt
of his gun, pistol-whipping the droopies who came,

but our efforts didn't matter. The ETs swarmed us, beat us down, and soon they had us.

"Sons of Atom, are you?" one of them said through its ears. Its cannonball hand was raised for the kill, and I felt sick. I didn't mean to die like this; I didn't want glory or martyrdom. I wanted to die an old, happy man, with good memories of my time as a Son.

"Yeah," Mike spat, "and more are on their way!"

"When?" the droopie asked. "How many?"

"Mike!" I hissed.

"All of 'em," he said, "and soon."

The ETs paused and looked at each other. Their cannonball hands melted away.

I felt a thrill, the genius of survival, before I wondered what it meant. And then they dragged us inside.

● ○ ●

It dawned on me that the droopies were not unlike us. No: They were not unlike *Kel*. It had been Mike, Tommy, and I that moved carelessly and quickly and broke an order that had previously existed. The droopies, on the other hand, had been biding their time. They only need to make one move, ordered and complete. *Together*.

Order, I realized, moved everything. Chaos—like Tommy's shenanigans—made the headlines, but it was order that squelched it.

They took us into one of the rowhouses, and from inside we saw they had all been connected: walls knocked out, made into single giant rooms. There were not all that many droopies, but they all acted in

concert and they seemed to have no need to speak.
I became afraid. I was used to an ET here or there,
clearing dishes at the diner or working in the big
lumber mill outside of E-Town; but I wasn't used to
being surrounded, being a minority.

The sun slowly sank and night came over the
lakes.

"Don't worry," Mike told me. "The club'll come
soon."

"What the hell is your problem?" I snapped at him.
The droopies were all bustling around; they'd left us
alone for the moment. "You're an idiot! We shouldn't
be here at all! They're going to kill us! Do you see
what's happening? They're going to *ambush* them all
now."

Mike shrank back into himself. The droopies
looked at us, then turned away without saying
anything. It wasn't even in their nature to laugh.

I hung my head. I think I'd really been yelling at
myself.

At some point, when I was wishing I could fall
asleep, the droopies picked us up and carried us
downstairs. As we went down, I saw another droopie
climbing the skeleton staircases that still rose
between the empty shells of the row houses and
climbing out onto the roof through a trapdoor before
we went into the basement.

What was there made me freeze up.

It was one of those alien ships, the ones they use to
come down from space. PRNA Immigration Services
are supposed to confiscate them all; that's pretty
much the only thing we've got over them. Somehow,

these droopies had managed to pull their ship out from under the rug of Immigration.

It was a disc sort of thing, with a big hatch on top that was clear as glass. It was nearly as big as the house we were in, and I could see now that the floors had been modified—with scrap metal and bits of old dinosaur-burning engines—in such a way that they could be peeled back to let the thing fly out. It was like they'd been at it for years, but they'd only arrived a few months back. I looked around at their little crew, not even ten of them I saw now; when they'd swarmed us, and when they held us inside the upper stories, it had felt like hundreds, a whole herd.

They were just organized, I guess.

Two of the droopies walked towards their ship. Below it was a table, and on it some sort of case. They opened the case and one of them pulled out a hunk of iridescent metal. I knew it from the smell right away: uranium.

"The last of our fuel," the droopies said, and for the first time I thought that maybe it wasn't just one of them speaking, but all of them.

"How much do we require to get to the target?"

The droopies began splitting the uranium with little knives, practically switchblades, that seemed to poke out between their knuckles. I wondered if they had any weapons of their own, or if they just copied ours. Soon, they had made two piles, one much larger than the other and mostly of big chunks; the other consisted of many slivers, and was small.

"We will need all our strength to defeat the Sons of Atom," they said. The noise hurt my ears. Then the droopies came forward and started to pick up the slivers of uranium.

My eyes bulged. They started eating them.

I've been a rad-head for a long time; in fact, everyone in Athabasca Lakes is a rad-head. There's two reasons, I guess: The first is that the whole area was blanketed with nuclear destruction when the Nuclear Holocausto occurred. I've heard that in some parts of North America and the rest of the world people still get sick from radiation; but, here, in Athabasca Lakes, it just makes us high. Plus, we've got tons of the stuff to spare. There's half-degraded radioactive material all over the countryside from the war, and plus a whole lot in the mines in the ground. So, we've got a reason to be rad-heads.

But eating uranium pure? That's just sick.

Then I realized that was just what the droopies— the radiation-eaters—wanted.

They started to shudder when the stuff touched their tongues; and then they started to split. It was just like when Tommy had shot them with the ray-gun. They split right in half, and then, where there had just been one droopie, there were two.

It was insane. Mike moaned.

Soon, there were more than twice as many droopies in the room—nearly thirty, by my count. The only difference, it seemed, was that all the ones that duplicated were a little shorter than the others. The two droopies that had done the cutting hadn't eaten any uranium, like they were the leaders or something; and the others were all just half a head smaller.

"There will be much more fuel when we arrive at

the target," they said. "And the Sons of Atom will not
be there to stop us."

I realized, then, why the droopies—more than any
other ETs—weren't allowed in any of the bars in town,
or in the liquor store, or why they'd been kept out of
the mines vehemently. They were trying to *reproduce*.

Suddenly, all the droopies cocked their heads, like
they were getting a message from somewhere else,
and I remembered that one droopie on the roof.
Nodding in a little wave of bobbing heads, they picked
up me and Mike and carried us into their ship. We
tried to fight them off, but there were too many now.
The cockpit of the ship was spacious, and they tied us
to a couple of chairs that were backed with what
seemed like leather, but made from the wrong kind of
skin. I tried not to think about it, and instead watched
the two leader-droopies stoop down and put the rest
of the uranium in a little engine compartment. With a
flutter, the ship lifted off.

I gasped. Maybe the floors and the roof had been
made to peel back, but they didn't bother to open
them. They just smashed right through. And the other
droopie, the one on the roof? He got smeared all over
the windshield.

Mike screamed.

I looked out the cockpit and saw, in the street
below us, the Sons of Atom. They were on their bikes,
glowing softly in the very early morning light. They
had stopped and looked up at us. It was a little earlier
than they were supposed to come, but I thought I saw
fury on Kel's face, down below, and I knew that me
and Mike had been found out.

His face and the rest of the Sons disappeared as we soared over Athabasca Lakes. The whole town, all its little boroughs and stores, spread out in miniature below us. The trees and hills and lakes and rivers whipped by, but it wasn't half as fun as riding on a bike. No: The air wasn't for me.

Neither were droopies.

I saw the clubhouse and the reactor leer into view, and felt my whole body shake. We touched down in the parking lot, and the droopies climbed out and carried us along with them like the prisoners we were. I was surprised they hadn't killed us, but I knew there must be some reason. Probably bait. The droopies wouldn't do anything stupid or emotional; they wouldn't care about offing us, just like they hadn't cared about wasting Tommy. Everything had a purpose. It was all done with a reason. They were like Kel in the supreme.

They were taking us toward the big, steaming tower of the reactor when Silent Shiny came out of the clubhouse. In his hands was an old automatic rifle, hauled from some storage bin somewhere. He had a look of real determination on his face, the kind of determination you only see on the faces of the already-dead; but the droopies were on him, fast. I heard the gun explode with a chatter of fire and saw some of the ETs drop, their gray guts spraying, but all too soon old Shiny was crushed by the weight of the enemy. They pulled back, and I saw the scene of Tommy again, sprawled out on the curb—only this time, it was someone else.

"Oh, God," said Mike. He was tearing up, and I

thought I might do so, too.

The aliens picked us up again and carried us to the reactor. We went up the outside staircase to the big lip around the smoking green caldera of radio-active sludge. There, we were forced to watch as the droopies started slurping big heaps of the stuff into their mouths—and splitting, just like before.

It was awful. I knew that, sooner or later, the boys would come back, and there would be this whole army of droopies to attack them. And the droopies didn't care about their individual members, either: I'd seen what had happened to that lookout on the roof. They fought for the whole.

It was going to be bad. They weren't like Kel, actually; they were sort of like us, but the difference was our whole was all about individuals: It was an organization, not an organism.

Soon, there were at least a hundred of the droopies standing around the lip of the reactor. They'd grown shorter; they were nearly half the height they had been. But I knew that didn't matter. A dwarf could still kill you, especially if it could metastasize its hands into bowling balls and knives.

Then the Sons arrived.

They rolled into the parking lot on their bikes, silent and deadly. They were all armed with ancient guns: Kel knew that ray-guns wouldn't do a thing to these monsters. But when they saw the army poised on the lip of the caldera above, they all stopped. It was like Kel knew it was lost.

"You cannot win, Earthling," the droopies chorused. "Your emotional outbursts have defeated you. Now we control the resource that makes us invincible. We are legion. We are innumerable. When one of our number falls, two more shall spring to fight you."

Suddenly, I realized the absurdity of it. They'd just been slurping little handfuls of goo and getting smaller; more of them, and more overall, but smaller. A hundred shorties would be hard to fight; but ten thousand insects wouldn't be.

I got up and ran, starting to push the droopies into the reactor. They hadn't seen it coming: They were too fixed on the guys below. Mike caught sight of what I was doing, and, realizing what I'd figured out, followed my lead. Soon, we had half the droopies in the tank. They were splitting at an insane pace, ripping and tearing apart and becoming two, then four, then eight.

The other droopies split and tried to get down the ladder. They knew, too. But Kel saw what I'd been doing and he gave the order to open fire.

Bullets ripped the droopies to pieces. It also tore holes in the tank of the reactor, and the shit started to spill everywhere. The other droopies were climbing out of the reactor, pint-sized now, literally. Me and Mike began stepping on them, and the squelchy splatter was the most satisfying thing I've ever heard.

It took us a while to kill all the droopies; there were a lot, now. But a jump from the reactor would kill them, so their only escape was to come down the stairway where we crushed them. There was radio-active waste spilling everywhere, making our heads light, making us laugh as we killed. It was awful.

When it was done, I was sure the whole town of Athabasca Lakes would be high for days. Weylan and Sheriff Ichibara appeared, swaying back and forth. Weylan giggled, and Ichibara started laughing, too. The rads were hot in the air, and there was gray and green waste all over the ground.

"Don't ever," Kel said, coming to put a weak hand on my shoulder, "disobey my orders again."

I grinned. I was feeling really hot. "Why, boss?"

"Because this is too funny," Kel said.

"Hey, Kel," said Mike, coming up. "What do you think about making me a prospect?"

Kel laughed hysterically. "What did I say about spending too much time with hangarounds, Jack?"

CHERRY BLUE

Matt Edginton

As the guests entered, Pol noted the obnoxiously expensive designer clothing worn by all; it was presumable that no suit or dress or fur-jumper had cost any less than ten thousand SCs.

Some of the pretty maidens wore them well—*very* well—and a handful of the gentlemen were still young and debonair. To Pol's distaste, however, most of the forty-seven guests were as old and tattered as aged parchment and looked to be on the verge of fossilization. Pol thought them a better fit for display in a museum of artifacts.

He smirked at the thought, and nodded at an especially pompous and overweight man who was waving confidently in his direction. Attached to that

silver-studded arm, like a lamprey, was a lovely but
stupid-looking girl young enough to be his daughter.
Pol knew from his extensive client files that Evan
Crowitz, president of SkeleTek Industries, did not
have any daughters. But even without that knowledge,
the girl's obscenely provocative shred of a dress and
jackal-like eyes would have been clues enough to
deduce that she was a mistress of some form or
another.

The lavish clothing and gaudy jewelry was a
display expected of the world's elite—Pol's own silk
three-piece was a one-of-a-kind *Vega Loricella*, and had
cost somewhere in the fifteen- to twenty-thousand
standard credit range. A laughable price for a man of
his stature—but in contrast to many of the others,
Pol had never been one to become fascinated with
fashion. He wore the most exclusive designers because
it was expected of him, but in truth he would be
perfectly content in a laboratory smock, plain pseudo-
cotton shirt, and loose, well-pressed slacks.

The elite were being shown to their designated
seats by Pol's selected group of handsome (or beautiful) escorts. The expansive chairs and tables were
more items of lavish fabrics, materials, and designs,
and drinks of rare vintage were served in gleaming
crystal glasses—all on the house, of course.

Ensuring the security of the location and transportation of guests had been thorough, exhausting;
all of them had come to the private auditorium by
means of unmarked, cloaked jets that had stopped at
multiple "dummy" locations. Some of the elite had
been flown in from the opposite end of the planet and

had just spent nearly a full day in transit. They would return to their homes and countries the same way—never knowing for sure where the private display had taken place.

Pol hoped it was enough.

He had seen to the security and public-evasion maneuvers himself, but despite his efforts to keep the assembly private and unknown to anyone but a select group of VK6 employees, he had his worries. If there had been even a small leak . . .

Well, no use in dwelling on that now. If there had been a leak in the staff, the bombs would be exploding any minute, or the lower level of the building would be swarmed with mercenaries, and Pol and his guests would all most likely leave the party dragged lifelessly behind a mob of protesters.

Pol had plans for such contingencies, but unfortunately they did not include securing the safety or escape for many but himself and his family.

C'est la vie.

The lights dimmed, and at the front of the auditorium a soft spotlight centered on the neatly posed man with emerald cufflinks. Pol, his hands gently clasped, stood regally before a large holo-screen. He switched on the Avoldexi *Luminance*, a compact verification pod to his right. Its green lights flickered, then stayed fully on, indicating the device's ready mode. Pol always had been impressed with the gadget: Running, the fist-sized orb perched on a sturdy set of tripod legs would absorb any film or audio material present in the room. At the slightest hint of forgery or tampered footage, the device would start spitting out warnings and codes and references to any cloud-linked input device in range. The guests could check the status of the pod's findings at any time by the consoles embedded in their seats.

In other, less demanding circumstances, they could have checked the film's authenticity status via their personal phones and tablets. However, any and all phones or communication devices had been confiscated during transit.

The irony of employing the expensive piece of equipment was not lost on Pol; Avoldexi Corporation had vehemently condemned his clone research and production from the beginning. The megacorp had been quick to confirm their role (along with five other giant corporations) in the hiring of private-militia firms that had been responsible for bombing two of his South American facilities.

And now, to his amusement, one of Avoldexi's greatest innovations was going to be present for one of VK6's greatest unveilings—it was Pol's personal retort to one of his most capable enemies. That, and the Avoldexi *Luminance* bore a widely recognizable trademark. Synonymous with factual assurance, it was good for the presentation. Good for the guests.

He paused for a dramatic moment after silence in the room had been established, then began his introduction.

"Good evening. I am Pol Blue, president of VK6 Enterprises. I know that the security precautions for this unveiling have been relentless; unfortunately, it was unavoidable in order to make possible your attendance tonight. I hope you understand the need for such measures and accept my apologies for any discomfort. I know that you are all here with some inkling to the nature of our unveiling, and so I will not dally on trivial introductions. Aside from the essence of time that we all understand too well, our product will need very little introduction; I believe you will find its implications to be immediately apparent."

Pol gave a genuine smirk. He was excited, but confident. He met eyes with a particularly gorgeous guest in the second row who was also smiling and lazily twirling a seductive finger across her prosthetic cleavage. Pol's eyes sparkled. "This evening we will be showcasing our latest model—the LOPAN R9."

There was a murmuring of excitement among the world-giants. Nearly everyone had heard some rumor or bit of teaser information on VK6's latest project, and they knew that the commotion over the project was not just hype: This was going to be a model that would revolutionize the world.

The VK6 emblem flashed on the screen and then a series of videos began. The first showed the basic design of the LOPAN R9: the egg-like main chamber that was cushioned with durafome and large enough to comfortably accommodate a small child. Then, pretty cutaways (simplified, of course) showed the different layers and materials that made up the smooth exoskeleton. From the titanium alloy body extended two electromechanical arms and legs, each highly polished and composed of the same specially treated titanium sandwich that made the unit's limbs and casing so effectively rugged.

Footage was shown of tests that proved the

interior of the bulbous chamber to be shock resistant by means of acoustic stabilization: Soft melons were inserted into the main chamber and then the entire unit was dropped from outrageous heights, battered with common projectiles, and generally abused in countless other ways. The melon was always removed intact and unscathed, and the audience gave murmurs of their approval.

At the film's end there was footage of the final test run. VK6 technicians stood around a LOPAN R9 in their tightly fitting gray suits, diagnosing the machine's vitals with proximity-link handhelds. From behind a door appeared a man in a black smock with a male toddler holding his hand. The boy was ushered into the R9's cockpit with smiles and nods from the techs and the man in the black smock, and then the unit was sealed and directed to an outside enclosure.

Under a blue sky, there was a long, narrow field of shortly cut grass. Tall walls and gates, studded frequently with capable-looking gunnery, lined the test field on all sides.

The technicians flanked the LOPAN unit and brought it to stand by a white line near a main wall. One of the techs placed a small, remote-controlled vehicle (of obvious military grade) onto the ground and sent it racing down the testing field in a wild zigzagging pattern.

It wasn't ten seconds before the little vehicle hit a sensitive trigger buried under the grass and exploded into nothingness; clumps of dirt rained down around the smoking crater that was left.

The LOPAN with the young boy inside was now

brought to stand against the white line that had been painted on the field. The narrator of the film explained that this line signified the termination of the "safe area."

Techs fiddled with their handhelds, and the machine lurched forward, seemingly against its own will. The small red lights between its joints lit up, filling the crevices between its limbs with brilliant, pink luminance. The techs continued to punch away on their small computers, and the R9 continued to protest against the commands. Again, the narrator explained that this particular unit's security features had been previously removed, but the inherent core safeguards were still giving the technicians a workout. (Pol hoped this display would serve to impress the audience with the unit's resistance to hacking. It was a gamble, though; they could just as easily see *any* successful tampering with the unit as a weakness.)

The safeguards were finally bypassed: Suddenly the LOPAN R9 dug its titanium heels into the dirt and shot forward down the field, leaving the white line behind it.

When the first mine was triggered by the galloping foot of the unit, a blue blast of light preceded the explosion. The ARCs (*accelerated-repellant charges*) had sensed a close-contact detonation and created an explosion of their own to negate it. This caused the unit to fly upward nearly twenty feet, but with little or no apparent damage. Cushioned by a subsequent, smaller ARC explosion, the R9 fell to the ground, and with its red lights still blazing, righted itself and began forward.

The innards of its cockpit were not visible—a smoky sheen had rendered the egg-front opaque.

The LOPAN R9 had not quite completed its third step when another blast from the earth sent it flying through the air, again preceded by the unit's own blue discharge.

The initial explosion after the LOPAN had left the white line had been surprising; Pol assumed the audience was just now remembering there was a live child within the R9. He watched their faces grow grimmer and more concerned with each successive explosion.

This collision course endured for a full two minutes, with the R9 encountering a total of thirteen land mines. Finally the R9 unit reached another white line at the opposite side of the field, and by means of hover-planks the techs bypassed the mine field and flew to the other side. The camera never stopped filming.

The techs could be seen exchanging bits of jargon between themselves as they poked away on their handhelds. The R9 unit was standing completely still. It was covered in dirt and grass, with small but clearly visible dents and dings covering its alloy exoskeleton.

Thin wisps of white smoke spilled from its joints and vents.

Quite abruptly, the red warning lights shut off and there was an audible hissing of released pressure. The cockpit broke seal, opened. The young toddler could now be seen inside; his head was tilted to the side and his eyes were closed. The man in the black smock approached the open chamber and gently shook the boy's shoulder. His eyelids fluttered. He sat up lazily, rubbing at his eyes but visually amused with the attention. He had been sleeping; the heavy blasts from the outside had initiated stability forces within the cockpit that created a kind of acoustic cusion. As the multiple explosions had jolted the R9, the child had essentially been rocked gently into sleep by the womb-like inner atmosphere.

The techs were exchanging handshakes and pats on the backs, congratulating one another on success.

It could have appeared that this was the first run involving human subjects (it was not, however, and Pol would never be made to comment on previous runs). Someone brought the man in black a small, rubber car—a toy—and he handed it to the toddler. The boy's eyes lit up, and clutching at the toy he smiled a prize-winning grin.

After a short epilogue, the film was over. The lights in the room came back to life to illuminate a crowd of pleased faces—some were still visibly shaken, but impressed. Some of the world-giants were already punching banking codes into the consoles embedded in their seats.

A couple of the men had left their seats and their mistresses to join Pol on stage, to vigorously shake his hand and slap his back with gusto.

Pol's wife, Terra, had entered from the left and taken her husband by the arm. She was exceptionally beautiful, as was expected; but because they looked to other parts of her anatomy, none of the men took much notice of her perpetually dreamy eyes. She insistently touched and rubbed at the oblong stone hanging around her neck, at times almost becoming completely immune to the conversation.

After more drinks were served, Pol initiated the final display of the evening. In the front of the room next to Pol and his wife there was a satin curtain that was drawn back to reveal a shining R9 model. Pol gestured and it came forward; the hatch opened.

Inside there was a small child, much like the boy in the film—no more than two or three years old. A beautiful Ashera cat was curled up on its lap.

The child was severe in manner, and almost completely unisex in its grooming—the latest fad with children. The men and women in the audience were clapping and smiling at the cute child snuggled protectively within the unit's cockpit.

Most of the world's elite automatically assumed it was one of Pol's clones (*surely* He *would have more than one*), and the resemblance was obvious. It was not a clone, however, but a naturally birthed child—and it was a *girl*.

She was Pol Blue's singular offspring, and her name was Cherry.

● ○ ●

Six months later, Pol stood in his extravagant study sipping aged bourbon, reflecting on that night when his LOPAN R9 model had been unveiled. It had been a good evening; VK6 sold thirty-some R9 models that night alone, and steady purchase of the unit had continued since.

Pol thought about the hurdles he had jumped to make it this far, about the struggles that his cloning process had endured.

A decade ago, cloning had been effectively mastered, and two years after that the restrictions and laws against it were abolished. The rigid laws had disintegrated, partly because *law* in general seemed to be decaying, but mainly because of the outrageous cost of cloning a single pure human. Only a *fraction* of a percentage of the world's population would ever have been able to afford such a thing, and at the time there was no real inclination to. Clones of the early years were nothing more than bags of duplicated flesh; the well-built ones grew and learned like any other human, and created almost totally different emotions and memories in contrast to their DNA-parents. Medical companies invested in the business for expensive transplant materials, but the private sector quickly lost interest in the cloning process.

Then came VK6 with its dashing and brilliant front man, Pol Blue. His team was the first to successfully transplant brain matter *and* consciousness into a willing clone body.

Essentially, a person with enough funds could have a slice of their brain removed, without losing the delicate strand of thought-continuation, and inserted into a suitable body with only minor side effects.

There were restraints to the process, though, and Pol had capitalized on them: Foremost, the transplant process would not "take" unless the body was of original tissue and DNA (a clone), and then the body needed to be of mid-pubescent range (eleven to thirteen years of age) in order to retain all transferred information and consciousness.

Observing this "Goldilocks" range was especially important to the process; implants that occurred before this range, being blended with so many other new stimulations and experiences, wore off and quickly dispelled. Implants made after held on even more briefly due to conflicts in personality.

Naturally there were special cases in which implants had held when applied a year or two before or after the Goldilocks range due to variances in maturity, but for the most part the prime range for swapping consciousness was but a small window.

And so, with the VK6 process, a slim percentage of the world's elite could have themselves cloned, and eventually they would be able to transfer their mental beings into these younger vessels. The process equated to a degree of immortality.

Eventually there was a desire to protect the clone against natural dangers and hazards, and as the elite-cloning business grew, the disapproval of the general population likewise increased and became more apparent on such procedures. Clone-bearers quickly desired additional protection against the onslaughts of kidnapping and vehement destruction of their "copies" and themselves.

VK6 set to work on the LOPAN prototype.

A few years later and the project was a success: The tough R9 suits were more than capable of protecting the tender brood of the aging world-giants. The carrier units could be submitted to extreme abuse with no damage to a clone awaiting its coming of age and right of passage.

Pol himself had two clones, as did his wife, Terra—

but they were kept at almost opposite ends of the world from each other, and surrounded by security greater than one could begin to imagine.

Like the others, Pol did not like to release information about his personal clones; his inherent distrust of humans had led him to surround his precious clones with nothing but artificial overseers and caretakers. The closest humans to his clones were a constantly rotating set of guards, set up with a small barracks in a corner of an undocumented island, and they were under the impression they were overseeing the security of a wildlife preserve. They were there to watch for and report any unauthorized aircraft or boat that approached the reserve—that was all. Metal-clad and heavily armed robotic sentinels would take any security issues from there.

Like the personally designed caretakers that watched over his clones on one of his islands, Pol had constructed a special suit, modeled after the LOPAN, for his beloved daughter Cherry—as she was *nearly* as important to him as his clones.

Pol was taken away from his reverie; there was a soft thumping outside of his study. He turned to see his daughter's R9 turn the corner of the hall and stand in the doorway.

He could see her small body and her solemn face through the mostly clear glass. Cherry didn't ever make it completely reflective for him, which made him happy. It was a small sign of her trust for him.

For Terra, her mother, it was a different story . . .

The large snow falling outside cast shadows through the window onto the smooth titanium body of the R9.

Pol smiled at Cherry, but suddenly felt the urge to cry. Here was his daughter, his own flesh and blood—a miracle if there was one—and she was terrified to leave the world inside her robotic carapace for any longer than a few hours.

Like a premonition, he could see the future reports coming from his research groups; the clones were safe from bullets and bombs and knives and mobs—but were they safe from *themselves*? Would the children be protected from their own fear and emotion when they were continuously trapped inside of the LOPANs with them?

Pol didn't think so. He could see the signs of un-healthy agoraphobia already emerging in his daughter.

Cherry spent nearly all of her post-womb life inside of the mechanical carapace, often accompanied by her loyal Ashera cat, Calypso. At one point in time she had expressed a desire to escape the machine's restriction, and had been allowed to wander free from her suit for a matter of weeks. But after a bloody, vicious, and well-documented assault on a fellow elitist's clone by a mob of rioting commoners, Pol had insisted that Cherry remain in her suit almost exclusively.

The image of the clone hanging from an inter-section's stoplights had given him nightmares for months; he would not allow someone to mistake his daughter for a clone and do her harm (or know full well that she was otherwise and do *worse*).

Encased in her R9, Cherry stood by her father and

watched the snow fall. Pol gazed at her and could not shake the feeling of guilt that was multiplying inside of him. He was beginning to wonder if he was effectively crippling his daughter rather than protecting her.

Aside from her daily exercise routine that demanded her release from her suit for three hours, Cherry had been confined to her unit for nine straight months.

Pol gulped the rest of his bourbon and poured another.

● ○ ●

The condition of the world had quickly deteriorated. It was good for business, Pol considered—his money was now of such a great sum that it was laughable. And still, all of the money in the world would not stop the riots and the mindless, barbaric destruction of clones and their parents. *At least*, Pol mused, *not in any reasonable ideology.*

Pol had decided in the previous weeks to jet his family to one of their private islands for a few months until everything cooled down. He had already moved his prized clones to even remoter locations for fear of their discovery.

He tried to convince himself it would only be months, but the dark half of him knew it would be years—perhaps even more than could be planned for.

He made arrangements to accompany a load of materials and supplies to the island. He planned on personally observing that the conditions of his island fortress met his strict standards, as well as the other strongholds for his younger selves. Then he would return at once for his wife and daughter.

● ○ ●

Cherry had opened her cockpit long enough for her father to kiss her goodbye. Two of his personal guards stood tensely outside of her nursery. He told her that he would see her in a couple of days.

Cherry watched him leave with a sick-sense that

only children know well. He was leaving her with her mother, and Cherry dreaded it. Her father wasn't around *all* of the time, but when he was he was kind and loving—unlike her cold and strange mother.

In recent weeks her father had become so fully immersed in his escape plan that he had not been able to see how quickly Cherry's mother, like the world, was deteriorating.

Terra had become so frail and thin in the recent chaotic months that she appeared skeletal, mostly due to overuse of the stim-stone that hung around her neck at all times now.

One of VK6's subcompanies had developed the neural jewelry line, which had also been a great success. Upstanding citizens of the world no longer smoked or injected their drugs; they wore the small polished stones of nano-circuit technology around their necks or as tiaras, and as of late even embedded under their flesh in wafers. At the slightest touch they could receive mood-altering frequencies and chemicals straight into their cerebral cortexes.

The staff knew full well the cause of Mrs. Blue's condition. Cherry's small but bright mind was only beginning to figure it out.

●○●

It was December and Cherry's father had been gone for two weeks now. She overheard worried rumors and suspicions from the staff; nobody had heard from Mr. Blue since his departure, and the worst was feared.

All conversation on the subject would stop when

Cherry or Terra came within earshot. Some of the staff had taken abrupt leaves without giving promise of their return. Others appeared to be on the verge of walking out at any moment.

The atmosphere of the Blue manor had degraded into static tension. Cherry made it a daily practice to stand outside of the large room where staff members met and listen to the most recent news of the outside world. She did not understand most of it, but the words *riots, military firms,* and *social chaos* were constant topics.

Her mother had become erratic and frighteningly outgoing during the days, and then she would sink into near catatonia in the evenings. Cherry was only two years old, three in a month, but she was smart enough to deduce that her mother's condition was related to that oblong, gray stone she had seen Terra rubbing against the back of her neck more frequently as of late.

After her mother left on a wild shopping spree one morning, Cherry resolved to set in motion the simple plan she had devised to separate her mother from the terrible necklace.

After her exercise time, she climbed into her R9 suit and secured the softly cushioned hatch. Then she went upstairs and waited in the kitchen hall.

When Terra returned carrying an armload of intricately wrapped parcels and looking even more strung-out with her wind-messed hair and bizarre choice of designer clothing, by means of neural suggestion Cherry maneuvered the LOPAN to reach out and snatch the necklace from her mother's pale neck.

Terra's eyes widened and her slender hand reached up to caress her now naked throat. The packages were dropped to the floor and one of them audibly shattered.

"Cherry, honey," she stammered, "give Mommy her necklace back."

The woman's face was twitching between fear, anger, and the attempt to hide them both with a lousy reassuring smile.

Cherry did not speak. She only gazed at the too-thin creature that was supposed to be her mother, who was now visibly beginning to hyperventilate with anxiety.

"Cherry . . . give Mommy's necklace back NOW!"

The woman made a swipe at the dangling necklace, but the pneumatic reflexes of the LOPAN suit quickly swung the bobble out of reach.

"Damn you, Cherry!"

Terra curled her fist and slammed it into the convex bulb that separated her and her daughter. The hit made Calypso rear back and hiss and Cherry flinched. The machine registered the blow as something other than common impact and tiny red warning lights glimmered across the titanium body's surface.

A faint humming had begun somewhere in the rear of the suit; it sounded like a very small turbine winding up—

It was a *warning*.

Cherry spoke quietly inside of the bulb and her voice passed through the sound-proof encasing by means of electronic speakers.

"No, Mommy, no. Let's play. Please—*please*."

The words were pleading and sincere, near weeping. Usually Cherry was a quiet and standoffish child, but she had cracked her cold shell for this one attempt to make contact with her mother.

Terra was surprised that Cherry had spoken so many words to her at once, and it showed in her face. Still, her eyes kept flickering to the dangling necklace.

"Honey, you and Mommy can go play! We can! Just give me the necklace back and—"

Again Terra swiped for the necklace, but was too slow. The necklace was brought even further from her reach, and this time it swung around the glossy metal fingers and the stim-stone came to rest in the palm of the carapace's fist.

The strong fingers crushed the stone without any resistance. The shards that were not reduced to dust fell to the floor, now only useless bits of hydro-boards and processors.

There was a growling sound coming from Terra's mouth and even a bit of foamy drool.

"You little brat, look what you have done—*look what you have done!* I hate you!"

The ferocity was so great that Cherry backed up in her suit. Her mother's eyes were something terrible now, full of predatory wildness. Through the hatch she saw the two white-knuckled fists coming at her face but could only manage a wailing *No Mommy!* before they made impact.

The suit registered the impact to be beyond unusual and immediately hostile in respect to the previous warning. The unit did not discern between relation—it only knew Threat or No Threat.

No other warning was given.

In a matter of milliseconds a wave of highly-charged plasma had exploded around the suit in a blue sphere expanding twelve feet in every direction.

What had been exotic wood in the kitchen area was instantly set to flame or incinerated, and the stainless steel surfaces could be heard warping . . .

Terra would no longer be needing her necklace.

Pol had never considered installing protective functions into his daughter's suit that would differentiate between assaults made by himself or his wife, and assaults from other, more *dangerous* individuals.

Pol would never have dreamed of striking or attacking the suit, and he had unconsciously assumed it would be an equally absurd notion to his wife. He had not considered the mood- and logic-altering effects of his wife's precious stim-stone.

Cherry was frightened, and the hurt and fear were escalating to levels she had never known. What had been a simple desire to entice emotion from her mother had turned deadly—Cherry did have a small understanding of *that* concept, only it lacked a grasp of duration. In her child's mind, Cherry knew her mother was hurt, badly—but there still may have been a chance that she could spontaneously reappear, perhaps at another time.

She stared at the necklace pieces scattered on the floor; the chain was melting from the heat and making a small puddle.

Because the fire and smoke sensors had been instantly destroyed in the plasma blast, the kitchen was now engulfed in flames. Crying, but instinctively knowing she must find *some* kind of help, Cherry walked through the flames and down the hall to the front entrance of the mansion.

Outside, the day was deceptively pretty: A smooth, marbled sky and bright sunshine towered over the white, rolling hills, but a frigid northern wind bit relentlessly at the landscape.

It was cold in the open, but that did not affect the climate inside Cherry's protective suit.

The young girl looked across the extravagant grounds and saw a plume of smoke near the front gate. Beyond that she could see a scene that was not immediately understood—but a thing she instinctively knew to fear.

There was a swarm of armored vehicles and many men in dull black masks and suits blasting their way through the guards and stone walls. Something inside of Cherry's LOPAN suit began to wind up, and the tiny red warning lights cascaded along the surface.

A group of black flying machines had descended from the sky and fired missiles into the steel building that was a primary guard post. Cherry could feel the ground around her tremble when the mighty blast devastated the garrison.

Burning shrapnel and fodder were blown across the grounds. The flying machines began to circle the mansion. Cherry did not need any further warning; she was already maneuvering her unit through the forested area behind the house.

● ○ ●

One of the sleek black helicopters had hovered around the mansion like a wicked wasp and then began slowly scanning the snowy meadows and trees through which Cherry had fled.

It must have registered some sort of heat or movement signature and decided to investigate.

Cherry's escape almost surely would have been discovered if a projectile hadn't pierced the air by the flying death machine . . .

Presumably a group of the Blue family's in-house bodyguards had made a final attempt to thwart the invasion, and were focusing on the most dangerous pieces of the assaulting party.

The pilot of the black wasp turned abruptly to re-engage the mansion's security. A blaze of light tore through the winter air and ended in a large explosion at the area where the projectile had been fired from. A quarter of the mansion went up in flames.

The mercenaries either became so involved with the fighting, or eventually succumbed to it—which was doubtful—but regardless of the circumstance, no one gave further chase to the rogue LOPAN unit.

● ○ ●

The gentle roll of the snow-covered countryside was beautiful, and the sky was a magnificent blend of white and blue. Cherry was not taken with the view, however. It was something alien to her, and she was sad and lonely. What was only half a day in hours seemed like forever to the little girl.

The LOPAN initiated a kind of self-assumed

preservation mode and continued to jog into the wilderness with no apparent direction. The unit's simple objective only knew that it had to go *somewhere,* and the direction opposite from the mansion seemed the most mathematically sound— the direction away from the weaponry and elevated aggravation that the LOPAN had detected with its specialized sensors.

The R9 suit could withstand nearly anything less than being dropped into lava and close-contact nuclear affronts—and even with those scenarios the outcome was unknown, never tested. It could provide shelter and protection, maintain favorable inside temperature regardless of the extremes outside, was equipped with a plethora of anti-assault devices— it could even camouflage its exterior to fit its surroundings within an eighty-percent likeness.

The suit could not, however, produce food. Or company.

Cherry's father had been investing great time and effort into the next model's design that would include "long-isolation" provisions; quaint things like micro food-tabs and water-suckers that could siphon moisture from the surrounding air . . .

Sadly, though, it appeared her father would never bring that model to fruition.

●○●

Snow crunched under titanium feet.

Nestled in her metal and polymer womb, Cherry was beginning to succumb to a mixture of shock and overstimulation. The internal speakers were set at low, but it was enough to hear the constant sound of snow under foot and the wind blowing by. It was a small comfort, but it was better than dwelling in complete silence.

Cherry would sleep for hours and come to long enough to see the soft glow of the R9's internal lighting keeping the darkness of night at a safe distance. Then she would nod off into a wave of fitful sleep and scary dreams. The R9 trekked on.

Calypso would be content to sleep for a while, curled up protectively next to the little girl, but eventually she would grow restless and pester Cherry until the girl opened the hatch and let her out.

Cherry would leave the hatch open for a moment, and take in the cold and fresh air. She wondered what the snow tasted like—her stomach was feeling very empty and the loneliness was making it worse. Then the expansive landscape would become too overwhelming, and the agoraphobia would kick in.

Cherry would shut the hatch and doze fitfully until Calypso came trotting happily back to the LOPAN.

The cat had tried to bring a fresh kill into the unit, a small furry animal with long ears, and Cherry had refused to open the hatch until the cat had finished its meal and was pawing and meowing frantically at the view plate. Calypso had enough instincts to hunt; she was from an ultra-expensive breed that had been genetically altered to manifest a great deal of wildness. It was part of her beauty. But despite instincts, she had lived most of her life indoors and on jets. Calypso was a faithful animal, but it was apparent that the Ashera cat had a bit of agoraphobia, too.

Cherry had been roaming through wilderness for almost two days. The machine, the cat, and the girl moved through a white forested land that to her was as much another planet. She began to fever and shake from dehydration and untreated shock.

The LOPAN R9, aware of Cherry's severe condition but unable to solicit help, continued forward.

● ○ ●

The Mallow family was packing their car with a small collection of clothing, food, and family documents.

Nolan, the two-year-old son, had been making mountains in the snow and marching his toys up them while his father and mother made trips in and out of the country home. His father, Jacob, had snatched him up and placed him in the luxurious back seat of the family car, where he began to protest mildly from a combination of sleepiness and aggravation at all of the hurried hubbub.

Jacob placed his hand on his wife's back as he was entering the home for the last of the supplies. Peg had her arms crossed, staring off into the snow-crusted copse of trees that encircled their property.

Her eyes were moist, and they would surely spill over any minute. Jacob felt a pang of anguish and had to exhale away the sourness that was growing in his chest.

"One more left and we can get going. Aunt Cynthia just called—she said the jet is ready and Job will be waiting for us at the gate."

Peg squeezed her husband's hand and took a breath. "Oh Jacob. Our home. Our *home*."

Jacob wanted to comfort his wife, but knew they must be going. This area was not safe anymore; reports of military activity had been reported from only a few miles away. Jacob knew it was probably from the larger homes in the eastern district—but that was still too close for comfort. He knew that in situations like this, proximity to persons targeted as guilty was as good as admitting association. The Mallows still understood that life was more important than material things; so, as much as it hurt, it was time to leave.

Peg watched her husband enter the house for what would probably be the last time. She allowed the tears to come, now, and the cold made them sting.

She was about to turn around and take her seat in the car when she saw a large object plodding through the foliage. At first she thought it might be some kind of attack drone, but no explosions or bullets tore through the silence; then the thing stopped at the edge of their field and a parade of lights flashed across its smooth, bulbous body.

"Jacob! Come quick!"

The Mallows stood motionless, staring at the robotic form. They did not know that their emotional signatures, voice patterns, and chemical excretions were all being silently studied by the machine. Jacob's mind kept going to the rifle that was buried in the back of the Horizon. The only thing that kept him from running and digging it out was the lack of aggression from the visitor; he did not want to be responsible for instigating an attack that could put his family in danger.

Also, he did not think the rifle would do much to the obviously sturdy exterior of the metal creature.

Unknown to the Mallows, the LOPAN R9 unit had quickly checked dozens of prime variables for the current situation and deduced *them* as being the most logical chance for Cherry's survival. There was a sixty percent chance that the Mallows were not hostile (*yet*), a seventy-eight percent chance that humans of that rating would be scarce for a hundred miles, and a ninety-seven percent chance that Cherry would die from lack of medical assistance if it was not procured within the next fourteen hours.

The LOPAN unit began forward, toward the Mallow mansion.

As the machine crept through the snow, Jacob again resisted the urge to leap and dig for his gun. Peg must have been equally frightened; she grabbed him by the coat and directed their bodies in a direction away from the car—away from their son if there should be gunfire.

The LOPAN came to a stop not ten feet away from the Mallows and sank back into a squat. The front hatch opened with a hiss. What Jacob and Peg saw surprised them both: a young girl that looked dead or unconscious, and a very large breed of cat lying behind her with its ears folded back.

Peg instinctively began forward. "Oh God, Jacob—"

Despite her hesitation to approach the menacing bulk of the machine, she quickly ran to the girl. The cat did not seem to mind her approach, and even purred a bit when Peg moved the girl's hair away from her neck to check her pulse.

It was there, but fluttering, and when Peg opened one of the girl's sticky eyelids and saw the dilating pupils, it was obvious that the child was in trouble.

Peg had been a nurse for ten years at Saint Christopher's—if left untreated, she knew the girl had a day to live if anything.

"Jacob, we have to bring her with us."

Her husband was breathing hard and cramming a large square container into the back of the Horizon, already returning to his task of packing now that any imminent threat from the machine seemed unlikely.

Nolan, having not yet been automatically secured in his safety-seat, was peering through the open hatch at his father, then his mother—then curiously at the large metal contraption that seemed to have a little girl and a very large cat curled up in its humongous, open mouth.

"Pegs," said Jacob impatiently, "it's probably one of those God-damned *clones!*"

The comment made the woman pause. Part of her wanted to take a step away from the machine and the girl, as if they were suddenly diseased.

Clone. That word had been the source of so much discontent and violence within the last decade that it was impossible not to be affected by it.

The married couple had been successful (though they were quite modest, the expansive grounds and large house attested to as much), but purchasing clones had never been a topic even contemplated. It was not a matter of funds—the Mallows could surely have scrounged up a large portion of the price if they had so desired. The simple truth was that Peg and

Jacob had never approved of the idea of clones. Like most of the populace, they felt it was something unnatural and frightening—but that was not to say they would stand together with the savage majority of the country whose hatred for the clones and their creators had produced so much bloodshed.

No, they did not necessarily approve of *that*, either.

If the Mallows had their way, they would have continued to live quietly and peacefully, with little in the way of technology and even smaller portions of politics. They had thought they had found a sanctuary on their bit of land, which until recently had been a slice of paradise; unfortunately, the world of privately funded war had crept up to their doorstep and was forcing them away from their now-shattered dreams.

That made Peg burn with anger.

The little girl momentarily resembled everything that Peg and her family had come to despise. Had Peg been a different person right then, the little girl's fate almost surely would have been sealed with the land-scape's icy endorsement.

As it happened, though, Peg managed to unearth within herself a bit of compassion and humanity for the stranger—things that were nearing extinction in the world of humankind. She supposed that even Jacob, good and honest man that he was, would have difficulty seeing the poor child as anything but a threat or a menace.

Her mothering instincts seemed to swell with every thought of prejudice or harm that could befall the girl; clone or no clone, she was a child, and she was going to die alone in the middle of the Mallows' field if someone didn't help her.

"Jacob—she needs help or she's going to die."

Her husband had loaded the last of their emergency provisions and lowered the back hatch of the Horizon. Jacob pressed a button on his vehicle's remote tab and Nolan was gently nestled into his seat and strapped in.

Jacob looked at the mountains in the distance, then looked slowly from left to right at the home they had worked so hard for and were now being forced to abandon in order to ensure their safety.

His own personal anger began to swell, making his throat harden and his teeth grind. He did not like being scared in his own home and his own country.

And now, on his own property, in a monster of a contraption, was one of the slivers that was causing the infection of the world—

And his wife wanted to take it *with them* . . . No way.

"Get in the car, Peg."

Jacob stepped through the snow and made his way to the driver's seat, never meeting his wife's eyes. Aside from anger casting its shadow over him, there was a bit of shame as well. He was having a hard time convincing his heart that it was not a dying little girl in the cockpit of that walking pile of metal—a little girl who couldn't be much older than his own son.

It was hard to get past these things . . . but he was trying his best.

Peg had expected as much from Jacob; very rarely did he allow his emotions to overshadow his logic. It did not change her resolution, however, and she clenched her fists. Her face became hot and her feet stayed firmly planted in the snow, next to the open hatch of the LOPAN. She had given birth to Nolan two years ago, and there was still a bit of raw, postpartum instinct looming within her. It flared up suddenly.

"Jacob Morgan Mallow! If we don't help this little girl so help me—"

It had not been shouted, but the way in which her voice had seethed surprised even herself. It happened from time to time.

Jacob cringed. Perhaps it was his wife's eerily calm voice mingled with certain emotions implanted during his childhood in relation to his mother. Or perhaps it was the universal ability of women to demand such subordination at times like this . . . but, regardless, the implications were clear. At this point, disregarding his wife's attitude or protesting against her feelings would only incite an insane reaction with unimaginable consequences.

At this point, there was just no use in arguing.

He stared at his wife, making one last attempt to assert his stance on the subject. It was short-lived, though. The fire in Peg's eyes burned so fiercely that he dropped his gaze.

"I talked to Boris Leggar an hour ago," said Jacob, finding an interesting corner of the roof to inspect. "He said there's another squad coming in from the west—"

Peg crossed her arms and raised her chin.

Jacob studied the roof. Then, finally, with clear intention to bring the child: "Let's load up and get the hell out of here."

Jacob grabbed a blanket from the car and tossed it to his wife. She quickly wrapped the girl into a bundle and removed her from the cushioned cockpit of the mechanical suit.

Calypso watched the woman grab a satchel from the back of the car and then take Cherry into the passenger seat with her. The cat meowed once and leapt to the ground. It made its way through the snow and pawed at the door behind Jacob.

"You have got to be kidding me . . ."

The door behind the driver's seat popped open and the cat jumped in. Jacob pressed a button on the steering console and the door retracted, locked.

Little Nolan stared wide-eyed at the very large cat now squatting in the seat next to him. Calypso gave a quick head-turn in the boy's direction, touching his cheek with her cold nose. It made him giggle nervously.

In the front seat, Peg had removed a hydration unit from the satchel and attached the hypodermic band to Cherry's forearm. Her pulse was still faint, but almost instantly a bit of color blossomed on her face.

Peg met eyes with her husband and both pairs shared a flash of worry.

To be in a machine like that—how important is this little girl? Important enough to issue search teams? . . . Important enough to set up road blocks?

Jacob smiled reassuringly, committed now.

No matter, now—it's done.

Jacob accelerated and banked away from a snow drift, sending a spray of white powder into the air.

The Mallows drove away from their home in the

woods. Unknown to them, the R9 was keeping rigid surveillance of the area—making sure no harm would come to the vehicle until it was out of sight.

The streamlined Horizon hovered over the white-covered earth and silently sped off into the distance, toward its blue and pink namesake.

TOUCHING FROM
A DISTANCE

Alex J. Kane

The welding torch blazed in Kael's hand, spitting flecks of scorching plasma that chewed away at his blackened armored work suit. Behind the flaring face shield, beads of sweat dribbled across his blistered forehead. Nine hours of laboring felt a hell of a lot longer in a low-pay, low-gee working environment.

Kael had been shuttled into lunar orbit wearing the pins and medals of a distinguished soldier, but not long after arriving on-station at habitat Leonov he'd discovered the real truth of the UNE Spacebound Corps: Instead of keeping humanity safe and moving further outward into an increasingly wondrous galaxy, the SBC was really just a clever ruse to get able-bodied persons into a factory ten hours out of the day.

A fucking robot's job.

The assembly unit wasn't all bad, he supposed. It kept qualified warriors working jobs, which was an astonishing feat in a solar system presently free from the threat of war. It also, unfortunately, sent a lot of good men and women back home to Earth with a surprise or two—cardiac arrhythmia, most often—in addition to the unavoidable muscle atrophy that was the shared bane of all UNE soldiers living on the curved inner surface of the massive cylindrical station.

The flightless, newborn starship Kael had worked on for the better portion of his shift bore the trappings of an unarmed commercial vessel. Emblazoned on its smooth, rounded sides were the markings of some ridiculously influential megacorp conglomerate. The heat-resistant paint artfully depicted the long-feathered head of a mythical phoenix next to a stylish mess of bold Chinese glyphs.

The plasma torch let out a *whoosh* as it powered down, and its brilliant light vanished.

Kael slapped his suit's mask open, winced as the naked luminance of the fluorescent tube lamps overhead struck his eyes. The rush of oxygen-rich air, however, felt incredible against his warm face. He heaved a few long breaths, and then trudged across the hanging support structure that wound like a snake amid row after row of unfinished craft within the spacious facility.

He stood in line for a good twenty minutes or so, waiting his turn for retinal scan at the time clock.

After the red lens atop a thin metallic pole had flashed a point of light across his eyes, he exited the assembly area and stepped out into the vast central hub-tower of the colossal station, strode on in his cumbersome welder's attire.

When at last he reached the cramped, lozenge-shaped tram capsule beyond the factory, he hunkered down inside, sinking deep into the soft aerofoam. With a flick of the console beside him, the tiny door slid shut, sealing him inside. Kael punched in the designation code for his living quarters, and the capsule rocketed through the kilometers-long vacuum-shuttle tube en route to the residential zone of the habitat.

Where, from his private quarters, he could temporarily escape.

The military came with a basic set of advantages, not least of which was the cutting-edge tech that civilians back home could only fantasize about. Aside from his underground app sales business getting phased out during the recession, that had been one of the biggest draws for Kael to enlist. Access to the most awesome technology in known existence . . . and credit.

●○●

Kael flushed the remains of a hearty vegetable broth and a soggy, half-eaten soy roll, took a revitalizing piss, then crossed to the broadcast throne that sat at the center of his apartment's tiny living area. He stepped over the tangle of electrical cables and fiber-optics that surrounded it, then sat down in the reclined chair. It enveloped him, caused his implant to tingle in anticipation.

The Net was a realm all its own, with its digital epicenter in the heart of North America. Kael had been fortunate enough to befriend some of the more skilled programmers on Leonov, who let him in on a well-guarded secret: that atop the pirouetting cylinder-world stood an impressive array of pulse-beam laser transceivers. The secrecy that surrounded the tech made him wonder whether SBC might be searching for extraterrestrial intelligence, but no such rumor had ever surfaced. Regardless of their intended purpose, they allowed for a direct connection with Earth's own vast network of telecomm satellites. Whenever the station moved beyond the moon's dark nightside, the relays enabled instantaneous passage between worlds for the habitat's more . . . *privileged* individuals.

As Kael positioned himself securely in the broadcast throne, magnetic stabilizers guided the transdermal uplink of his implant into the chair's hyperfast zaibatsu router.

A message alert bleeped, then a fuzzy string of bright green alphanumerics scrolled across the corner of his vision: *Establishing feed . . . Success.*

He punched in the proper access commands, then: *#//_Leonov.lun.orb/@kstaten. Link byway transfer: unoptimized. Welcome to UNE WorldNet. Please consider upgrading your firmware and/or system equipment for best experience.*

Darkness flooded Kael's field of vision, and then sensation faded from his extremities. Like entering into a deep sleep, the universe seemed to crawl gently out of bed and flee from existence.

Touch of cold moonstone. Total, unbounded dark.

And then Kael drowned in neurosensory stims, feeling himself swept up by a tide of intoxicating perceptions—sprawling matrices of mesmerizing light and smell and thrumming, buzzing electrochemical distortion—until he found himself washed upon the stiff-grassed shore of an icy lake.

●○●

Earth.

Kael felt the warmth of homecoming underfoot, despite the frost that speckled the chalky soil and the cloud of foggy breath that spewed forth from his mouth each time he exhaled.

Winter already? How hastily time slipped by unnoticed when you lived in a place with no seasons to mark it.

His omni displayed in red text his present location: *Outskirts of Lachiga, North America. 3.6 kilometers to inbound Magnetrak station.*

Great, he thought. *Dropped wherever the hell is convenient for the off-planet mods. Thanks, bastards.*

The pleasant thing about the cyberspace render-ings of Lachiga and the industrial sector to the south, the *old city*, was that the programmers had omitted certain undesirable characteristics from the envi-ronment entirely. Pollution, notably, as well as the less attractive neighborhoods of the sprawling megalopolis, were virtually nonexistent in the world of the global public Net.

Instead, the air smelled of lively earth, rich forestation, and the gorgeous aroma of humankind's inescapable presence. The evening chill also carried with it the landward-falling wastes of the eco-city that dominated the mirrorlike expanse of frozen Lake Michigan. For Kael, the scent was only mildly repugnant.

The flowering colossus of Lachiga protruded into the misty night sky from a lily-pad-shaped foundation that ran off in metallic veins for kilometers in every direction. Its rounded walls spiraled up and outward like the bell of a brass instrument, disappearing into the gray-white veil of the clouds.

A suitable monument to humanity's everexpanding reach toward the stars.

He'd have to make the walk in realtime; the tiny device in the back of his skull was a purely civilian model, and therefore couldn't manipulate the flux of experienced time. No matter—Kael recognized that the addictiveness of the Net was the way VR enhanced and perfected life on Earth. The trek, despite taking almost half of the night, would be an enjoyable one.

●○●

The wind at his back urged Kael onward, and he wasted no time as he made his way around the upper commercial district toward Club Valhalla, the all-night bar he'd made a habit of frequenting ever since he'd started dreaming his way across the distance between Earth and Leonov.

A few small clusters of individuals in winter coats, arms crossed and beers in hand, stood just outside the entrance. Their hushed voices resounded as whispers down the winding street. Breath fogged the air above their heads like halos of steam.

Kael slipped between two distinct groups of patrons, tapped the touchscreen beside the door. The entrance irised open, and he stepped inside.

The club was smoky with atmospheric fog and a kaleidoscopic display of pulsing, multicolored lasers that danced about the room, which was wide and deep and filled with the stink of drinks, artificial pheromones, and urine. The stench, thankfully, was weakened considerably by the poor connection strength. Music thundered from the belly of the room. Basso heartbeat flavored by equal parts traditional Caribbean reggae and the potent, hypersexual culture of modern youth.

Faces, bodies, and bare skin glowed like infrared heat signatures within the rainbow-lit dimness. Muscles flexing and working, mouths agape, they rode the tidal rhythm of the music.

Breath of sweet, sensuous life.

I must be the only gay man on the planet who hates dancing, Kael thought as he drifted through the sea of dazzling forms.

He scanned the faces of the young men throughout the bar, many of whom were remarkable, but each pair of eyes met his with a glimmer of revulsion. They were all focused on the soft, heart-shaped asses of lovely young women. Doubtless his own avatar was in need of a fashion upgrade.

How many nights had he wandered in here, ghost-like, only to leave feeling empty and unwanted? It wasn't his sexuality that was the problem, but his hesitance to publicize it. Military life, he felt, hadn't strengthened him; it had only made him uncertain, timid. Unwhole.

He could go without sex—if that was all he wanted, he could find it in abundance throughout cyberspace via pay-per-play sims. No . . . he lacked interaction, companionship.

In truth, he came for the conversation.

At the bar, he noticed, sat a goateed, dark-skinned man with a clean-shaven scalp, a face unmarred by troublesome acne. The man wore a jacket of faded brown leather that fit his large biceps snugly and revealed broad, powerful shoulders.

Kael took a seat in the swivel-chair two places to the man's right, waved to the female bartender.

The young girl smiled at him, leaned close.

"What can I get you?"

"Gin and tonic, please." A symbolic gesture; drunkenness was impossible to realistically simulate, and moreover all drinks were free in cyberspace. Or at least the legal ones. The bartender, he knew, was almost certainly a disguised mod assigned to monitor the club.

The drink materialized in Kael's hand, and right away he took a sip. It tasted of pine and bubbly tonic, but the alcohol was nonexistent.

He cast a casual glance at the attractive man to his left, nodded hello.

"Ira Maalik," the man said as he held out a rigid hand.

Kael smiled and shook it. "Kael . . . Staten." There

was no point in keeping his identity a secret; his signature was all over the place, like footprints of fragmented data.

Then Ira subvocalized: *You must be looking for something. Maybe something I could help you with?* His unabashed nature caught Kael off guard. That upfront hypersexuality was something not found in military life, especially not on Leonov, where Kael estimated that virtually everyone wasted their weekend holiday with a pitiful series of on-and-off masturbation, or at least plugged in, fantasizing.

In an earthly, instinctual sense, Kael found the man's directness pleasant, refreshing. *Maybe so,* he sent. A quirk tugged at the corner of his lips.

"Where you from?" Ira asked aloud.

"Habitat Leonov," Kael said.

"Ah, military boy. In outer space, no less."

Something about *boy* stung. "Yeah, you got it . . ."

"Impressive. How you like the view from up there?"

Kael hadn't ever given it much thought, not since he'd first arrived. "It's okay. Pretty marvelous, I suppose, although I rarely have time to do more than glance at it. The moon's a lot less beautiful when you're hovering right over it, studying all its blemishes and imperfections. At this point, I've come to think that everything looks much better from Earth."

Ira raised his dark eyebrows, slowly nodded.

● ○ ●

With one finger, Kael traced the smooth, warm outline

of the larger man's body. Ira's bare skin gleamed like polished wood in the serene, moonlit semidarkness. With each slow breath, Kael's finger rose and fell until at last his hand reached Ira's shoulder and collapsed onto the bed.

Over the past five and a half years, Kael had given in to fleshly temptation on two or three occasions, seeking refuge in the comforting arms of others—who, he had to constantly remind himself, were almost 400,000 kilometers away. But, he often reflected, the body was little more than a prison of the mind . . . each had its own unique set of needs and desires. Such thinking served as apt self-justification for all the time he spent aimlessly exploring within the grand artifice of the Net.

A cycle rife with sorrow, but it put him at ease in an otherwise tiresome period of his life. And who knew for certain that, some day, he might not return home to Earth to find one of his transient love affairs had grown into something more, something *everlasting*? This dream enabled him to rise from bed each morning, march to drill and then on to a job he abominated.

This man, Ira, with whom Kael had experienced one of the most incredible nights of his life, outshone any taint that might have been inflicted on his soul by prior heartbreaks. The future looked hopeful indeed.

"I enjoyed that," Kael whispered.

Me too, Ira subvocalized unnecessarily. *We should . . . see each other again.*

Quiet ecstasy took hold of Kael.

"Absolutely. I'll come looking for you."

A pair of moist lips pressed against Kael's forehead, and then the muscular body that had lain next to him for over four hours flickered, phased into a shimmering pool of pixelated cubes, and then with a splash fell away into nothingness.

● ○ ●

The bed felt desolate. Kael was painfully certain that he'd at some point unplugged, returned to reality, but to wake for a long day of work seemed an unreasonable expectation following such a heavenly night. Despite this, he pulled himself upright and stumbled toward the airtight shower. He felt grimy with cold, stinging sweat as he stood inside the cramped chamber and reached for the dull metal release lever.

Water drizzled down his body, spiraling in broken streams of transparent silver into the black vacuum drain between the balls of his feet.

He washed the scent of glorious deeds from his skin, knowing with sadness that there was, in truth, no scent at all.

● ○ ●

The light of the Earth flared into being, and Kael felt a sharp jolt of pain course from his eyeballs inward along his strained optic nerves. The lengthened, efficiency-based day cycle aboard the habitat wasn't entirely without logic, but it disregarded the twenty-four-hour cycle of Earth. As a result, one never really knew what to expect when spawning into the Net via the distant lunar satellites; daylight and fair weather, though, were always a welcome surprise.

Ira had been alarmingly vague about his occupation, although he'd admitted to dwelling online for the majority of the time, as his job relied on the convenience of cyberspace access.

A salesman of some kind? Kael couldn't recall.

Either way, it would be difficult to track him down in daylight. Luckily, Kael had been given a full forty-eight hours of holiday time.

Freedom.

With a gentle roll of his eyes and a quick succession of blinks, Kael accessed the public matrix of logged data signatures, searched: #/_@imaalik. Maalik, Ira.

A stream of brilliant alphanumeric entries pinged across the field of his vision, and he focused for a full second on the correct feed: *insecure.WorldNetlog/ dat/recent(*)*. And then an instant later: *@imaalik: Ira Maalik. last location logged 1.2 hrs ago via anonymous satellite encryption string—cerebrospinal implant 'OMNI' _offline—Lachiga, UA North; traveling on foot (approx. pace: walking), residential bowl 11, upper-middle level.*

So Ira wasn't hurting for money. Not if he lived at that elevation.

But, dammit, he was unplugged. Kael wondered how long it would be before that changed, before they'd see each other again . . .

Above, the immense inner walls wrapped a circular band of glimmering silver that framed a pool of blue, starless sky. Like a grain of pollen on the stamen of a flower, Kael had spawned somewhere inside the central spire that served as Lachiga's main commercial district. Magnificent though it was, he knew with a pang of bittersweet joy that Lachiga would undoubtedly be far more beautiful in reality. Like being employed as a space monkey for the UNE military, VR had its inherent limitations.

Any second, Kael thought, the WorldNet system would log his location. With any luck, Ira would be tracking the ping via his own implant.

He set out toward the nearest bridge, a massive arm within the complex framework that held the inside of the city together. Its walkway would take him to the luxurious upper-middle level of Lachiga's residential tier, where he could likely intercept Ira.

You around? Kael broadcast directly to Ira's omni.

A few minutes later, as Kael was making his way across the lengthy bridge amid the chaotic bustle of bodies, he received Ira's reply: *Ten minutes. Meet you outside apt. 913.*

● ○ ●

Ira drew closer from along the unending sidewalk that encircled the inner platform of the upper-middle skyline subdivision. Silhouetted by broken rays of glaring sunlight, the man looked godlike among the tranquil people of Lachiga's wealthy middle-class installations.

"Glad you could make it," he said on approach.

Kael smiled, shrugged.

"Yeah, okay, good to see you too." Ira waved his palm over the door console, and it clanged open. He led them into the dim apartment, and light gradually found its way inside soon after.

"I can't stand this," Kael said, and he felt the truth of it add weight to him. "The being apart, I mean. It's early, sure, nothing serious—but *damn* it's hard. You know?"

"Yeah," Ira said as he removed his jacket, tossed it onto the black leather couch. "It's hard on me, too, no lie. But you probably get leave sometime soon, yeah?"

Kael grunted. "In six months," he hissed.

"Damn. How long you been up there, anyway?"

Kael clicked his tongue, calculated. "Oh, about . . . five years, six months."

"Almost six years? *Shit* . . ." Ira shook his head. Then he came forth, took Kael in an embrace.

"You'll —you'll get your leave soon," he whispered. "And then you can come live with me in Lachiga. I'll get you a job here, big guy, and we'll have everything. Everything."

Kael felt the man's warmth run into his own flesh, relax his muscles. His nerves seemed to go numb, ease into a state of unfeeling bliss. Blood, for contrast, ran to his core. He felt his pants tighten; felt Ira's groin grow hard against his own. The tension of the opposing organs mounted, beckoned them into the bedroom.

Breathing heavily, Kael took Ira's smooth face into his, kissed him passionately as they stumbled across the living area floor toward the large bed in the adjacent room.

Together they collapsed onto the bed, still locked in a continual exchange of tongues.

And then Ira, with a strong, knotted hand, pulled Kael by his belt into the darkness beneath the cool bedsheets, pushed his face deep between the soft, white pillows at the headboard.

Kael bit his lip as Ira entered him.

● ○ ●

Dreary, silent space.

Kael showered, dressed, and plodded out of his living quarters, dreading the work day.

On his way to the vacuum-shuttle, he noticed something peculiar: There was no line in which to wait for a capsule. In fact, the whole damn habitat seemed quiet . . . somehow *off*.

Had he missed an alert of some kind? A drill, maybe?

He halted, scanned the station. Activity was inexplicably minimal; the entire arm of the habitat looked deserted. He accessed the time display via his omni, which showed that he was right on schedule. Why, then, the emptiness?

Something whistled, rocketed through the air, and slipped into the flesh of his neck. Simultaneously, an alarm began to bray.

Sharp bite of a needle, spreading of warmth . . .

Dark.

● ○ ●

"You've been busy," a voice declared, muffled by a shroud of numbness and blurred vision.

"Huh?" Kael murmured, and then coughed. His lungs burned with the toxin of whatever had knocked him out. "What the hell are—"

"Oh, wake the fuck up," the voice said.

A hard slap across the cheek rattled Kael's skull, stirred his equilibrium.

Slowly, like the dribbling-down of rainwater upon a windshield, the fog cleared from his eyesight and he could at last make out the form sitting across from him. His heart thundered.

Gustafson, the station administrator, eyed him with an icy glare of contempt.

"Staten, I gave you broadcast permissions on the condition that you stay the hell *out of trouble*. Tell me, Ensign, about the son of a bitch you've been making contact with."

He was talking, of course, about Ira.

"What do you want to know, Sir?" Kael asked.

"You've been plugged into the public Net every night for weeks," Gustafson said. "Every time, it's Lachiga. Same map, same destination. Or thereabouts. Care to enlighten me?"

"Just a healthy friendship. Sir."

"Don't bullshit me, Staten. You're fucking the guy, and frankly, I don't give a damn. What concerns me is the man's *motive* in pursuing a rendezvous with you each and every night of his life. Sure, your needs are clear; you're stuck cold and flaccid in orbit, which is reasonable cause for you to want to wander . . ." His voiced tapered off as he waited for Kael to elaborate further. His gaze was sharp, imperious.

"Sir—*Admiral*—his name's Ira Maalik. Works logistics for a Net security firm, something like that. Zero threat, Sir."

"Oh, yeah? That so?"

Kael hesitated, considering, then nodded. "Harmless. We mean to . . . unite upon my return. Truth of it is, if you'll pardon my enthusiasm, I've never been more in love, Admiral."

"Well, Ensign, congratulations—*but!* Let me stress this: Keep wary of the man. We're getting cryptic laser and radiocomm whispers like never before ever since our feed shows you started seeing this guy." He paused, blinked for emphasis. "I smell the stench of a leak. Now, I'm not saying it's you—"

"Sir, I assure you that I would never tell *anyone* about the cloning operation. I will take that knowledge to my *grave.*"

"I don't doubt that, Ensign, but there are those who would snoop. Would have you sell your information regarding the nature of that contained installation to the public. Should that ever happen, no matter how righteous the interloper's intentions, humankind's very foothold in space would be lost forever. Centuries of study, hard work—hell, the very *blood of fallen soldiers*—would all be rendered meaningless."

Kael understood the Admiral's predicament all too well. He also partially agreed with the administration's thinking—but so many laws were broken in the SBC's otherwise noble project.

The hell of it was, testing starships built for antimatter propulsion was just too unpredictable, too utterly dangerous, to assign to good, well-trained soldiers. The odds of a naked singularity forming, rupturing the warp field and pulling the vessel's passengers straight into oblivion, were dishearteningly unfavorable. But the reprogrammed minds of

soulless, mass-produced human clones could be
shaped into expert pilots, who could then take off and
get ships up to almost the speed of light, without
needlessly risking the lives of honorable men and
women.

Gustafson was a genius when it came to trouble-
shooting, but there was little doubt about what the
UNE would do if his test flight methodology ever came
under the scrutiny of internal affairs auditors: He
would disappear. Right into military prison . . . or the
crematorium.

"You have my undying loyalty, Sir," Kael said,
feeling a pang of pity toward his heartless superior.
"I'll be careful."

"Er, well, no. You see, it's not enough for you to
tread carefully. I wish that were so, but I'm afraid it
isn't. I've already ordered a team of technicians to
your quarters to disassemble and confiscate your
computer broadcast equipment."

Kael felt stunned, immobile. *"What?"*

"I'm sorry, Staten, but I had no choice. Think
about it! Place yourself in my vantage point, and I'll
think you'll understand that this is a military habitat.
Because of your knowledge regarding the legal
conundrum of our facility, you were granted access to
privileges far above the clearance level of your rank,
but I can't play the cards on this one. The pings and
static we've been picking up escalated tenfold since
you met your little boyfriend. The correlation may be
an imaginary one, but I sincerely doubt it. I'm sorry."

"Sir." Kael rose and saluted, forcing himself to
restrain any urge to protest. Anger warmed him like a

fresh kindling of flickering, burning flame. His eyelids twitched.

"Dismissed."

● ○ ●

The next few months dragged by in a blur of despair. Kael spent most of his time more or less in total isolation, counting the minutes until the departure of the shuttle that would take him home to his long-distance lover. Most nights were sleepless, and the few exceptions were agonizing and dreamless.

Work grew hellish. Kael became convinced that Gustafson had orchestrated an off-record plan that once set in motion would drive him inexorably to the point of suicide. Coworkers and supervisors would pester him about his poor productivity, even though he unfailingly found himself assigned the worst, most dangerous duties on a daily basis. If it wasn't intended to kill him, it was certainly meant to show him that Gustafson hadn't been fucking around about the cloning intel.

If Kael talked, he would be a dead man.

He might've even succumbed to the lure of a cowardly end, had it not been for the promise—the mere *possibility*—that Ira might be sharing his suffering. The hope that Ira, too, might be clinging to the ambition of a more fulfilling relationship kept him moving forward.

What had Ira said? *We'll have everything. Everything.*

Surely that sort of dream persisted, if there had been any basis of truth behind it. And indeed such a fierce love could outlast even the brightest-burning stars, in such instances. Truth, trust, and the ultimate giving and sharing of oneself was to Kael the penultimate goal of human life.

Not a belief held by all, but certainly a powerful one.

● ○ ●

At last the day of honorable discharge from active duty came, and Kael wasted no time in gathering his few material belongings—a collection of a few earthly trinkets, his clothes, and his toolbox—and sealing the door shut behind him. His bulky backpack slung over his shoulder, he ran the full distance of the cylinder's lengthy bottom ring-section to board the shuttle home.

As he ascended the gangplank, a flight attendant nodded grimly and handed him a personal Net-synced reader.

He found the news that greeted his embarkation disturbing.

The headline of the *Chicago Tribune* said it best: *Contact With Outside Intelligence—UNE Call for Mobilization of Orbital Weapons Array to Prepare for Aliens' Arrival.*

A WorldNet mod's private feed had another proposition: *Say no to bloodshed! Don't point a gun you're not prepared to fire . . .*

Another warned, *Nothing is ever inevitable! Protest the deception!*

Shit. No wonder the pilots and attendants all looked so grave. The whole Earth was damned.

Hearsay quickly overtook the readers as the

primary source of information—and misinformation, undoubtedly—once the shuttle prepped for reentry and started the long dive through the glowing heat of the atmosphere.

Some declared the interception of an alien transmission to be false, little more than fear-mongering military propaganda. Others claimed to have actually spoken with the unfortunate individuals who had been quarantined, having been suspected of coming into contact with alien tissue on one or more of the Sol system's pulse-beam comm buoys or weapons platforms.

Thankfully, habitat Leonov came under no such accusations.

The vessel set down in a spaceport outside of New York City, UA. From there, Kael took the vacuum-shuttle all the way to Chicago, where he linked up with the Magnetrak.

En route to Lachiga, he trembled in anticipation of his reunion with Ira.

All of their plans, all of their hopes, were now minuscule afterthoughts in the context of a much larger, potentially apocalyptic threat.

Kael supposed he lacked faith in the nature of humanity.

● ○ ●

Gloomy gray of cold concrete and overcast skies.

Ira had told Kael to meet him on the upper-middle tier of Lachiga's residential zone. Apartment 913. Light flakes of silvery-white snow sailed landward from the abysmal, moonless air.

The sidewalks of the colossal flowering eco-city were comparatively barren, almost *empty*, in the corporeal world. Kael had assumed talk of an alien invasion would enliven the planet, yet somehow it seemed to have had the opposite effect.

The Net, no doubt, overflowed with the simulated, soundless voices of a thousand panicking souls. Screaming, speculating, pointing weighty fingers in every direction but space.

Almost there, Kael sent via his omni.

His brain stem vibrated when the reply came, winked across his vision: *Door's unlocked. Come on in.*

When he reached his destination, he did so.

The apartment, only marginally familiar, was lit solely by the light of a slatted window beyond the spacious bedroom down the hallway.

"Hello?" Kael called out, jittery with unaccountable nervousness.

He stepped into the bedroom, crossed to the window, and turned. Before he could scan the room, he saw a woman—standing, arms crossed—leaned against the wall.

"Hello, Kael," she said. Her long dark hair flowed in curled waves over her shoulders. Eyes the color of lush forest. Skin the color of the earth.

"Who—where's Ira?"

The heart-wrenching quirk of a frown. "*I'm* Ira."

Kael's mind swam, his throat filling with the bitter, acidic poison of his stomach.

"You . . . you're *lying.*" Unless, all too plausibly, Ira —if that was his/her name—had crafted an attractive male avatar for the purpose of getting to Kael. Lured in like a hunted animal.

"No, I'm sorry—it's no lie."

Kael drew in a deep breath. "Fuck," he sighed. "But . . . *why?*"

"I would've confessed sooner," she said, "had you not gone black on me the way you did. Just doing my job, Kael. You of all people should understand that."

Had Kael, in a fit of foolishness, intimated to Ira the unlawful secrets of Leonov? No, he was sure he hadn't. Ira never talked business, and so neither did Kael.

"You—you *evil* . . ." Kael felt his knees grow wobbly, and he sat down on the neatly made bed.

"The UNE does its best to keep the world safe," Ira explained, her voice beginning to sound shockingly like the man with whom Kael had spent so many ecstatic nights.

"How did any of it have to do with protecting the world?"

Ira shrugged. "Maybe some of it . . . didn't. But there was truth in a lot of what I told you. Almost everything, really. I was in love with you, the sex was phenomenal; it was just doomed from the beginning. Unfortunately—" She chuckled, twisted her lips. "—I don't have a penis. But Kael, I . . . it never could've worked even if I, you know, were a man. My job entails doing some pretty terrible things when the occasion calls for it, and right now the call is echoing round the *world*. Aliens, Kael. Fucking *aliens*!"

"So I've heard. But . . . what did you have to gain by linking up with Leonov, listening in on a military installation? Doesn't that violate international law?"

"No law is inviolate in the face of extinction." She took a seat on the end of the bed next to Kael, and her hand looked as if it wanted to wrap around him in a comforting embrace. Gravity, or some other great force, held it motionless in her lap.

"Everything," Kael whispered gravely. "Everything I've waited for is . . . a lie. All that hoping, longing for a normal life, *wasted*."

"I'm truly sorry," Ira said, turning her gaze up to

meet his, then allowing it to fall back to the luminous sunlit floor. "I never would've done it if I had been thinking, if I had known how hurt you'd be. It was more than just a mutual back-scratching, Kael. You know that."

Kael grunted, shook his head. Unbelievable.

"Goodbye, Ira," he said as he rose.

She made no attempt to stop him. The doors opened as he neared them, and he strode out into the light of the fearful, paranoid world before she had a chance to glimpse the tears that streaked his face.

With his implant, he accessed the SBC-Comm secure broadcast channel.

Admiral Gustafson, he sent to begin the transmission, then: *I'm re-upping.*

ПЧХ

Jasmine Michaelson

Willa leaned back from the small toilet and wiped the vomit from her chin with the back of her hand. She stood and washed her hands and face at the basin and rinsed out her mouth with the lukewarm water that came through the spout in jerky spurts. She pushed back the flimsy accordion door that separated the bathroom from the kitchen and dining area of the pod. Vivian and Ulrike looked up from their breakfast.

"I'm sorry about the eggs," Vivian said. Worry drew her features downward with invisible strings, making her look older, like Ulrike. "I had forgotten what the smell does to us in the third trimester. I made some toast for you. Would you like some oatmeal?"

"No," Willa said. "The toast is fine. Thank you, Mother." She took her seat at the tiny collapsible square table, beneath which all six knees touched.

"What's wrong with the water pressure?"

"I don't know," Ulrike said. "Energy levels have been fluctuating this morning. I'll check on the reactor after breakfast." She brought a spoonful of oatmeal to her deeply creased lips with a quivering hand that was knotted and ridged like the bark of the apple trees. She chewed slowly with the same side to side motion as a sheep and swallowed. "It's healthy, you know. The nausea. It shows the host is trying to protect the fetus from contaminants."

"Mother," Vivian said, "when you refer to Willa as a host, it implies that your great-grandchild is a parasite."

"They are not dissimilar."

"There are a few dissimilarities."

Vivian took her last bite of oatmeal and stared at Ulrike, who swept her wispy silver hair into a knot at the back of her skull and offered no response. Vivian turned to Willa with her features now exaggeratedly upturned, but still pained.

"Have you settled on a name?" she asked brightly.

"No," Willa said.

"A name is not essential," Ulrike said. "Anna said it herself. Just the letter to differentiate from the other generations would be sufficient."

"You think I should call her X?" Willa said.

"Of course not," Vivian said.

"Why not?" Ulrike scooted back from the table and stood. The rubber feet of her stool scraped across the aluminum floor producing a sound like the ram made when a ewe was in heat. "It would serve every practical purpose a name serves. The child will be Generation twenty-four, corresponding letter X. Anything beyond that is superfluous."

Vivian followed Ulrike to the basin with her bowl.

"But in twenty-three generations every daughter of Anna has had a name."

"We are not her daughters. We are her clones."

"We came through her loins. We *are* her daughters."

Ulrike shook her head as she rinsed out her bowl from the coughing spout and went to her bunk, where she sat down and pulled on her boots. "You will soon see it as I do."

"Am I not *your* daughter?"

"You are the zygote that was on top of the stack in the freezer."

"That's our relationship?"

"We are tools sent to perform a task, Vivian. I am wearing out. You will take my place. When you wear out, she," she pointed at Willa, "will take your place. You will soon see it as I do."

"All she's saying," Willa began to say and was cut off by a wave of Ulrike's hand.

"When will you understand?" Her coarse voice was sharp but laced with something almost like sadness. "I know exactly what she's saying. Better than you. Better than she does. I had every thought and made every argument she's making. I, however, have pro-gressed beyond that, and neither of you can relate to it now. But you will. After I am dead."

The light over the table suddenly brightened and went out with a soft pop. The three women stared at it. Vivian turned on the faucet and a deep gurgling ensued, but no water came.

"I'll see to it," Ulrike said. Vivian and Willa watched her pull her wide-brimmed hat down low over her eyebrows and hoist her oxygen tank onto her hunched shoulders. She threaded the tubes into her nostrils and went to the airlock door.

"Don't waste your energy on sentimentality," she said and flipped the heavy latch on the door with a soft grunt. The seal hissed, and she pulled the thick door open. She did not turn around to finish the thought, but rather mumbled it to the tools hanging on the walls in the airlock as she closed the door behind her, as though they were the only ones capable of understanding it: "There's too much work to be done." She pulled the door closed without looking at either of them. The latch reset, and the door sealed.

Vivian cleared the rest of the breakfast dishes and dumped them in the sink. Willa heaved her enormous torso up from her stool and walked to the porthole. She chewed the last of her toast and watched the red dust cloud around Ulrike's boots as her bent frame shuffled to the nearby outhouse that sheltered the reactor. Beyond it the algae bog stretched out across the plain, as far as she could see, disappearing over the curved horizon, glistening green in the morning light.

"You left the house last night," Vivian said.

Willa's gaze jerked away from the porthole and down to the crumbs resting on the shelf of her belly.

"You are never supposed to leave alone at night."

"I'm sorry."

"Is the baby keeping you awake or is it the dreams?"

Willa walked over to the kitchen basin, picked up the dishtowel, and began to dry the dishes that Vivian had washed before the water had gone out. "When I became pregnant and stopped the pills . . ." Willa began and trailed off. "I know you warned me but I didn't expect them to be so vivid."

"You must be very careful right now. You must tell us if your thoughts turn dangerous."

"What do you mean?"

Vivian pressed her lips together in a tight line and tilted her head slightly in a half-shake.

Willa set the pot and towel down and stared at Vivian. "Why would my thoughts turn dangerous?"

Vivian sighed and leaned against the basin. She looked up at Willa with her Ulrike-face. "Claire," she said. "I'm talking about Claire."

"You mean Clarice."

"No, I don't. I mean Claire. Before Clarice, there was another Generation Three."

"What?"

"She—" Vivian sighed again and sat down on her stool at the table. "Anna had not yet developed the pills that we take now. For some reason, the dreams had not affected Beth. But they were strong with Claire. We don't know any details. Anna's log says very little about it. Beth made no mention of it at all. Perhaps it was removed. Claire's log was destroyed, so we don't know what was in her mind.

"She was nearing her impregnation when she left the pod one night without a suit. Of course there was almost no atmosphere then. Anna and Beth found her the next morning just outside the door. Thankfully Beth was still able to become pregnant or Nyx would have ended there."

Willa watched a droplet of water grow on the tip of the spigot. It wobbled and swelled and began to pull away from the lip, but clung there, as if by a single chain of atoms.

"It sounds so preposterous to me now," Vivian said, running a hand through her steadily salting hair. "But I remember. I remember when I was pregnant with you and having the dreams myself and Ulrike told me. I remember *understanding.* I can't recall now what I understood." She looked up at Willa now with eyes like wet, black moons. "Do you understand?"

The strand broke and the droplet of water fell, a perfect sphere, through space until it smashed into a dozen smaller droplets on the bottom of the basin. The baby shuddered in Willa's womb. She idly stroked her drum-tight abdomen and avoided her mother's eyes.

"Maybe Ulrike's wrong," Vivian said. "Maybe the greater knowledge was lost to her and to me, but is in you." She stood and put a hand on Willa's shoulder. "Please be careful."

Willa kept her eyes on the toes of her boots and nodded once, almost imperceptibly. Vivian kissed her forehead. She had just turned back to the sink when the atmospheric condenser cut out. Vivian and Willa froze in the eerie absence of its perpetual hum.

"I'd better go help her," Vivian said. "You stay here. Keep your tank close and lie down." She was at the door in three strides, snatching her tank along the way without pause. She was out the airlock before Willa blinked again.

Willa stood in the dim silence, awestruck at how much the change in light and sound had altered the house. She didn't remember leaving it last night. She remembered waking early, before the others, as the first gray rays were coming through the porthole. Her heart had been hammering in her chest and her bedclothes had been soaked in cold sweat. As with most of her dreams she couldn't recall the details of last night's, only the overwhelming residual emotion it had left lodged in her chest. Normally it was a sense of tightness, of the *smallness* of everything around her. Like waking with her feet jammed into her childhood boots. The homestead. The routines. The thoughts in her mind. The air. Even Vivian and Ulrike. They didn't fit.

But that morning in the dead light as she had shivered in her damp bed, the feeling had been different. It wasn't fear. Not exactly. Her eyes glazed over as she searched for the right word. *Finality.* That was the feeling. A sense of the End.

Her mind was still gnawing this out, standing in the dim kitchen, when her body, somehow independent of her mind, jolted into action. She felt the adrenaline tighten the muscles in her legs as she rushed around the pod. She watched her hands, like frenzied claws, rip the leather pack from its hook and ransack the pantry. They stuffed the pack full of water bottles and tins of mutton and beans and bottles of fruit. Her right arm swept a shelf of medical supplies into the pack and onto the floor. Her body clamored through the mess she had made, crushing bottles and syringes under her boots as she went. Her thoughts fumbled behind her body, worrying about the ruined provisions and the scolding she'd get from Ulrike. Her arms flung the heavy, jaggedly stuffed pack onto her shoulders and laced through two oxygen tanks on her way into the airlock.

She caught her reflection in the porthole window as she pulled open the door and found that her face was wrong. Her eyes were narrow and wild. Her lips were twitching furiously and her tongue was writhing in her mouth, flinging saliva onto the scratched plexiglass, like an external force was attempting to draw out speech. *Stop it*, she thought as bewildered terror built in her gut. *Just stop.*

"N-n-n-nyx," her mouth spat at the window, "m-m-mother of d-d-d-death."

Her hands stuffed the tubes from one of the tanks up her nostrils, and she was out of the house, leaving both doors ajar behind her and running half-blind out under the white-yellow sky. Her legs pumped hard under the weight of the gear and the baby. She ran past the reactor house and around to the back, past the chicken coop where the hens were chattering for their breakfast. Dully, through the thumping of her own heart and the deafening roar of her breath she heard Vivian call after her, but her head would not turn, her vocal chords would not scream for help, and her feet would not stop.

Her back wailed in agony as she cut across the vegetable garden and ran into the apple orchard. She got about three-quarters of the way through it before her abdomen seized around its cargo in protest. The wind went out of her, and her knees buckled, throwing her down to her hands in the dirt. As she waited for her lungs to take on air again, her swimming vision fixed itself on a brown apple between her thumbs that had ripened before the others and grown too heavy to cling to its feebly drooping branch. It had split on contact with the hard ground, squirting its mushy flesh through the soft skin.

An apple, she thought, her mind catching up now that her body was down, *I dreamed of an apple.*

Everything around the apple in the dirt began to glow white as the blood drained from her head. Her skin grew cold. *An apple.* Not brown, though. Red. Dark red. Shiny and hard. She had brought it to her lips. Her teeth had pierced the skin, and juice had bled, frothy and clear, from the wide white wound. The taste. Like nothing. Like ecstasy.

The vice around her torso released, and she snorted a slug of cold dryness from her tank and hacked it back out with a belch and dry gag. As the blood rushed back into her brain, her vision briefly went black, and that reminded her of something else. Her hands groping through the dark. Her fingers closing around a long, slender handle. Heavy. The pick-axe. The cold night. The stars. The reactor. *Oh, dear, Mother Anna, the reactor.*

No, no, no. The word ricocheted around in her head,

growing louder and overlapping itself. It must've been a dream. Just another dream. But it wasn't. She knew.

She'd killed them all in her sleep.

Something else seized her torso. Something black and heavy. Horror and self-loathing reached their cold tentacles down her throat, wrapped around the half-digested toast in her stomach and yanked it up hard and fast. It splattered on the brown apple between her hands.

She wiped her mouth on her sleeve and pulled herself up with a spindly tree trunk that bent under the dead weight of her. She wanted to run back and scream at them to leave it and run. Even if they found her work in time, the reactor couldn't be fixed. Not before the End. But against every plea of mind and body, her right leg tripped forward, away from the house, and her left foot dragged itself out to catch her.

That's all walking is, Vivian had told her once when she was small, after she'd stepped on her own boot-lace and sent herself face-first into a pile of sheep droppings. *Just falling and catching yourself over and over and over.*

Wincing and tear-streaked, that's how she emerged from the orchard, falling and catching herself, over and over and over, in a staggering, hideous half-run. In the corner of her eye she glimpsed the cemetery where twenty squarish red stones stood in a row, marking the graves of twenty bodies. Generations A through T. In all her life Willa had never seen a grave marker for anyone named Claire. Where had they buried her, the defective daughter, the error? The thought stumbled to the forefront of her swimming brain: *Where will they bury me?* And then that black nausea again as she realized that no one would bury her. In moments she would be ash. They would be ash. *It* would *all* be ash. The End. Lifelessness would reign again on this sphere falling through space, and no one would ever know that she, Generation W, had rendered meaningless the existences of twenty-three individuals. Twenty-four counting Claire. Twenty-five counting X. And the zygotes still in the freezer. Did they count? And the sheep. And the plants. And the algae. She had killed all life on this rock. The thing inside her, the thing that spat at her reflection, it was right. She was the mother of death. She was Nyx.

Vivian had taught her the ancient human myth when she was a child: Nyx, shadowy goddess of the night who stood at the beginning of creation and for whom the project had been named. Mother of death and doom. Of blame and deception. But also of dawn and day and, most significantly, of atmosphere. *What a silly story*, she'd thought at the time. *What a stupid, silly story.*

Her boots slogged over the scrubby grass of the pasture. Her withering lungs sucked in and let out air in shallow wheezes, and the muscles along the sides of her torso felt as though they had been sturdily flogged. But her heavy legs would not stop, and in fact, somehow, halfway across the pasture, sped up.

By now she was weeping openly in the ugly, unabashed way she hadn't done since she was a toddler. Some part of her was humiliated by it, ashamed that she would face death like that. What would Mother Anna think? To set out alone in an effort to save her race and then to see it end here with a defective, subliminally murderous and suicidal clone lumbering through the grass and bawling like a sniveling child. The shame, however, did not slow her.

She finally reached the stone barn and flung back the wooden door. The black-faced sheep regarded her momentarily with their strange horizontal pupils before casually filing out past her. She pushed her way over and between them and was nearly to the back of the barn when it happened.

Light consumed everything. It blew the door off its hinges and sliced through the gaps between the rocks in the walls. It flooded the place and picked her up and threw her against the back wall of the barn with a sound like time and space splitting apart, a sound so loud that Willa only knew she was screaming by the feel of her constricting lungs and the vibrations in her throat and the ache of her jaws stretched as wide as they could go.

When she began to come to she was on her back at the rear of the barn wondering why no one was tending to the toast that was obviously burning on the stove. The acrid smell rapidly swelled and thickened in her mouth and nose. She flailed in the debris with the only arm that would respond until her fingers brushed the smooth aluminum of one dented tank beneath splintered eaves and straw. It wasn't until she had downed several deep breaths that her body allowed itself to acknowledge the absence of her hearing and sight and to recognize the presence of other pains. They slogged into her consciousness, dull throbs at first that rapidly escalated into something so massive that her mind could not name it.

She lay in the straw and let it roll over her. She turned onto her side and whimpered in the dirt as her body writhed beneath it. Eventually it ebbed and left her shuddering in the hot wind blasting through the doorway. She rubbed her aching eyes until they began to make out shades of light and dark and pushed herself onto her knees and good arm and crawled toward a lighter rectangle she took as the doorway. Her left arm dragged through the dust beside her. She pulled herself up with what was left of the door jamb. Her right ankle collapsed under her weight and sent a scalding shock up her shin. She cried out and almost heard it. She fell back to her knees and located a piece of blown-apart roof long and sturdy enough to lean on and gave it a second try. With the makeshift crutch under her good arm and all her weight on her good leg, she hobbled out into the smoke and wind.

Her mouth filled with the full force of the smell, and her stomach heaved unfruitfully in protest. She righted herself, looked out over the scene, and waited for her eyes to adjust. Shapes gradually shifted into focus, but color did not. It took a moment for her to realize that this was not due to her eyes. The world was shrouded in soft gray ash. The sheep's bodies were strewn across the pasture along with the smoking remnants of the orchard and the garden and the house. Where the house had been there was only a charred gaping mouth with some mangled strips of metal jutting from it like frozen strings of spittle flung out in mid-scream.

It hit her again. The pain yanked her to the ground and slashed at her abdomen. There was a warm gush between her legs and the pain subsided somewhat, leaving her lying on her side in the puddle gasping, her back to the smoldering crater. Through her water-filled eyes she saw something emerge from behind the barn. The eldest ewe tottered toward her. Blood oozed brilliant red through the white wool on the sheep's back. It meandered around Willa and came to rest in the crumbling grass behind her. Willa leaned back against the soft body. She closed her eyes and felt the ewe's deep, labored breaths.

The pain crawled up onto her again, and she pushed.

As the baby's head began to crest and Willa's screams filled the lifeless silence, the smoke overhead thinned enough that she could see the sky. It had changed. It looked green and close. It squeezed out a drop of cool water that fell for miles and came to rest on her cheek. Another landed on her hand and another on her throat. Then there were dozens of them. Hundreds. Alighting on her as softly as down feathers with a sound like rice pouring into a pot. She clawed at the wet grass as a force within her but somehow separate dragged her deeper.

In the strangely telescopic focus that came to her then, she watched the droplets dissolve the ash and roll black down the thin blades of grass. They beaded in glittering specks on the hard dirt. Willa looked up, and through the billowing translucent sheets of it she watched the smoke roll away toward the mountain range. It engulfed the monstrous atmospheric condensers that had come with Anna and were now lichen-encrusted relics that rivaled the mountains themselves. The black cloud parted at Miriam, the tallest of the peaks, and began to dissipate.

Her gaze settled and narrowed on a rock below Miriam that was larger than the others. As her body shook like it would split apart, the rock's strange shape became familiar. The smell of wet dirt made pictures in her mind of things she could have never seen. Of a pasture so green it was nearly blue and a great animal, the same shape as the rock, with a coat as shiny and black as oil taking a firm, crimson apple from her hand with its lips.

And the air. The air is so big.

In a final, blinding rush Willa's sobs were joined by another's. X shouted her arrival with raspy squawks that, in spite of their tininess, rattled with effort and urgency. Willa gathered the blood-slippery infant from the puddle in the grass between her legs with her good but quivering arm and lay back against the ewe. Gradually they both stopped crying. The infant had nestled against her breast and nodded off before Willa even realized it—X could breathe.

Like the sheep and the chickens and the plants, she thought first. *She's adapted. She's modified.* But no, that was impossible. She was a clone. Willa pressed the little body to her chest and felt the umbilical cord pulse inside her. Was that it? She was still attached to the placenta, was that why X could breathe?

But it wasn't, and Willa knew it with a sudden inexplicable certainty. She looked up. Squinting through the shimmering veils of falling water, she could see the sky was changing again. Fading from green to a pale blue. Cradling the baby in the crook of her functioning arm, she brought her trembling fingers to the tubes in her nostrils and removed them. She closed her eyes and inhaled. It was thin, but it was there.

Words came out with the exhale that were not hers, but unlike before they came without effort or accusation: "Nyx. Mother of Atmosphere."

An invisible hand caught her chin and turned it, gently, toward the rock at Miriam's base shaped like the great and mysterious animal, and it came to her as a recalled memory.

All of it.

Behind the rock the water trickled in muddy streams off a silver ship that waited for its rider, who, having forgotten the beginning of things, would one day remember and return.

FOR ZANNA

S.C. Wade

I shifted around documents on the holographic
computer screen. "The Wall is seven feet thick."

"Does it say anything about the other side of the
Wall?" Belle asked, her concerned voice emanating
over the communicator fixed inside my ear.

"No, but I didn't expect it to. What's strange is that
the Wall is a cavity. The Dassters don't keep sensitive
material on their shared networks so I can't find out
why it's hollow unless I have more time to break their
encryptions."

"How much more time would you need?"

I looked at the Dasster who lay dead on the dull
metal floor. His laser rifle I used against him had
seared his oversized, wormy body in half.

"How much more time are you willing to give me?" I asked. "It's not a problem on my end." I fought to keep my gag reflexes under control, but the feces stench of the dark green liquid that escaped the pudgy carcass was potent.

"What did you do, Angel?"

"He's unconscious. That's all I meant."

"Using the Teleporx without approval is enough guilt on my shoulders," she said. "I would prefer not to add accomplice to murder."

Belle's implication that I was capable of murder didn't faze me. I only wondered how much time would pass before she saw me as a murderer and not just a man who was capable of it.

"The Dassters are the murderers, Belle." I skimmed useless files. "The way they forced us into subjection, making so many people sick?"

"Wrong is still wrong."

It was irritating how Belle was steadfast in her morals no matter how bad the Dassters treated us. She showed no hatred. She even chose to garner employment in one of the Dasster-sponsored institutes. While her managerial service in their teleportation sector allowed me to execute the mission, I still felt like Belle and everyone in her company was a sellout without backbone. In order to do such scientific research, they had to give the Dassters a portion of the profit.

"I think I have all I'm going to get," I said. "Did you get the upload?"

"Eighty-five percent complete."

"Let me delete my tracks." I made sure to

obliterate all records of the data I had sent to Belle's office.

I had shunned Belle so many times in our relationship it was a miracle she agreed to help me. She realized, far before I admitted to myself, that romance and marriage weren't priorities for me. My focus was getting my sister healed of Bleeding Eye Syndrome.

"Done," Belle said. "I'm teleporting you out."

"I'm ready," I said.

My loafers and black slacks were the first to vanish. While it was weird for me to see part of my anatomy dissipate, it was a weirder feeling because each part of my body progressively became numb. When the effects reached my neck, I felt as if my lunch was about to surface.

I blinked, and the eight-by-ten room I'd been seated inside disappeared, replaced by Belle's lofty office. She held a trash bin in front of my face. Before my body was fully rematerialized, I vomited.

I hunched over in the chair while my body recovered from the numbness. Belle yanked the communicator out of my ear, pushed my forehead for me to sit up, and then shoved the trash bin in my arms. She walked around to my side—her long, taut skirt clinging to her hips nicely—and began typing on the console that was connected to the chair I sat in.

Her cheeks had reddened since I was teleported into the Dasster station. It was a sign of her anxiety. I knew so much about Belle, sometimes I wondered if I could get her back. I found it rare for someone so attractive to have the charisma and intelligence that she had.

"You can stand up." Belle stared at me from over her maroon-rimmed glasses.

I set my regurgitated lunch on the floor and retrieved my briefcase from Belle's desk. It was an odd accessory. Although Belle had her own office, I had to appear as if I was doing business, just so no questions would be asked.

I watched Belle enraptured behind the Teleporx. It was her turn to wipe the memory.

In its beta testing stages, the Teleporx was only used by company employees for quick travel to meetings and such. So when the Dassters reviewed their station's security footage and discovered that no one walked the halls, it wouldn't take long before realizing someone in Belle's company had used the machine in an unauthorized manner.

After knowing how the invasion happened, all the Dassters had to do was sift through the company's surveillance footage to find out who used the machine. Thankfully, Belle had a friend who worked surveillance who'd cover up the tracks.

"Straighten your tie," Belle demanded, glancing up from the console.

I obeyed her command. "I appreciate you doing this, Belle."

She stepped away from the console and inspected everything onscreen. "Everything looks good." She handed me the computer chip that held the information I had sent over. "Send Zanna my best wishes."

When I got home, I inserted the computer chip into my holographic adapter so my laptop could display the information I had gathered. It was primitive compared to a holographic-screened console, but it served its purpose.

I studied the anatomy of the Wall and reintroduced myself to the Dassters' medical scheme via articles, reports, and briefs.

The only doctors the Dassters allowed to practice were those who would forfeit a percentage of their income. The more funds humans provided, the more business the Dassters could do with other planets.

My sister and Jared were forced to feed into the Dassters' payment ploy, as they required certain medicines for their conditions. And every medicinal request needed to go through Dasster Hall for processing and approval.

The Dassters had to resort to such behind-the-scenes efforts because they were not a race of physical might. Apart from the addition of arms, they possessed the same anatomical makeup as a human-sized worm.

It was a while before I heard the fingerprint scanner outside the apartment door activate. Seconds passed and the door slid to its side, allowing Zanna and Jared entrance.

"I didn't expect you two to be back so late," I said.

"We got caught up talking to my cousin. He just got a position at Dasster Hall," Jared said.

"Good for him," I said, looking back at the computer screen.

"How's Belle?" Zanna asked as she sat at a stool in the kitchenette.

Neither of the two saw me roll my eyes. "Good."

"How did it go?" Jared sat across from Zanna and set his cane on the counter.

Jared's instigating was often annoying, but I tolerated it because his commitment to my sister was surpassed only by my own.

Jared and I had once taken an air sample and broken into a doctor's lab because we were trying to pinpoint the cause for all the ailments suddenly occurring among humans. Jared was a lab tech for years, and there was a mixture of chemicals he didn't recognize. We were discovered; Jared was nabbed and physically reprimanded for trespassing. His leg had suffered from nerve damage ever since and he needed pills to control the spasms and pain.

Because of that recon mission we learned that the Dassters changed the breathing atmosphere to take advantage of humans' impressionable immune systems. With many humans sick, and the Dassters controlling the doctors, the Dassters profited from the vicious cycle.

I turned in the chair to face Zanna and Jared. "There's still no proof that sanctuary is on the other side of the Wall," I said, "but once the Dasster schematics reach the Wall, all records end."

"Like there's no outside world?" Jared asked.

"It's actually not even a wall," I said.

"What do you mean?"

"We're inside a dome. The Dassters project the illusion of a sky. That's how the chemicals they're pumping into the air don't thin out. It's trapped in here the same as we are."

Zanna said to me, "We need to get through that

Wall."

I rubbed my forehead. The only reason I sought out this information was because of her.

"Where's your faith?" Zanna asked me.

My faith had been in her since I was a child. In school she was my protector. In life she was my confidant. In my relationship with our father, she was my savior.

When I had made mistakes, he'd slap me around in an effort to toughen me up and teach me lessons. The week he lost his job, he gave me a couple physical lectures an hour. A busted lip and a bruised arm wasn't anything, but when I got a gash in the side of my head from being pushed into a desk, Zanna came to my rescue.

She and Dad had argued. I threw in a few unflattering words and ended up on the floor. He was at me while I was down, and Zanna took a lamp to his head. Rest assured it wasn't Zanna's intention to kill him but that's what she ended up doing. I owed her my life.

"Angel," Jared said firmly.

I came out of my daze and noticed that Zanna gripped the countertop with one hand and held onto Jared's wrist with the other.

I stood and maneuvered my way around the kitchenette, grabbing a rag from the rack and then wetting it beneath the faucet. Looking over my shoulder, I watched Zanna's pink eyes transform into a bright red. I wrung out the rag and applied it to Zanna's eyes just as the blood started to seep out. She put a hand over mine and applied additional force.

She screamed, and I shut my eyes.

Bleeding Eye Syndrome was just one disease caused by the Dassters' chemicals. Zanna always had a weak immune system, and although having a decent immune system didn't make one exempt, she was especially susceptible to the effects.

I often wondered why it was me that had the health when it was Zanna who carried us both through life. Why did she have to suffer?

The rumor that the human race outside the Wall made technological leaps sounded good. It sounded better when added to the fact that the Dassters never expanded their territory. People assumed the humans outside the Wall kept the Dassters from planetary domination.

Not knowing the base of those assumptions was my only problem. If anyone had escaped, why would he venture back to his prison to tell his former fellow inmates that there was hope on the other side?

I opened my eyes and saw the horrendous scene before me. I leaned into Zanna's ear and whispered, "I'll get you on the other side of the Wall."

● ○ ●

"I thought I told you not to call unless you had good news," Belle said.

"I just need to search through their databanks to find if there's any record of a human crossing through the Wall," I said, wearing the teleph-headset. "That's it."

"You make it sound like nothing to invade the Dasster station and hijack one of their computers. Do you really think I can give you the time to decrypt what it is you need?"

"This isn't going to work without you." I paced my room.

"That sounds like something I said to you once."

I ignored the jab. "Zanna is dying. The fits are coming more frequently. If you don't let me back in—"

"You have no right to place her life in my hands," she interjected.

"But—"

"No! You are asking me to do something that I despised doing the first time. I want Zanna better too, but the way you want to go about it, I cannot support. It makes no difference to you who you use, does it? As long as it benefits Zanna, everything is okay."

"I'm sorry," I whispered. "What can I do to change your mind?"

"That sounds like something I asked you before, too." Belle sniffled before she ended the connection.

I whipped off the headset and pitched it across the room. It hit the wall and broke in two.

I collapsed on the bed and covered my face with my hands. It was only a few seconds before I heard Jared's heavy footsteps arrive at my bedroom door. He was without his cane.

"I guess it's a no," he said, seeing my demeanor.

Every time Jared tried to walk or stand without his cane, I wanted to punch him to remind him he didn't carry the strength in his legs to do so. I motioned for him to sit and he joined me on the side of the bed.

"I don't know what to do," I said. "We can't waltz into a Dasster station."

"Well, what about Dasster Hall?"

I cocked an eyebrow. "With the security that place has?"

"Zanna and I do it all the time."

"Unfortunately," I grumbled. "Jared, you two can go in, but you wouldn't know what to look for."

"You do," he said. "You can get a temporary pass as a Guider."

I kept quiet.

He bit his lip; he didn't appear to want to say it.

"All the medical experts say that Zanna's condition can render her blind any day now. We can use that expectation to push up her next scheduled visit to the Hall. They won't question it."

"So, we pretend Zanna's blind to gain access to Dasster Hall. If I go in with her, I'm stuck by her side. If I leave a supposed blind person, that doesn't look good."

"I'll be there."

"How?" I asked.

"My cousin. I'll act like I'm visiting him. I'll bring a congratulatory cake, chitchat a little, and then you and I can unexpectedly cross paths. Then you pretend you need to use the restroom."

"Is there another way out of the restroom? We can't make plans unless I have the schematics, and the only way to get those is through a Dasster computer."

Jared smirked throughout my rant. "My cousin, Angel," he said.

My heart dropped. "You're going to trust your cousin—someone who is willingly employed by the Dassters?"

"Belle works for the Dassters."

I glared at him but quickly realized that was the only option we had. "Fine. But that only gets me inside the building. How will I gain access to private areas?"

Jared looked away. "I don't know. My cousin doesn't have a high clearance level . . ." He slouched. "It looks like we're at square one again."

● ○ ●

Later that night, when Jared was asleep, Zanna sat in the stool at the kitchenette again. She breathed heavily, dabbing the corners of her eyes with a clean rag. I washed the blood off of my hands.

She'd just had another attack. It wasn't as strong as the one prior but it still made a mess. I looked at the blood trail on the floor.

"You need to stop trying to handle this yourself at night," I said.

"I don't want to wake you or Jared. I don't need you two losing sleep because of me."

"I don't need you hurting yourself as you stumble into the kitchen practically blind from blood."

"I've never stumbled. I know this apartment." She smiled but it was a disapproving smile. "You can't live your life trying to be my white knight. You'll miss out on too much."

I shrugged. "I don't care."

"I do. I want to see you happy."

"I'll be happy when you're better." I banged the counter. "I need you to be better. I'm sick of this. These stupid Dassters all need to die."

Zanna clasped her hands. "I find myself wondering

what your life would be like if you and Belle were still together."

"Don't."

"I'm not naïve, Angel. I know my condition is what caused the tension between you two."

I stared.

"Sometimes I think if we would have accepted the Dassters and worked for them, we'd be living just as comfortably as Belle."

"They're slave drivers, Zanna."

"And I don't deny that."

"Then why're you talking like this?"

She slowly shook her head and said nothing. She stood from her seat and walked off to her bedroom.

I leaned against the counter and folded my arms. Jared must have spoken to her about us not having a plan to get through the Wall. Her mind appeared to be wavering, and if regret was getting the best of her, I needed to do something. Zanna wasn't herself if she wasn't optimistic.

But how could she think that serving the Dassters would have made a better life? We'd be their captives. There was no freedom. We would only be able to climb as high as they sanctioned us to climb, and Belle was a testament to that. She was only as successful as she was because she yielded to the Dassters instead of opposed them. Belle was helping them make money at the expense of everyone else. Belle gained more responsibility due to the years of service she surrendered herself to.

I unfolded my arms and placed my hands against the counter's bullnose. If she was entrusted with so much responsibility that she had access to the Teleporx—one of their most innovative machines— maybe her access card granted her admittance to Dasster Hall. Her job required her to go there sometimes.

The plan was back on.

● ○ ●

The next morning, I had Jared drop me off at the edge of Belle's ten-acre property. We couldn't risk her seeing me anywhere near her house. While he drove along the pavement to her driveway, I walked on the grass the rest of the way, taking cover behind trees from time to time.

When Jared parked and approached the front door, I was still about fifteen yards out. I crouched behind well-trimmed shrubbery and watched Belle invite Jared inside. I sprinted through the last of the grass and into her backyard.

Belle lived in a secluded area surrounded by woods, so I wasn't worried about anyone spotting what I was about to do. Me having to live with knowing what I'd be doing was enough. But I figured Belle was so fed up with me that she wouldn't let me borrow her access card. So Jared and I thought it wiser that he kept her occupied while I stole it.

The deck was large and the patio doors that led into the house were out of view from the living room, which was where I instructed Jared to keep Belle.

I opened the patio door just wide enough for me to step inside. Once inside, I softly closed it back and I heard Belle's faint voice asking Jared how Zanna was doing.

"Like you care," I mumbled, being light on my feet as I crossed through the kitchen, going for the back steps that led to the second floor.

Belle's way of showing concern was different than mine. I actually did something to help Zanna; Belle only asked and offered assistance if it wasn't too hard or if she felt it was "okay" according to principle. Using the Teleporx was a fluke. She never wanted to get dirty.

When I stepped into Belle's bedroom, I wasted no time going to her closet.

Since the bedroom door was just at the top of the front stairs, and the living room was at the bottom, I heard parts of the conversation between Jared and Belle.

"If we wanted to begin to work for the Dassters," Jared asked, stalling perfectly, "would Zanna be able to get the immunization?"

Belle paused. "For new personnel there's a provisional period of at least six months before the Dassters offer the antidote. And, honestly, even if Zanna were able to get it in six, I think her condition is too far gone, judging by what Angel told me."

"So getting her on the other side of the Wall is her only shot," Jared asked.

"She stands a higher chance, yes. The chemicals are unlike bacteria because they are incapable of multiplying. Zanna's disease is worsening only because of her continued exposure. If removed from the chemicals, she should gradually improve."

I sifted through Belle's purse and found her access

card in her wallet. I looked at the picture ID and smirked at the chin-length hair she used to have.

Belle was off for three days, so she wouldn't notice the card missing. Of course, after I used it to infiltrate Dasster Hall, she probably wouldn't be in a position to need it anymore.

I slid the card in my pocket and made my exit.

● ○ ●

It didn't take long for Jared's cousin to get us the schematics. There were no alternate exits in any of the restrooms, but there was an *Employees & Doctors Only* door that sat adjacent to one. It was near the doctor's office where Zanna went for her checkups.

Jared had gone ahead to visit his cousin, so Zanna and I were left in the apartment alone.

I finished putting on my suit jacket just as she entered the room. "They better not ask any questions to verify your blindness."

"They won't," she said. I looked in her hands and saw the patches that blind people wore. My breathing became rigid because I didn't want to see her wear those, even as a ruse. "They're all wondering why I haven't gone blind already."

Zanna walked to my mirror and affixed the patches over her eyes with a swift delicacy. I knew she and Jared had learned how to put them on, but Zanna's speed made it appear like she'd mastered it.

"You know I love you, right?" My stomach was knotted up.

She turned around, and the white blots over her eyes made me bite my lip to keep from screaming.

"Angel, that's a stupid question," she said and walked toward me. "The question is do you know how much I appreciate all that you've done for me?"

"You're the one who saved my life," I said.

"But you gave me yours." She placed a hand on my cheek and started to feel around my face, as if she was really blind. I pushed her hand away and pulled her in for a hug.

After we released, I held out an arm for Zanna to hook her arm through. As she did, validating my role as a Guider, my throat felt like it was full of marbles. I couldn't speak, could hardly breathe. As much as I didn't want to put my hope in it, going through the Wall seemed to be the only shot Zanna had at keeping her eyesight and, in the long run, her life.

● ○ ●

When we arrived at Dasster Hall, I received my temporary Guider pass and we began our walk to Zanna's doctor. Jared met us, we acted surprised to see each other, and I made my cue to walk down the short hall to the restroom. Zanna and Jared blocked the way in case anyone was watching.

I put my hand in my pocket and grabbed the access card. I hoped it worked or else we'd have to find another way.

Instead of walking into the restroom, I veered sharply left, quickly scanned Belle's access card, and the door slid aside. I smiled and strode through the doorway.

The hall was similar to that of standard Dasster architecture. The lights on the ceiling were in zigzagged rows of three. The walls were plain and dull. This section of the hall was near the meal room, so the faint smell of decomposed flesh made me shudder.

I was dressed in a suit so as not to look out of place in case I was spotted. Hopefully I'd be assumed an employee and not be asked for ID. But I felt naked. The hall was barren of any sort of cover, and there were too many doors for me to be relaxed.

A door a few doors down the hall slid aside and a Dasster slithered into the hallway. I held my breath before I saw him turn to travel in the same direction I was going. He didn't see me. I slowly exhaled.

I let him lead the way, ready to pounce if he happened to turn around, see me, and call me out on my facade. If only I had a weapon for backup. Anything. I remembered Belle's access card—it was relatively sharp around the edges.

The Dasster led me down the hall at a slow pace for a good minute, and I only had to make one more turn before I reached the nearest office and I could leave this hallway.

A door behind me opened. I turned around and looked at the Dasster. He stared at me with his beady eyes.

My pulse elevated and I wrapped my fingers around the access card in my pocket. He slithered closer, never taking his eyes off me until he passed. Being so close to a Dasster . . . It would've been so easy to . . .

He was yards ahead before I started walking again. When I approached the intended door, I looked through the window and saw a crowd of Dassters slithering by on their way to the meal room. With so many occupied with their road kill lunches, infiltration of a computer wouldn't be hard.

My heart pounded louder as each brown worm passed; my heartbeat hardly overpowered the spongy sound they generated as they traveled. It was despicable how they went about their days and prospered at the expense of our poverty.

I clenched my fist and waited out the rush. Once it had gone, I hurried through the door, walking in the opposite direction of the Dassters.

The office I needed was to the left. I stepped inside the open door and was met by a Dasster who hadn't yet left for his meal. I grabbed his plump body, positioned myself behind him, and applied a chokehold.

His neck molded to each of my finger impressions like jelly. His putrid stench was overwhelming. The temptation called out to me.

"Human, what do yo—"

I severed his neck and his head flopped a few feet away. His body slumped against my legs, so I stepped back. The majority of my attire was stained with his dark green blood.

"Not the smartest idea," I said with a satisfying smile as I stepped behind his desk. I locked the office door via a command at the computer console.

I sifted through the backlog files, sliding aside documents that didn't meet my purpose. Then I saw a record dated a couple years back of a young man who tried to escape. A Dasster guarding that sector had fired, missed, and the bullet created a hole in the Wall. I pulled up a photo of the gun used; it was a model I hadn't seen before.

Searching for information regarding the weapon

was difficult because a lot of it was hidden behind passwords and codes. I didn't have time to hack around the login.

There was one article that briefly mentioned how the Dassters chose to discontinue the use of that gun, in case there was another escape attempt and a Dasster made another less-than-perfect shot.

I heard slithering out in the hallway, which was normal as so many Dassters had to pass this office to go to the meal room. But this particular slither stopped in front of the office. The silhouette of a Dasster projected through the hazy door.

Then I realized—the blood of the Dasster wasn't hard to smell, as the green goo serving as their blood reeked like garbage. He was probably concerned and excited at the same time.

I resumed my search and found that the damaged section of the Wall was thirty miles from Dasster Hall and had been repaired with an inferior metal. A Dasster's laser gun could reopen the hole. I looked around the office. This Dasster didn't have a weapon, but a laser gun was easy to obtain with the right connections.

The Dasster was still loitering outside the door.

I gathered all the articles I had found and placed them on a chip I found in the desk drawer. I unlocked the office door because I knew I could take on the lone Dasster that stood there. It was the getting out of the building part I wasn't so sure I could do anymore.

I placed the chip in my pocket.

The door opened and the Dasster looked at me with wide eyes as I wrapped my arm around his neck and squeezed. The fleshy neck constricted until it broke. That Dasster met the same fate as the other.

"Intruder!" A Dasster had seen me murder his friend.

Scanning Belle's card, I entered the back hallway and tried to remember the schematics that Jared's cousin had provided. I had to remember what door would bring me to the office where his cousin worked.

The alarm sounded and I ran to the right. It wouldn't take long before I was met by armed opposition. I couldn't even blend in and pretend like I belonged as I had the green stains all over my clothing.

This was now a suicide mission, but my impromptu back-up plan would still guarantee it successful for Zanna.

That's all that mattered.

I approached a fork in the hall and took a left. I then took the second door on the right. When I stepped through, a Dasster was on the far side of the room, which translated to about five yards away. He pointed and yelled, but that's all he did as he wasn't security.

There was a human at the desk in the corner. There was a white box on his desk. A cake box.

I took the chip from my pocket and grabbed Jared's cousin by the collar and stood him up, backing him into the wall.

"No, let me go!" he yelled, gripping my arms and trying to make me release him, but he was puny and weak. His efforts worked perfectly for my plan, though.

Keeping one hand around his neck, I grabbed one of his hands and forced the chip inside his grasp, all the while making it appear like I was trying to keep him from taking a swing at me.

"Give it to Jared," I whispered and his eyes widened slightly. He realized who I was.

His gaze went past me and I knew security had arrived. I spun around and was met by three Dassters aiming guns at my head. Jared's cousin scrambled away.

"Live well, Zanna," I whispered before I was impaled by the lasers.

Party at the Phaedrus 5 Galleria

Rob Oxley

Through the pink-tinted tube, the asteroid scenery whizzed by: up to 63rd; left on Sybilia; straight for a quarter mile and then left after Shoop.

I stopped at the intersection of Kwail and 252nd to have a look at the Gamma-Tal megasection.

The massive structure was a tightly wound ball of tubes and their softly ribbed couplings squirming around a routing center. I watched as dozens of my fellow asteroid natives passed through the rippling orifices gently, seamlessly.

Admittedly, I was not fond of the newer cross-section style when the architects first presented the blueprints, but I have to say that the design is growing on me. And yes—even though it beat *my* proposed design during voting, I can see now that the overall efficiency is undeniable.

From behind the bubble, the view of Gamma-Tal was fantastic and I soaked it up. Scattered around the megasection like neon confetti, bots crawled over the rocky terrain, restlessly fusing new ports and tubes of the megasection together and erecting girders. The glittering lights covering their shells and wheels gave the impression of sparkling streams running through the valleys of mineral and metal.

There is something entrancing about viewing the caverns in their raw state. With their jagged hills and expansive craters, it never fails to conjure profound and humbling sensations—

And why shouldn't it? Really, it is the closest thing to a *natural landscape* that many of us in the rock will ever have the chance to experience. And once Central starts D-phase blasting and construction, the area will be off limits for miles. All of the tubes will reroute away from Gamma-Tal and the crude view of the asteroid section will be lost.

Of course we have our extravagant gardens and parks—dozens of them, and every one different—but for all their beauty, I can never get past the idea that they are only things that we have created; that they are in many ways inferior to the marvels of the natural cohesion and melding of metals and minerals of our drifting home. The parks are something . . .

Trivial. Manufactured. *Synthetic*.

But, unlike them, this asteroid could very well be older than our *species*.

To me, *that* is just such a beautiful notion. Sobering, sure. Even intimidating at times—but still, absolutely beautiful.

I could have stared through that pink bubble for hours . . . but I had a party to attend.

I jumped back into the tube: a right to Lagpin; a left onto Haroo; and then straight for two miles—and *then* I got stuck in Chinatown for twenty minutes while the transporter glitched and rewired itself.

"WE OFFER OUR SINCEREST APOLOGIES," the sultry digital voice assured. "THIS SYSTEM WILL BE FUNCTIONAL IN THREE—*bzzzzzt!* . . . TWENTY. THREE. MINUTES. THANK YOU FOR YOUR CONSIDERATION. WE OFFER OUR SINCEREST APOLOGIES. THIS SYSTEM WILL BE FUNCTIONAL IN—"

So naturally I grabbed some jiaozi with iced dragon sauce and slouched into a bench to watch all of the hustle and bustle. Little Krane was sleeping—and at such a productive level, too!

According to the alpha wave graph on his capsule, he was content and dreaming. Happy. Healthy. *Perfect.*

It was something of a poetic contrast, watching Little Krane floating comfortably in his green goo, sleeping and dreaming with no sense of stress or worry—and then looking in all directions around me at the swarms of people jabbering constantly, swapping goods, gliding by on magnetobikes, selling hybrid fruit—

Does naming something "Chinatown" automatically induce it to perpetually fold into itself and become overwhelmingly cramped? Every time I come here (which in all reality is rarely) I find myself equally entertained and baffled. There's plenty of room in Phaedrus 5, even with it only being ten percent developed—so why do the occupants of these particular areas always insist on cramming themselves into the smallest space imaginable?

I guess that *new ideas rarely last* and *old habits hold fast*. I think someone dead and legendary said that.

Oh, well—it was a semi-interesting tangent, but then the bulb over the tube-port flipped to lime green and I jumped back in, awaiting my reintroduction into traffic. Little Krane, his capsule tethered to my wrist, glided through the air and came to a bobbing rest at my side.

I smiled at the fetus and emotionally sent him my fatherly love. Because the shield that separates us keeps all but the most trace amounts of light and definition from reaching his sensitive forming eyes, I know he doesn't *see* my smile—but I know that he *feels* it.

We have that deep kind of connection now. Maybe you understand—probably you don't.

The port door closed with a wet, sucking sound that preceded ejection, and then we and the capsule were jolted gently back into the biotube system that served as Phaedrus 5's main mode of long-distance transportation.

I was still making good time. The party was probably just starting, and—barring any more glitches in the tubes—I would be arriving in another fifteen minutes. That was fine with me; I preferred to be on the fashionably late side.

Racing through the tubes, neatly packed inside my transport pod, I stretched out on my cushion of air and listened to the non-engaging muzak. I watched the mini-towns fade into the more commercialized section of the city. The housing blocks and apartment clusters covering the asteroid walls and ceilings like lichen soon became malls, outlets, and stores, all beginning to blur together when the tube abruptly changed directions.

Sometimes tube rides are like being trapped in a kaleidoscope. Dizzy, I started to nod off.

Without any obvious reason—save to maybe pass the time in the tube without falling asleep—I thought about Phaedrus 5 and its history.

●○●

Ten years ago, Berry and Serg Partners—a *goddamned* KolaDak subsidiary: *We Control the Stars, We Navigate Your Destiny* (as I always liked to emulate their commercials and include the obvious and asinine association)—had purchased the asteroid in a bundle and begun immediate action to populate.

The rock was a good size, especially for the price. It had been projected that at least three megacities could be successfully formed in its bowels. That may not seem like much nowadays, but Phaedrus 5 was never intended to be a "Super-Rock"—merely a good chunk of estate to bring in some working folk who could operate the mining facilities at the center of the asteroid, and eventually steer the rock toward Fevval-Boges.

Berry and Serg must have been near elation when they found out that their little purchase was a class-U teven geode; what they could mine from it would surely triple in return what they had paid for the whole bundle. Not a bad stroke of luck, I should say—too bad it was wasted on soulless conglomerate inbreds.

Then came the flood of homestead requests. Everyone knows that pop-positions like these filled quickly, and even though hundreds of rocks are being homesteaded yearly, people still feel they have to push and shove their way to the front.

I think it was D'arcy who told me about the latest and greatest prospect. I had been moon based on Dhava when the rock became open to submissions, and I was in roster for the next 4k leap. I had been writing landscape simulation code for months and was ready to rip open the access hatch of my console and forcefully jam my head in just to have a change in scenery. So when D'arcy confided to me about B & S's greatest new catch, I hurried over to dispatch and handed them my green slip (having the supervisor owe you a favor for covering a math-fuck pays off heavily in such situations). I found myself as close as could be to the front of the line.

Thirty-two hours later and I was deep-sleepin' my way to asteroid 3233 Plu: the rock that would soon be formally known as Phaedrus 5 and later become my permanent home.

Why such a wacko name? Why *Phaedrus 5*? You may assume it could be contributed to the Roman philosopher as a kind of noble dedication—but no. It was because giving planetoid habitats bizarre names has been the fad for close to a century, and after our asteroid-buster had burrowed into the rock, the first asshole to set his foot down—thus gaining entitlement privileges—had been a devotee to a cult revolving around alter egos. Apparently the name Phaedrus has some significance, but it is lost on me.

Actually, I know that "asshole" quite well. Huck Marocaf and I have been drinkin' pals for as long as I care to remember. I haven't seen much of him since we smash-landed—well, except for those crazy few weeks when . . . but I'm getting to that—but lord knows that his luxurious women and exorbitant habits keep him plenty busy. And then of course he has his quasi-administration jobs to fill in the rest of the cracks . . .

Lousy bastard is just perfect for appearing competent and getting far too much credit for far too little.

Don't get the wrong idea—Huck and I are as tight as friends get, you see. But because he has a shiny diamond-shaped pilot's card and a flat in the lavish New Praan section, and I don't, it's mandatory that I affectionately smother him with crap when we do meet up. Stuff like: "Really, ass-hat, how hard is it to crash a thirty-megaton capacity missile into the broadside of a B-type asteroid? Chimp work if you ask me. It is a skill that I hardly understand requiring a vigorous five-year instructional—"

Huck *hates* that one.

So anyway, the asshole smashed us into 3233 Plu nearly eight years ago. After our initial set-down, the buster released its army of bots and drones into the surrounding caverns to install Central's main nest, which took about three agonizing months (just ask anyone who's ever had to wake from a 3k sleep or higher and live in a buster for a couple months—that's the longest three months of your life).

Once Central was set up, a special group of bots began mining the precious teven and using the metal to construct the refinery. Everything after that was pretty common protocol: The standard bots shot outward in hundreds of directions, scanning and documenting our new home and planting the tube hatches. Coaxer-bots set up posts. Then the biotube system began winding itself through the rock and metal of the asteroid, setting up small blips of housing here and there.

Once a suitable percentage of homestead was complete, the buster's restless occupants were released into the *wild*.

Talk about combustion! From the way people partied for weeks straight you would swear they thought they were the last of their species . . .

Oh, to be out of the buster! Such freedom, some space to really *live*, man. *Party at Sully's Place!* and *I've got two cases of 151! Who's a lucky lonely-bunker tonight?*

I didn't have to bunk with anyone for those months after sleep, but trapped inside that hunk of tin, just knowing that there was some body less than a wall's width away—it was enough to drive me bonkers.

Immediately people were issued housing instructions and told to report for work—and they even rejoiced at *that*.

I settled in to my comfortable four-room suite in Alpha-Roger Section: *alone*, and loving it. Dhava had been so cramped that I had shared a room with four other men, which (despite them being rather nice and courteous fellows) quickly grated on my nerves.

I had enough status on the buster to earn a private studio (barely), but this was different. I had finally found some space of my own here.

In truth, it was simultaneously exhilarating and horrifying. I knew the stats on Alpha-Roger: It could be years before I was assigned a neighbor. So different from what I was used to that it was kind of scary, yes—but it was perfect.

For some time I had a view bubble just outside my apartment, and I would spend hours there watching the bots fly around. Their little lights would illuminate the cragged peaks and valleys surrounding the main nest, and the tube systems snaked restlessly around hills and into caves, running out of sight into unknown areas of the massive rock.

With the continuous and well-coordinated movements of tube systems and bot-assemblies, it was like watching a kind of symphony. I had been fascinated with the process since I was old enough to crawl through the tubes back on Shinobi Atari. Hence the reason I had become a surveyor and eventually dedicated my life to helping populate giant flying rocks.

Others may consider it a boring job, but there are few that would ever complain about the benefits: a bitchin' four-room suite, unrestricted tube privileges, and enough pseudo-administrative powers to satisfy even the boldest of egos.

For the exciting first years I had been content.

Then—as I guess it always does in times of

tranquility—the blues came.

And it came hard.

● ○ ●

A sharp u-turn on Galtor and then it was straight down to the Galleria. I looked at the time-pix under my left wrist: *right on time . . .*

Well, *my* time, at least. Being punctual—even if it is to my own design—has always been important to me.

Little Krane was awake now. He was moving his tiny hands in front of his softly featured face. On the stats his beta waves fluctuated gently—*beautifully*—and his large eyes were bugged out.

I think that the little guy really enjoys these fast-drops in the tubes.

I patted the capsule lovingly. "Here we go, little man! Wheeeeeeeeeee—"

● ○ ●

So bachelor life had been great for a couple years; after our landing in Phaedrus 5 I was busy enough to not notice any loneliness for quite some time. I had my job, which was equal enough parts cake and hell—which was nice—and I had my own kind of venturesome frolics into the social stream of Phaedrus. You know how things go on these kinds of rocks . . . *any way you want.*

Then, as the planetoid eased into monthly and yearly rhythms and the workload started to slow down, the loneliness hit me like a brick.

I had tried partnering with other occupants in my area—not just nighters, but *really* trying for long-term

—but they were always short-lived excursions and failed to pacify the void growing inside of me.

The counselors confirmed what I had already suspected: I was not a socially dependent person. I was fine being alone. And I would be happiest if left to my own privacy and personal space. Well, "No shit," I told them—

but then why did I feel so hollow?

So mating and social-pairing was not something I had a need for. That was all fine, like, really. But still, *something* was missing . . .

Suddenly I found myself fully submerged in sticky depression. I missed work constantly and my excuses were ridiculous. Without shame I spent great bouts of time with ol' Huck and began to feel even worse. Shortly thereafter, even the binge-drinking and the random pill games wouldn't help and I knew I was in some big trouble.

When the *good* meds only made it worse, I went back to the quacks. One of the genius counselors suggested that it may not be AHCS—Abrupt Habitat Change Syndrome—at all. They ran some more tests and numbers and told me a couple days later that I was, apparently, just "At that age . . ."

As if *that* explained everything.

My next session with the counselors was pretty profound. Before then I had never even considered the notion of becoming a parent. But as soon as it was suggested, I was obsessed with the idea. Those damn quacks . . . *of course* that was what I was missing!

Someone to carry my legacy.

Someone I could teach and help grow.

It was my ticket to purpose; my golden key.

I was standing in the Reproduction and Census office the next day, smiling and fidgeting like an idiot.

Two weeks later, a large package came through the mail chute.

I must say that I was disappointed when I unwrapped it. I unlatched the outer casing and just stared—inside was nothing but a cylinder the size of my travel beer cooler filled with green *goo* and hundreds of sensors crawling through it like spider legs!

I tried to be positive, I really did. I read through the *What to Expect* files that came with the package. They explained that it was normal to feel disappointment for the first four months until the fetus took on a more recognizable shape. Not so . . . mutant-ish, I guess. I read some more: ". . . The first-stage nutripack is capable of delivering sustenance to the embryo/fetus for a period of three to four months. It is fairly common practice to place the capsule in a safe room or cupboard for this duration, and then to bring it out when the nutripack is depleted and needing replacement. Reminders will be sent to you beginning a week before depletion (see 3.75). If you fail to replace the pack in a suitable time frame, the R and C office will be contacted and criminal charges for neglect (Section 455-G-C-5) may be filed—"

Disgusted with the disappointment and feeling the claws of depression returning, I shoved the capsule into my closet and shut the door for three months.

I was *really* deep into the blues the day a private alert popped up on my work screen. I choked on my coffee—which was really just some rum with coffee flavoring. The message was from the R and C office. It was time to change the nutripack . . . and I had nearly forgotten all about the capsule sitting in the dark of my closet!

With a bit of newly kindled excitement I left work early and rushed home. My eyes must have looked like two big, puffy bot wheels when I pulled the capsule out and looked upon the tiny life growing inside of it.

Why . . . it was a small piece of *me* in there!

Kinda skeletal; kinda creepy—but *me* nonetheless.

At that moment, the depression was obliterated. I will admit it: I cried for hours without shame.

Little Krane has not left my side since.

●○●

The transport tube had become transparent apricot and I could see the giant palace of the Galleria come racing upward from under my feet.

It wasn't anything exceptional: The gallerias on Shinobi Atari dwarfed this one by a hundred times. Of course, my home asteroid was a major software and gaming manufacturer, so it was not unbelievable that we had boasted some of the greatest entertainment arenas in existence.

From that came a bit of irony: Growing up in an environment that revolved around gaming and enter-tainment had eventually repelled me from it. Before the depression monster began stalking me, I would prefer to go over stats and diagrams for days in the quiet comfort of my simple quarters than to spend a couple hours at a galleria where every sensation was amplified and over-the-top.

Even now it made my palms begin to sweat. China-town was different, I guess. I was just an observer there. Here I would be expected to *socialize* . . . but I had Little Krane, and he gave me confidence.

You see, I wouldn't have come of my own accord. The people thing, yes, and the fact that I grew out of gaming and amusement parks decades ago. Really, I was only going now because Roxanne had asked me to, and I hadn't seen her for close to a year now.

● ○ ●

Roxanne had been my second attempt at a pairing, and even though it had lasted less than a hundred hours, I had become quite captivated with her.

Unfortunately, it was not in the purely sexual and healthy fashion. Huck had laughed and told me that, once again, I had let my feelings get in the way of good, meaningless sex . . . I told him to shutup; I staunchly maintained that I was free and clear of any of *those* feelings. Asshole.

Roxanne was completely understanding when I confessed my lack of interest in further involvement, and in retrospect I believe she had a suspicion of my condition even before I did. God, was I weirdo then. And she just talked to me like everything was dandy. She didn't get angry and throw things, or laugh and blow me off. She just seemed a little sad, but real supportive. It was . . . weird.

She remained a good friend for a time; we met for walks and drinks or food and drinks regularly—

And then I heard that she'd paired with another man. Congruently, I heard less from her.

It didn't really bother me—I assured myself of it regularly—and at the time I was busy planning for the asteroid's arrival at the J3RR8D sling-station, scheduled to come to fruition in six years.

From J3RR8D, Phaedrus 5's trajectory would change by ninety degrees and we all would be home-bound for the Fevval-Boges quadrant—the largest asteroid cluster ever assembled. Once in Fevval, our little rock would be mined for generations and our descendants would eventually shoot out and away from it in search of new prospects.

Descendants. *Children . . .*

It was kind of scary imagining what would happen after J3RR8D. Once en route to Fevval, my life's work would be all but complete. It would be hundreds of years before Phaedrus entered Fevval boundaries, and we would be too far out at that point to jump to another rock.

Phaedrus 5 was going to be home, for good.

The thought had begun to rattle around in my head: *Was I doomed to be forever alone?*

Being busy with the job helped, but even still it wasn't long after I heard of Roxanne's pairing that I fell into thick, vulgar depression. I will admit that it may have even contributed to it; replacement is replacement, whether between close lovers, or between loose friends, or between . . . well, whatever the hell Roxanne and I had been.

But after I found myself with child, my bitterness toward Roxanne dissolved.

I had been empty, void—and no pairing of any sex could have changed that.

What finally did was my little man. My big guy.

I finally embraced the fact that this giant rock was where I would spend the rest of my days, and I decided that it was too small a world in which to harbor any ill feelings. With the visions of Little Krane running around—maybe even one or two more!—life had never looked better.

So when Rox called up and invited me to the party, I wasn't in such a blue mood. I said "sure."

●○●

The Galleria was exactly what you would expect: non-stop rides and game arenas, endless halls of vendors and entertainment vaults.

The first thing I saw when Little Krane and I exited the tube was the giant hydro-orb centered in the main conjunction area.

There were dozens of children and perhaps a handful of adults floating around in the clear, no-g liquid. The adults seemed to congregate toward the middle of the orb, some gyrating slowly and then jetting through to the other side at super speeds. Some of the chiseled stags were obviously racing each other—but the ageless goddesses drifted around them lazily, mostly oblivious to their displays and more interested in sensually rubbing against one another.

The children zoomed around in the mazes of piping and fort-like walls that lined the rim of the orb.

I approached the surface and smiled; a boy with long black hair sped past me with his arm propellers blazing. In the froth of white bubbles that was left behind him, what was apparently a pet dolphin followed, squeaking happily.

I thought about Little Krane growing up, and when he would be ready to take swimming lessons and eventually come play with the other kids here in the orb. The idea was actually pretty likable.

Perhaps I would be coming to the Galleria more in the future after all . . .

I was daydreaming pleasantly when a fist dug into my ribs from behind and startled me. I made some shrilly noise that was unbecoming of a man my size.

"Eghhhrlll!"

Instinctively I pushed Little Krane behind me, away from harm. I put my fists up.

When I turned, Roxanne was there. The chances of us bumping into each other in this crowd were pretty slim—but Rox and I just seemed to have that strange, non-romantic kind of natural attraction. We could probably bump into each other in a crowd twice this size. She looked surprised, then giggled . . .

Then she began laughing hysterically. It's quite amazing, really; she's the only person I have ever met that can bray like a wild jackass—like the cartoons, of course; the real ones are extinct—and still maintain an attractive quality.

I let my guard down.

"Jesus, Rox! You scared the shit out of me!"

She grabbed my upper arm and leaned in for a kiss. The first thing that I noticed about her was the large, protruding belly that was encased in her tight shirt. Her breasts were fuller and she had a bit of pudge in her face. She always was kind of into the *natural* thing—I should have known she would choose to carry in utero rather than artificially.

I put my arm around her. With my other hand I reached out reflexively and rubbed her stomach.

"Holy shit, Rox! You look like you're ready to pop!"

Her demeanor changed abruptly: She nudged my arm away and stepped back. As her back arched and her smile fell south like a broken door, one eyebrow raised in confusion and the other curled with anger—over all, it was a very frightening transition.

"What the fuck are you talking about, Krane? I'm not *pregnant*—"

I cannot explain the terror that gripped me. It was something total and eclipsing. I swear that my temperature increased by fifty degrees, and my forehead and neck sprouted giant beads of sweat just like the condensation sheets that covered the plant labs a level up.

I ran through useless refutals in my mind. I was ready to just bow out and turn around and shoot myself back up the tube—

Then came that beautiful braying and she brutishly slapped my shoulder.

"Holy shit, Krane," she managed between gasps. "You should see your face! I am *so* fucking with you!"

My stolid stance relaxed and I shared a nervous laugh with her; she was having a hard time containing her giggles. Before her laughing got offensive, though, she calmed down. She wasn't *that* mean.

She kissed my cheek and then placed my hand back onto her stomach. She patted her strangely erotic belly with our hands. "Any day now and Joolee should be breakin' out," she said, still smiling mischievously.

Little Krane bobbed his way forward from behind my back. I waited for a reaction.

Roxanne eyed the capsule tethered to my wrist but did not immediately say anything about it.

She pointed to the chamber beyond the swimming orb and said that the birthday party was down that way, but that most of the kids were busy swimming and racing magneto-bikes. "We've got some time before cake and presents," she said.

She took my arm and we strolled down toward the eatery. Kinda like old times.

I'll be honest: It felt good to have a bit of human contact, especially with someone as good-looking and outwardly radiant as Rox. I didn't mind the second looks that some people threw our way. *Stare on, fellas.*

We chatted openly, cheerfully.

As it turned out, Roxanne had broken it off with the man she had taken up with after me, and eight months ago she had become involved with a younger woman named Gustel.

The couple had fallen quickly for each other, and Roxanne claimed she woke up one morning two months pregnant and with only a vague memory of becoming artificially inseminated. She said that Gustel had that effect on her: She was in a constant state of bliss and love. So fully, in fact, that she lost track of time constantly.

I knew that trends such as this were common in newly established rocks: In a subconscious attempt to populate the hollowed asteroid, natural birthing would be a raging fad for decades. Phaedrus 5 would be a category three settlement for at least another fifty years, and that meant that reproduction would be allowed to continue at a loosely managed rate. Sure, eventually the census would anticipate some crowding, and then mandates would dictate all reproduction by introducing permits and contracts—but for now, there was no reason to exert any control over the populace.

It was one reason that people were so excited to jump on asteroid busters and pioneer new rocks: The freedom was like a drug.

We meandered through the Galleria and talked. I asked her how the party was going. She said she was having a blast.

The party was for Gustel's niece's sixth birthday. When Roxanne had called me up and invited me, she had made it sound like it was for a *friend's* niece's party—not a *lover's*. Not a *soon-to-be parent* and *spouse*. Had I known the truth, I probably wouldn't have come. I think Roxanne knew that and had made it a point to keep the subject vague.

Roxanne said she was hungry, and from the stories I've heard I knew better than to prolong the cravings of a woman in her condition.

I paid for two apple-buns, one for her and one for myself, and then we continued to stroll around. Roxanne devoured her apple-bun and we had to make another stop for synthetic pork-chop-kabobs. I hated eating that stuff, but Roxanne confessed that she'd had an embarrassing craving for it for the last half of her term.

"The more salt, the better!" she confided between bites. Adorable, even with a face covered in grease.

Hearing her talk about cravings made me feel a bit of that recently forgotten hollowness. I was *with child*, sure—but without those quirky and exciting side effects. Why couldn't *I* want pork-chop-kabobs, too?

She seemed to sense my introspection. She licked her fingers and finally asked about the floating capsule bobbing at my side.

"So tell me about your friend, there."

I had thought it strange that she hadn't asked before now. Rox was like that, though; sensitive to the right moment for things.

"Oh, Little Krane? Well—that's not what his name is going to be, but that's what I call him for now."

We stopped at an alcove. She cradled her belly and gently knelt down to inspect the tiny fetus in the capsule.

"Well, Krane, I think he's going to look just like you. He has wonderful eyes! *Lady-killer* eyes."

I felt some pride and I'm sure it showed. I had not opted for full-on clone; I wanted some flavor added to my offspring. So I had requested a "cocktail" of miscellaneous attributes—stuff that I knew was not included in my own DNA. I wanted the little guy to be something special, unique. The quacks had referred to it as *tiny surprises*.

"What made you decide to go *this* way, love?" Roxanne was wiggling her finger in front of Little Krane's big eyes and biting her tongue. All I could think was, *God she is cute.* And on the tail of that, *God I was an idiot . . .*

"I mean, you'll make a great father," she continued, "but I think you'd make a great *husband* as well."

I couldn't help but blush from the compliment. We found a bench to sit on. I went on to explain that my father had decided the same thing when he was my age, and since I had turned out so well, it had seemed like a logical thing to do.

"I mean, I know I'm intelligent and caring, and I'm confident that with enough dedication I could have effectively learned and executed the 'mommy-daddy' thing . . . but it just felt more natural for me to do it *this* way."

She seemed to understand, though she kept looking at my eyes in a way that made me feel like she was digging for something. *That* was something I did not miss about the partnering escapades. The way that other people could become so suddenly strange and foreign, like another species altogether.

"Oh!" she gasped suddenly. "*Careful* there, Joolee!"

I helped Roxanne up from the bench, and we made our way back to the party area. She looped her arm around mine, and I tugged Little Krane along after me. We made another stop for apple-buns and soda.

Along the way we stopped to collect some of the party-goers from the Turbo-Rings: vast, floating rings that riders would attach themselves to by means of frictionless vests, and then accelerate around going outrageous speeds that required minimal amounts of push. The children looked like blurs. The stand by the ride had a sign saying you had to drink a bottle of *Special-G* before riding. *Naturally*, I thought—without it, riders would become liquefied.

I remembered my first ride on the rings. So much fun! Roxanne was swearing that she would never let Joolee ride them. We both knew differently, though.

At the party, among the crowd of friends and relatives of the birthday girl, Roxanne introduced me to Gustel. She was beautiful *and* extremely outgoing. Friendly . . . I wanted to hate her on general principle.

Was I really so shallow? Yes, apparently. But alas, I couldn't hate her; I could see *exactly* what Roxanne was so enthralled with. She was sweet, and kind—not to mention she was as smoldering-hot as they come and looked like she could wrestle a bear. I think she was of NeoCanadian descent, actually . . .

I wish I could tell you otherwise, but in all aspects she appeared to be an amazing person.

She was also very busy helping coordinate a wild birthday party, so I didn't get to socialize with her for long. I managed to gesture at Rox's belly and tell her "congratulations" before she was pulled away by a seven-year-old. She nodded enthusiastically and then disappeared into the crowd. I lost track of Roxanne shortly after that, and eventually became tired.

Most of the other women present were well into pregnancies of their own or just starting to gain some pudge, and they formed large groups and chatted among themselves. I had seen another man with a glowing green capsule in tow, but I was unable to approach him and strike up a conversation before he dissolved into the Galleria's masses.

Aside from him, I was apparently the only single-male parent in the area.

That was something I knew would eventually change, too. The natural-pregnancy thing would crest and then start to decline in popularity, and then there would be a flux of single-parenting fads. This just goes to support my thesis that we are not as instinctually co-dependent as we like to believe: When it's beneficial to the species, sure—but when we don't have to mate for safety or security, I think we would just as soon not.

Just the ebb and flow of life in a rock, *man*.

I caught up with Roxanne and told her that I was leaving. Tired.

"Don't be a pussy, Krane! Go grab a stim and stick around for a bit." She was prodding me, and I had to laugh. So far there was very little that Roxanne could playfully say that I would take any offense to.

I insisted that I was coming up on a long week, and she realized that I was not going to be persuaded to stay. She made a wonderful pouty face.

We both said it was great to see the other— and it was true. She made me promise to be there when Joolee came—"two in the morning or not, Krane!"— and I agreed. It was a promise I fully intended to keep.

We hugged. She kissed me and kissed Little Krane's capsule, leaving a perfect imprint of her lips on the glass. I have yet to clean it off. Gustel managed to pull away long enough to shake my hand and plant a wet kiss on my cheek and half of my lip. I blushed. Rox slapped my ass on the way out and whistled loudly; I blushed even more and walked away smiling stupidly.

Then the little man and I left the Galleria.

●○●

Little Krane fell back asleep on the way home, and I was only half-awake when the tube brought me to my apartment door. Inside I didn't even bother to take my clothes off; I threw a box of pizza-crammers into the ThawPro for breakfast, and fell into bed. Little Krane followed the tether and I threw the cover over him in bed, snuggling him closely next to me.

Lying there, rubbing my eyes, I verbally accessed my recent messages. Go figure; Huck had called only a couple of hours ago.

"Hey, dickweed, it's Cho—"

Huck got the nickname Cho Cho when we were both rowdy kids—I have no idea why. Probably because he was an asshole.

". . . Give me a call and let's grab a brew tomorrow. If I remember right, it's your turn to buy anyway—"

The message ended.

Exhaustion was settling in.

"Kiss it, asshole."

I leaned over and rubbed Little Krane's capsule.

"Sleep tight, big man."

I was beyond exhausted—being a single parent was rough!

But I was content, and happy, and eager to wake up in the morning. I would probably even call Huck tomorrow night. He wasn't aware of me being with child, and even though he was for sure going to give me some shit about Little Krane, I knew that under it all he was a true friend and would support me.

More than likely he would have one of his own in a couple months anyway . . . he's one of those people that just *has* to keep up on current trends.

I yawned and told the lights to dim. I smiled in the peaceful dark.

I will admit a lot of my recent nights I have spent lying awake, staring at the ceiling, worried about the days leading up to when Little Krane will make his entrance into the world. The *What to Expect* files had explained some of the final process: The capsule will receive alteration codes that will begin simulating the contractions and stresses of a normal human body in labor. Discomfort will increase. And once certain biochemical levels have been reached, the capsule will simulate the final contortions and pushes of birth. It will be horribly painful for Little Krane—and myself (as I will be receiving nerve-stimulation as well). Hard to consent to, but it is very necessary. It would be easy enough to just pluck Little Krane from his synthetic womb, but it has long been known that the pain and trauma of birth are essential for us humans; it kind of calibrates the body's pain threshold for the rest of our lives.

But these things were not eclipsing my positive thoughts tonight. It had been a long, fun day, and I was still amped from seeing Rox again.

Tonight, there was no denying it: Life in the rock was good.

I rubbed the shield by Little Krane's forehead, next to the pink lip imprint. He did a somersault and then settled against a blob of goo.

"Sweet dreams."

We drifted off to sleep.

Martin L. Shoemaker is a software developer and a science fiction and fantasy author. Software helps him think about technology and its impact on our lives, inspiring his fiction; fiction lets him explore how people work with new technologies, inspiring his software. His work has appeared in *Digital Science Fiction* and the charity anthology *The Gruff Variations*. Two of his stories have been finalists in Writers of the Future. His story "Not Close Enough" will appear in an upcoming issue of *Analog*.

S.C. Wade resides in the sunny state of Florida, where he is working diligently to make writing his profession. As a writer, his goal is to make fiction that is believable, relevant, and entertaining to his readers. He can be found on Facebook and also on his website, scwade.com, where he offers free fiction critique services. In addition to *The Glass Parachute*, S.C. Wade's work has been published at *DailyScienceFiction.com*.

Jasmine Michaelson grew up in Idaho Falls, Idaho, and earned her BA in print journalism from Utah State University. She currently resides in San Diego, California, with her husband, Jake, and their three-year-old son. She is a full-time stay-at-home mom who, like many stay-at-home moms, spends her spare time noodling on a cyberpunk novel. "Nyx" is her first published work of fiction. She can be contacted at jasmine.michaelson@gmail.com.

David Tallerman's short fiction has appeared in around fifty markets, including *Lightspeed*, *Bull Spec*, *Redstone Science Fiction,* and John Joseph Adams's zombie best-of collection, *The Living Dead*. His first novels, comic fantasy adventure *Giant Thief* and its sequel *Crown Thief*, came out this year by publisher Angry Robot Books, with *Prince Thief* scheduled for late 2013. David's first chapbook, *The Way of the Leaves*, is due to appear in December via independent British horror press Spectral. David can be found online at davidtallerman.net **and** davidtallerman.blogspot.com.

Ben Godby writes mysteriously thrilling pseudo-scientific weird western adventure fantasy tales. He lives in Ottawa, Ontario, Canada, with a girl, two dogs, and a cat, and he blogs at bengodby.com.

Alex J. Kane is a speculative fiction writer and critic whose work has appeared in *Digital Science Fiction* and *Foundation*, among other places. He lives in the small college town of Monmouth, Illinois, where he recently earned a BA in English. Visit him online at alexkanefiction.com.

Rob Oxley hails from Lufkin, Texas. He lives with a domesticated red skunk, some emus, the cremated remains of a goldfish, and a good woman who attempts to make sense of it all. When he's not fishing or writing short fiction, he frequents "work" from time to time: a materials testing company for which he heroically feints qualification. Contact him at rooblixo@gmail.com (spam only, please).

Grayson Bray Morris was born and raised in eastern North Carolina. Since 2002 she has lived in the Netherlands with her husband and three children. She earned a BS in mathematics in 1989, then went on to study the technical side of computer graphics before leaving academia to program assembly on parallel digital signal processors. For the last ten years she has worked as a freelance translator. Visit her on the web at graysonbraymorris.com.

Matt Edginton is a machinist by trade and lives in Idaho Falls, Idaho, with his wife and two daughters. He has been an artist all his life, and he is currently focusing on writing and publishing. He started Villipede Publications as a humble press intent on producing professional and exciting fiction combined with fine artistic support.

SERVA ANIMUM CASTELLUM CUSTODITUM · HORTUM BENE CURATUM · FLUMEN NON OBSTRUCTUM ·